Stephen Ainley was born in Birmingham U.K. in 1952. He served in the British Airborne in the 1970s before emigrating to Australia. He has written short stories and articles for many years but this is his first novel. He resides in Western Australia with wife Jane and Irish terrier O'Malley.

For my wonderful wife Jane, children Holly and Tim, and a heartfelt thanks to my grandson Stevie Rayy for all his encouragement and support.

Stephen Ainley

THE DENNIS BISSKIT ADVENTURES

AUSTIN MACAULEY
PUBLISHERS LTD.

A CIP catalogue record for this title is available from the British Library.

ISBN 9781786294050 (Paperback)
ISBN 9781786294067 (Hardback)
ISBN 9781786294074 (E-Book)
www.austinmacauley.com

First Published (2017)
Austin Macauley Publishers Ltd.
25 Canada Square
Canary Wharf
London
E14 5LQ

PROLOGUE

JANUARY 1964
JUST OUTSIDE KAMPALA, UGANDA

Dennis carefully placed the hat on top of the snowman's head, and then stepped back to admire his handiwork.

"There you go, all finished and it's a beauty, though I say so myself," he said so to himself.

Suddenly he heard a loud noise coming from nearby, he couldn't quite place it, but it sounded oddly familiar. When he looked back at the snowman he couldn't believe his eyes. It had half melted already. A blazing sun had appeared above it and within minutes it had completely disappeared, leaving a puddle of water with a hat floating in it.

"Come back, come back," Dennis shouted, then he shot up in bed, he was soaked in sweat and as usual had managed to get himself tangled up in his mosquito net.

He realised the strangely familiar sound he'd heard was the bugler, who shouted a chirpy "Wakey, wakey, rise and shine," before quickly disappearing to avoid the torrent of abuse coming from inside the tents. Dennis eventually managed to disentangle himself from his mosquito net and sat on the side of his bed, yawning and stretching his legs. He was wearing his army issue jungle green underpants, which like the rest of his army kit, appeared to have been designed for a person at least twice his size. Most of his body was its usual snowy white colour except for his face, neck, arms from the elbows down and legs from the knees down, which were burnt bright red. Dennis had initially thought that a beautiful tan would impress people when he got back home, but after about ten minutes of scorching heat and high humidity, he had suddenly realised that a ginger, freckly person was designed to avoid sunshine at all costs. Not only were parts of him semi-cremated but most of the rest of him was covered in red, itchy mozzie bites. He slapped his leg as he felt another bite and not for the first time muttered to no-one in particular,

"I was quite happy in Dudley, how did I come to end up in the middle of Africa…?"

THE EARLY YEARS

CHAPTER 1

ST. JOHN'S PRIMARY SCHOOL, DUDLEY JULY 1955

Dennis stared at the clock on the classroom wall and willed the hands to move more quickly. Three minutes, two minutes, one minute and that was it, the end of term and the start of summer holidays 1955. He hung back until the class was clear before making his way towards the exit. He peeped around the door and looked up and down the corridor but the coast looked clear. Being short, with ginger hair, and having one ear bigger than the other, meant that Dennis was often picked on by some of the rougher kids at school.

A few days earlier, he had walked out of the gates, attempting to keep a low profile, when all of a sudden, there was a huge explosion and his granddad's decrepit old Bedford van slowly came to a shuddering halt in front of the school. Every time the engine backfired, huge clouds of smoke would emerge from the rear.

As crowds of schoolkids gathered, Dennis's granddad had climbed down from the van, looked up, spotted him, and shouted "How's my little angel?" then he had approached Dennis, who by now was in shock, thrown his arms around him, and planted a big kiss on the top of his head. The last few days had been hell, but Dennis hoped that by the time the next term started, it would all be forgotten about. Just to be on the safe side, he'd explained to his grandfather that he could not come and meet him again until Dennis was at least 40. He stepped out through the school gates, relieved that his granddad wasn't there but then suddenly horrified to see his mother standing with her hands on her hips. She had obviously been baking as she was wearing her big apron that was covered in various food stains. She had curlers in her hair half hidden by a blue head scarf.

"Where have you been Dennis, daydreaming again?" she shouted; "I've got some nice bread and dripping for your tea," she added.

"Mum, you don't have to meet me from school, I am ten," he told her, but she just shook her head, and said "It's no trouble, I was over the road borrowing some flour off Mrs Whippet anyway." As they walked down the street she tried to hold Dennis's hand but he pretended not to notice. Just as he was thinking he'd managed to avoid anyone seeing him being escorted home by his mother, he spotted Stinky Blackshaw throwing stones at a lamp-post, Stinky was always in trouble at school and Dennis tried to keep out of his way. Before he could do anything Stinky glanced over the road, spotted him and started shouting,

"What's the matter Bisskit, are you scared to walk home alone?" and then singing, "Bisskit's a scaredy-cat, Bisskit's a scaredy-cat." Dennis's mother immediately strode towards him, saying "I'll give you a clip around the ear in a minute lad, any more of it and there'll be less of it." Stinky ran off down the road shouting "Bisskit's a scaredy-cat," at the top of his voice.

"Stay well away from him, Dennis," his mother told him, "he's a bad 'un, his mother was a bad 'un as well. I remember during the war, whilst her husband was fighting in the desert, she had far too many gentlemen visitors for my liking." Dennis didn't bother answering, he had every intention of avoiding Stinky Blackshaw. Little did he know that within a couple of years he and Stinky would become lifelong friends, but that was in the future, now it was the start of the holidays and he had more important things on his mind. Would his father help him build a new go-kart as he'd been promising all year? Could he find a new conker capable of beating the best? And most importantly, could he finally master the Bowline knot and receive his Wolf Cubs' Basic Knot-tying badge from Akela? He suddenly turned to his mother and asked "What's wrong with Stinky's mother having gentlemen visitors Mum?" She immediately smacked him top on the head and said "Never you mind lad, that's no concern of yours, now let's get you home for your bread and dripping."

His mother cut him a thick piece of bread and smothered it in about an inch of fat.

"Get that down you Dennis," she told him, "that will keep a growing boy nice and healthy." He took a large bite and strode out into the back garden to see his granddad. It was a beautiful sunny day, so he knew he'd be out there sunbathing, he did love a bit of sunshine. He'd told Dennis that ever since he'd visited Egypt during the Great War, he'd got a taste for it and sure enough Dennis found him sleeping in his deckchair, with his trousers rolled up to his knees, his shirt off and wearing a knotted handkerchief on his head. He was wearing an old vest, covered in burn marks where cigarette ash had fallen onto it. He awoke as Dennis approached and immediately yawned and smiled, he and Dennis had always been close.

"Hiya Gramps," Dennis said, "boy, it sure is hot today."

"Oh this is nothing lad," his granddad replied, "in Egypt, it was so hot you could fry an egg on the pavement." Dennis loved to hear his granddad's old war stories but was a bit troubled by this one.

"Didn't you have a frying pan Granddad?" he enquired. His granddad shook his head.

"Yes, we had a frying pan, but we didn't have any eggs, but you're missing the point Dennis" he told him, "The point is, had we not had a frying pan but had some eggs, then we could have, had we so wished, fried them on the pavement because of the extreme heat." Dennis wasn't convinced and said "Well I wouldn't have eaten them, you don't know what you could catch, there may have been camels walking on that pavement." Dennis's granddad was beginning to wish he'd never mentioned it, so he closed his eyes hoping he'd be left in peace, but Dennis had noticed something he hadn't spotted before, a faint scar on the side of his grandfather's left arm. He immediately asked him about it.

"Oh I did that digging a trench," he was told. Dennis hadn't heard this story before and said "Wow, I didn't know you were wounded in the trenches, was that France 1915?"

"No," answered his granddad, "it was Dudley 1936, down the bottom of this garden actually. I was digging a trench for the plumbing for the toilet, I fell in and landed on some broken glass." Dennis was disappointed,

"I thought maybe you had a war wound like Dad's," he told him. His granddad just gave him a funny look and closed his eyes again. Dennis's father was a war hero who had a round shrapnel scar in the centre of his forehead. Despite repeated requests he would never tell

Dennis how it happened, just that it was a top secret mission. In a few months Dennis would overhear an argument between his mum and dad in which she revealed that the scar was actually caused by a flying beer bottle, hitting his father whilst he was having a quiet smoke in a shop doorway. His father had actually been excused joining up for medical reasons and instead had spent the war as an Air Raid Warden. His injury had been caused by sheer misfortune, when a stray German bomber had dumped its remaining bomb on the empty pub across the street from where Mr Bisskit was having his quiet smoke. Of course that revelation was in the future, for now that scar was a source of great pride to Dennis and his dad's heroic war wound was normally the first thing he brought up when meeting anyone new. His granddad started snoring so Dennis left him to it, it was time to get changed into his cubs' uniform.

Dennis had been a Wolf Cub for nearly a year now. George Blunt, who had joined on the same day as Dennis, was already an assistant sixer, which meant he had a stripe on his sleeve and helped to teach new boys. The main problem for Dennis was the Bowline, a knot described by Akela as the King of Knots, seemingly a simple knot for every other boy who joined the pack, but unfortunately for Dennis, a complete mystery. No matter how much he practised, he just couldn't seem to get it right and until he mastered it, he could not get his Basic Knots Badge and gain promotion in the Dudley Wolf Cub Pack. Today was vitally important. He was off in a couple of days on holiday with his family and he was determined to enjoy it, safe in the knowledge that the Bowline was mastered.

The pack had split into various groups, but Akela beckoned Dennis to a corner of the room and handed him a short length of rope. Akela was actually Miss Plunge who, when she wasn't being Den Mother to the cubs, owned a local haberdashery shop. The lads, even if they met her in the street called her Akela; the main thing was never to call her Mrs Plunge. She would get very annoyed and shout, "it's MISS PLUNGE!" which sounded strange because she was about 60 years old. Dennis had never seen her with a man, in fact she didn't even seem to like boys and only appeared to do the job so that she had someone to shout at.

She stared down her spectacles at him and said

"Well, here we go again Bisskit, for the fifth time you will attempt to complete the Bowline in under two minutes. It's probably the easiest knot we learn, there are probably monkeys in Dudley Zoo who can tie one. When you tie up your boat on the docks, you will use a Bowline." Dennis didn't own a boat, he didn't know anyone in Dudley who owned a boat and he guessed there was very little chance that he would ever need to tie up a boat at the docks, but felt that now wasn't the time to explain this to Akela. She looked at her watch, and said "begin now."

Two minutes later she returned and looked at the knot Dennis had produced.

"I don't believe it," she said, "that's a Waggoner's Hitch, that's one of the hardest knots to learn." Dennis was ecstatic, somehow he'd tied a knot that he hadn't even been taught.

"Does that get me my badge," he asked hopefully.

"Well, not really," Akela told him, "that's not what I asked for is it?" Dennis looked confused, so she explained for him.

"It's like this, imagine you were Doctor Bisskit, and I asked you to remove a wart from a patient's nose, and you removed his left leg instead. Now, you might do a superb job on the leg removal, it could well be a faultless piece of leg surgery. Other doctors may arrive at the hospital, purely to see what a wonderful job you have done. Even the patient, on regaining consciousness may recognise it as tremendous leg removal. But, and I'm afraid this is why I cannot give you your badge, what we would have is a man with one leg and a wart still on his nose, and in all honesty, that is not what I requested. Now young Bisskit, I suggest you spend the majority of your holiday tying up your boat, using a Bowline."

The next day Dennis could barely contain his excitement. Only one day to go and the family would be off to Butlin's Holiday Camp Skegness for their annual holiday. Since Grandma Winn had passed away four years earlier and Granddad had moved in with them, it had become something of a tradition and was the highlight of Dennis's year. Still, as excited as he was, he couldn't help but frown as he stared into the bathroom mirror. He had thought he was imagining things but no, there was no denying it. His left ear was getting even bigger than the other one. Dennis had always been short for his age and now he had one ear bigger than the other.

"Just lucky I have ginger hair," he thought to himself, "it draws the attention away from my ears." Just then he heard raised voices coming from the sitting room. He went to check it out and there was his granddad with his trousers rolled up above his knees, in heated conversation with Dennis's mother. Dennis immediately knew what the conversation was about, the Butlin's Over 65's Knobbly Knees Competition. He had heard it many times over the last few years. As he entered the room, his grandfather turned to him, and said

"Ah, Dennis, I'm glad you're here, now be honest, do these knees look more knobbly than last year?" Dennis couldn't really see any difference but told his granddad that he thought they did indeed look a bit more knobbly.

"What's the point anyway," Granddad shouted, "That Cruskett woman will win it the same as every other year, it's just not fair, they used to have a separate competition for men and woman, but then came the great amalgamation of '52 and she's won it ever since. Women shouldn't even be showing their knees. I'll tell you something, I was married for nearly forty years and I've seen more of Mrs Cruskett's knees than I saw of your gran's, I very rarely even saw your grandmother's ankles."

"Dad! Calm yourself down," Dennis's mother said, "it's only a competition, you've done very well, second place for the last two years."

"I know that," replied Granddad, "but she hasn't even got proper knobbly knees, they are just deformed. Mine became knobbly through the sweat and toil of working down the coal mine." Dennis interrupted him,

"I thought you told me you only worked down the mine for a couple of days, then you couldn't stand it so you got a job in a shop." But there was no stopping his granddad now. "It was three days actually," he corrected him "but by then the damage was done. Anyway you are both missing the point, and that is, my knobbly knees were worked for, whereas she just had the very good fortune to be born with deformed knees. She should be banned for having an unfair advantage." He stood there with his hands on his hips waiting for further argument but Dennis and his mother had had enough and wandered off to carry on packing.

They had packed Granddad's bright red Bedford van with everything you need for a holiday, plus lots of things that Dennis felt were surplus to requirement. For example, the chalets at Butlin's already contained furniture, but for some reason the grownups insisted upon packing most of the furniture from their house into the back of the van. When Dennis had asked about this,

18

his mother had replied, "You can't be too careful Dennis." Also his mother had packed so much food, that you would assume food had not yet been discovered in Skegness. Still at last it was the big moment.

They all held their breath as Granddad rotated the starting handle, luckily the motor burst into life first time without causing any damage. A few years earlier, the handle had suddenly shot out and hit Granddad in the leg. He had screamed and hopped around on one leg for several minutes before slowly toppling over like a big tree. A massive bruise had immediately appeared on his leg. Today, no such problems and they all quickly boarded before the engine changed its mind.

Granddad sat in the driver's seat, with Dad next to him and Dennis, his mum and sister Gladys sat in the back surrounded by furniture and food. Granddad spat onto his hands and rubbed then together which apparently was supposed to be good luck; and said, "Right, 25 miles an hour, four toilet and cup of tea and food stops, should take us six and a half hours at the most. Skegness here we come." With that he slowly moved out of the driveway and started down the road. Granddad didn't drive very quickly, in fact sometimes people on bicycles would overtake them. Granddad would tut and say "The faster you go, the longer it takes to get there." Dennis could see no sense in that whatsoever, but still didn't mind; it was all part of the holiday experience, as was the van breakdown. Inevitably, somewhere along the journey, the van would suddenly start spluttering and come to a standstill. Then everyone would pile out, set up tables and chairs alongside the road, and have a cuppa and bite to eat, whilst the men worked on the engine. Normally they were back on the road within an hour, just as long as Granddad didn't say "my big end's gone," Dennis did not know what a big end was, or where it went but apparently, when it did go you were in big trouble. Today things seemed to be going well. After a while Dennis opened his Eagle Annual and started reading. For many years he had read The Beano, but now he was ten years old he felt that it was time to move on and had become a huge fan of The Eagle, and especially Dan Dare, space traveller. It was set well in the future, the late 1990s where Dan Dare explored the galaxy. It was hard for Dennis to even imagine life in the 1990s, "I'll be ancient, nearly 50," he thought to himself, "I'll probably be living on the moon." Just then the van started spluttering.

"You grab the chairs Dennis, and Gladys give me a hand with these sandwiches"

Ten hours later, at 8.30 that evening they reached Skegness. Dennis had been staring through the window for the last ten minutes, waiting for the big moment.

"There's the sea," he shouted excitedly, "it's still there." Before the family had started coming to Skegness, they had visited Southport several times and stayed at a B&B. Dennis had been assured that there was a sea there but had never managed to find it. There was a large plain of sandy mud covered in seaweed, as far as the eye could see. The locals referred to this as the beach, and told him that if he waited, the sea would eventually come in, but it never had. Once he thought he had detected a glint of something on the horizon, so he'd packed a lunch and walked off across the sandy plain to find it. He had walked for about half an hour, occasionally getting stuck in the mud, but when he looked up the glint was still on the horizon. He had come back exhausted, thinking everyone must be making fun of him, and really there was no sea at Southport. The next day, he'd walked down to the beach with his sister Gladys. She was so confident that she had actually bought a towel to dry herself off.

"You're wasting your time," Dennis had told her, "there is no sea," After an hour of staring into the distance Dennis had decided to go back to the B&B and leave Gladys to it. Not long afterwards, she had come in drying her hair on the towel. "You should have stayed' she told him "the sea came in just after you left, I went in up to my knees." Dennis ran and grabbed a towel but Gladys told him, "It's no use going now, it's gone again".

The van pulled into Butlin's and Granddad parked up near the Reception building, and entered... After a few minutes he emerged with a young man in a bright red blazer. Dennis knew he was one of the Redcoats. These were the men and women who worked at Butlin's, and helped you enjoy your holiday.

"Do you want to come with me Dennis?" Granddad shouted, "I have to check out the chalet." They walked off leaving Mum, Dad and Gladys standing by the van and made their way towards the Chalet Area. As they walked along, they suddenly heard a commotion coming from one particular chalet, lots of shouting and laughter.

"I hope you're not letting standards slip," Granddad said to the Redcoat. Just then as they approached the chalet in question, the door flew open and several women emerged, some of them with drinks in their hands. Dennis heard his grandfather let out a groan as he spotted his arch enemy Mrs Cruskett surrounded by her supporters; she never went anywhere without them; they were known as the Cruskett Mafia on the knobbly knees circuit. As soon as she spotted his granddad, she smirked and said,

"Oh no, it's Grumpy Bisskit, surely you are not going to try again. Why not just admit it, your knees are not knobbly enough." Granddad was fuming, he went red in the face and shouted,

"If you were my wife I wouldn't let you show those knees in public." Quick as a flash she told him,

"If I was your wife I wouldn't even show my face in public, I'd be too ashamed." Her supporters all cheered and laughed whilst Dennis told his granddad to take no notice. They walked past the group of women but before they had got very far, Mrs Cruskett shouted something. They turned to see she had lifted her floral dress up to her knees. She shouted,

"Oh no, the wind has lifted my dress up revealing my magnificent knobbly knees." Granddad immediately covered Dennis's eyes with his hand and said,

"Don't look lad," then turned towards Mrs Cruskett and said, "You don't impress me, flaunting your knees, anyway those knees aren't even knobbly, they are deformed," before she could reply, Dennis and the young Redcoat managed to drag him off towards their chalet.

Dennis did not sleep well that night, for one thing he was too excited, but mainly it was because, with his sister Gladys coming with them this year, he was having to share a bedroom with his granddad. Not only was Granddad a very loud snorer, but he obviously had a lot on his mind, because throughout the night he had kept shouting out in his sleep. Things like, "my knees are much knobblier than hers," and once he had suddenly screamed "get those deformed knees away from me." Dennis lay there wide awake, thinking he would be very pleased once this competition was over and he could enjoy the holiday.

Very early in the morning, before anyone else had awoken, he quietly climbed out of bed, got dressed and opened the front door of the chalet. He wanted to get a quick look at the sea, just to make sure it hadn't disappeared like it had in Southport. He looked across the gardens and between the buildings opposite and there it was, so still and grey that it was difficult to tell where the sea ended and the sky began. Just then he was startled to hear a cough close by. He turned to look at the chalet next door and there sitting on a deckchair was an old man with a big grey beard; he seemed to be staring out to sea just like Dennis. Dennis wasn't sure if the man had noticed him but out of politeness said "Good morning sir." The man didn't even bother turning but muttered,

"I've seen better mornings and I've seen worse." He didn't appear in the mood for further conversation, so Dennis went back into the chalet; he could hear movement, soon it would be time for breakfast and then at midday the Knobbly Knees Competition.

Dennis's mother had oiled and massaged Granddad's knees. He was very tense and had immediately gone off to the toilet.

"I'm not looking forward to this," she told the family, "it could turn nasty. Mrs Cruskett told me that he called her knees deformed and when she told him she'd never been so insulted, he said "I'm surprised with a face like that." Dennis's dad chuckled until Mum gave him the look.

"It's not funny George," she told him, "we must all be there to support your father." Gladys immediately said that she would be staying in the chalet to practise her walk for the Butlin's Miss Teen Contest. Dad said he'd be there but would be reading the paper, and obviously Dennis would be there for his granddad.

"Come on Dad, it's time to go," Mrs B shouted at the toilet door.

The crowd was boisterous, the Cruskett Mafia were out in force knowing that as she had won the previous two years, if she triumphed again this year, Mrs Cruskett would enter the Knobbly Knees Hall of Fame, joining the likes of Harold "The Beast" Fairclough, whose wife had donated his knees to science following his tragic demise at The Somme, not the battle but a camping holiday in 1950.

The crowd was so big that Dennis and his mother and father, were some distance from the stage. There were 12 contestants all together and Granddad had a large number nine pinned to his shirt. A young Redcoat approached the microphone, welcomed the crowd to the 15th Annual Butlin's Holiday Camp Knobbly Knees Competition and then, to great cheers turned to the contestants and said "Mrs Cruskett, and gentlemen, reveal your knees," The men including Granddad rolled up their trousers, Mrs Cruskett, ever the performer, waited until she was the final contestant, and then very slowly, inch by inch, as if she were doing some sort of exotic dance, raised her long dress, until her knees were presented in all their glory. There was applause from her fans, but Dennis also noticed a couple of the more sensitive observers gasp and avert their eyes. Dennis looked along the row of contestants until he reached Granddad. Something looks different, he thought; he took off his glasses and cleaned them on his shirt sleeve, put them back on and looked again.

"Mum," he said, "is it my imagination, or do Granddad's knees look knobblier than usual?" But Mum was telling his father off about something and at that moment the judges had started to move along the row, bending to examine the knobbly knees. One of them carried a large notebook in which he wrote comments and scores for various categories, including, look, size, and extent of knobbliness. When they reached Mrs Cruskett, there were huge cheers, the judges treated her like an old friend, smiling and chatting with her. Then they moved on to Dennis's granddad. They seemed to be bent in front of him for a long time, raised voices were heard and the crowd began to get restless, sensing something was going on. Mrs Cruskett left her spot, advanced towards Granddad and said something. Granddad reacted by shaking his fist at her.

"What's going on," asked Dennis's mother, "I don't understand." Just then, one of the Redcoats grabbed the microphone and tried to use it, but there was a loud whistling sound, everyone covered their ears, until he got the hang of it.

"Would Mr Head, the Events Manager report to the stage please, Mr Richard Head report to the stage," There was murmuring amongst the crowd and then a small man wearing a suit and trilby pushed his way to the stage and joined the judges. There was much arm waving and shouting, someone in the crowd began to do a slow hand clap, but then Mr Head walked to the microphone. He had to lower it to his own height, then he cleared his throat and began to speak in a trembling voice.

"Ladies and Gentlemen," he began, "in all my years in Event Management, this is the hardest decision I have ever had to make." One of the other judges ran towards him and handed him a large book; he muttered thanks and then turned back to the confused crowd.

"Ladies and Gentlemen," he began again, "may I draw your attention to the Butlin's Holiday Camp Knobbly Knees Rulebook 1938, amended in 1946, specifically Rule 12, Extension five, Paragraph three." Someone in the crowd shouted "Get on with it."

Mr Head removed a handkerchief from his top pocket, wiped his brow and said "Sorry, to cut a long story short, as I was saying, I draw your attention to Extension five, specifically the part that states, knees must at all times be in their natural state." Again slow hand claps broke out. Mr Head again wiped his brow and said "It's my painful duty to announce the immediate disqualification of Mr William Braithwaite Bisskit for illegal use of make-up to accentuate his knobbly knees."

The crowd went berserk, some screamed and then booing broke out. Dennis's mother stood up, and shouted, "Oh my god, the shame, the humiliation" then she collapsed in a dead faint. Luckily her fall was broken by landing on top of his father, who managed to save her, but irrevocable damage was done to his pipe when it fell from his mouth and shattered on the ground. Dennis could not believe what he had heard, he looked down at his mother and father and said "I never knew Granddad's middle name was Braithwaite."

After they got back to the chalet, Mrs Bisskit had wanted to pack up and go home. She said she couldn't stand the humiliation, but luckily they managed to get her to change her mind. Granddad said he didn't know what all the fuss was about, he'd only been trying to make the event more equal.

"You don't stand a chance against someone with deformed knees," he'd said, and then gone on to tell them where he'd got the idea. "I was talking to an old timer, he told me that years ago when knobbly knees was an underground sport, mainly frequented by the criminal classes, there was a lot of gambling involved and some of the lads, to get a bit of an advantage, had taken to rubbing dirt into the contours of their knees, evidently it accentuated the lumpiness." He looked at Mum and continued, "I thought if dirt worked, your make-up would work even better."

They felt it was best to avoid people for the rest of the day but the following morning, Mum said they should all go to breakfast together as a show of support for Granddad. Even Gladys took a break from her walking practice for the Miss Teen Butlin's event. They left the chalet, and walked past the old man with the big beard next door, he was still sitting in his deckchair staring out to sea. They all made their way to the large dining room. One of the things Dennis loved most about Butlin's was the food, they did chips with everything, He used to have chips for breakfast, lunch and tea. Egg and chips, fish and chips, mashed potatoes and chips, anything as long as it involved chips. Sometimes when he went up for dessert, he'd shove a pile of chips next to his apple pie. He was always worried that, like the sea at Southport, the chips may disappear at any moment, so he wanted to have as many as possible before that happened.

As usual the dining room was absolutely packed and very noisy. When they entered, it was like the baddie had walked into the saloon in a cowboy movie. It instantly went very quiet, everyone ignored them. They held their heads high, got their breakfast from the counter and found a table in the centre of the room.

"Just ignore them," Mum said, but then the quiet was interrupted by a shout of "Cheat!" from the back of the room. Granddad turned to say something but Mum hissed at him "Leave it Dad, you've caused enough trouble." He looked at Mum, who had a spoonful of soup in her hand. Just as Dennis had chips for every meal, his mum loved her soup, and even had it for breakfast.

"I don't think you're in a position to have a go at me, my girl," Granddad told her, "I fought in two world wars and you sit there eating that rubbish." Mum couldn't believe her ears and said, "What are you talking about Dad, it's just Minestrone soup."

"Exactly," Granddad said, "Italian soup, Mussolini invented it, they shouldn't even serve it here." Mum was lost for words and before she could answer, dad joined in.

"I think Dad's right, Edith." He rubbed the scar on his forehead and said "We shouldn't forget those who suffered." As usual whenever Dad mentioned his war wound, for some reason Mum raised her eyebrows and shook her head.

"I don't forget those who suffered at all," she said, "but I think you'll find that Minestrone was around a long time before Mussolini was born."

Granddad was in such a bad mood he then turned his attention to Dennis.

"And I thought you would know better Dennis, sitting there eating a sausage, don't you know the Germans invented the sausage under orders from Hitler himself?" Dennis was shocked but pleased when Dad defended him.

"I think you'll find those are Wall's Pork Sausages Dad," he told Granddad, "unless the pig took his holidays in Bavaria, I don't think Germany had a lot to do with them." Granddad had had enough, he loudly pushed his chair back, stood up and shouted, "You don't understand, it's the principle, we should do the right thing," then he stormed out of the dining room with everyone staring at him. Dennis noticed Mrs Cruskett watching him as he pushed his way through the crowded tables. Surprisingly, she seemed to have a look of admiration on her face. There was silence for a moment and then Dennis stood up and said, "I'm going to grab some more chips before they run out."

The atmosphere inside their chalet was a bit tense for the next couple of days, so Dennis kept out of everybody's way. There was always plenty to do at Butlin's, he spent time on the paddle boats, played some mini golf and came second in the 'Gingerist Hair Competition', winning a mug with 'BUTLIN'S SKEGNESS, SUN, SAND, AND KNOBBLY KNEES,' printed on it. Each morning he would take his length of rope, sit on the porch and attempt to tie a Bowline. It was so frustrating because he just couldn't get it right.

One morning he noticed the old man from next door watching him.

"I'm tying a Bowline," Dennis said, but as usual the man just grunted and turned away. He walked back inside and saw his mother.

"Has Gladys emerged yet?" he asked. The previous day after several days of walking practice for the Miss Teen Butlin's Contest, Gladys had confidently walked on stage, tripped, fallen flat on her face, and run off stage in tears. She had shut herself in her bedroom and not been seen since.

"Best to leave her Dennis," his mother said, "she'll get over it soon."

That evening was the last of their holiday. Dennis, with his mum, dad and Gladys, who had emerged from her room on the condition that the Miss Teen Contest was never mentioned again, made their way to the dining room for dinner. Granddad had told them he would go on ahead and get a good table. On entering they looked around and eventually spotted him, he was talking to a lady and as they got closer they were amazed to see it was Mrs Cruskett.

"Oh no," said Dennis's mother, "what's he up to now?" Granddad spotted them, stood up and said. "Mildred, this is my son, daughter-in-law, and, grandchildren; Gladys and Dennis." He then pointed at Mrs Cruskett and said "This is Mildred; I don't think we've all been formally introduced." Mrs Cruskett smiled and said "It's lovely to meet you all, William has been telling me all about you."

They were stunned by this turn of events and eventually Mum said "It's lovely to meet you, to be honest I didn't think you and William got along very well." Mrs Cruskett smiled at Granddad and said "Well, we didn't at first but that's just because we are both very competitive, but I've always admired a man who's

29

passionate about his knees like William is, in fact we've decided to pool our talents so to speak." They must have looked confused, but Granddad explained, "We are entering the Professional Couples' Knobbly Knees Circuit." Dennis blurted out that he didn't even know there was such a thing, but Granddad continued, "Not around here there isn't, but it's huge down south and there's big prizes to be won, Mildred won a brand new kettle last month."

Mrs Cruskett chuckled at their look of disbelief. "Yes, it's true," she said, "and take it from someone who's seen more than her fair share of knees, I can say with great confidence, when we put our knees together, William and I will have four of the finest on the circuit."

It was good to have the family all in a good mood again, even Gladys seemed to have got over her humiliating stage fall. Dennis slept like a log that night, then waking up early, he decided to get up and have one last try at the elusive Bowline. He took his rope outside and wasn't surprised to see the old man next door was up already, staring out to sea as usual. Dennis sat down and made a couple of unsuccessful attempts, then he suddenly realised the old man was standing next to him.

"I can't stand this anymore," the man said. He took the rope off Dennis and continued, "Is this supposed to be the Bowline, the King of Knots?"

"Y-Y-Yes," Dennis stammered, "it's very difficult."

"Difficult," the old man shouted, "difficult, I could tie the Bowline before I could walk, it's simple, now watch me." He held the rope, made a loop in the middle and said "Now, imagine one end of the rope is the rabbit, and the other end is a big tree, and this loop in the centre is a rabbit hole, now the rabbit goes up through the hole, around the big tree and back down the hole," he held up the rope and amazingly there it was, the Bowline. Dennis still looked baffled so the old man showed him again and then handed Dennis the rope. At first attempt, the rabbit went up the tree, second attempt the tree went down the rabbit hole but amazingly at third attempt Dennis got it right, and once he had it, he could do it correctly every time he tried, he couldn't believe it. He stood up and held out his hand, "I don't know how to thank you sir, my name is Dennis." The old man shook his outstretched hand and said "Captain Jackson, ex Royal Navy," with that he turned and walked back to his deckchair and recommenced staring out to sea.

Dennis raced into the chalet and spotted his mother holding the kettle.

"I've done it Mum", he shouted "it's easy, the rabbit goes up the hole, around the tree and back down the hole." With that he raced to his bedroom to tell his granddad. Dennis's father shot out of the toilet with his trousers and braces around his ankles.

"What's all the noise?" he asked.

Mum poured hot water into a teapot and told him, "Oh, just Dennis. I think he saw a rabbit run up a tree."

"That's strange," he said, "I haven't seen any rabbits around here."

CHAPTER 2

Akela could not believe her eyes. She had handed Dennis the rope, turned away to stifle a yawn, and when she had turned back, there it was, a perfect Bowline.

"Did you cheat, Bisskit, did someone else tie that for you?" she demanded to know.

"Certainly not Akela," Dennis told her, "it's only a Bowline, the king of knots, and yet probably the easiest of knots to do." He untied the knot in his rope and rapidly tied it again.

"Do I get my knot tying badge now?" he asked.

"Well, I suppose so Dennis," she told him reluctantly. "but we haven't got time for it now," and then turned and shouted "gather around wolf pack", and everyone formed a circle around her.

"Now, as you know," she told them, "next week is Bob-a-Job Week. I want to make it the best ever, I expect you all to get as many donations as possible, and the cub who collects the most money will receive a new badge." Dennis couldn't believe his ears, what could be better than that, the chance of a new badge, on top of his Basic Knot Tying Badge. One thing's for certain, he thought to himself, I'll be trying my hardest to be the winner.

By an amazing coincidence, as he walked home in his cubs' uniform, he spotted Rupert Fonsworth heading towards him with his mother. Rupert rarely spoke to Dennis; his family were the richest in the area. They even owned a television. Dennis had only ever seen one in a shop window. As they walked towards Dennis, Rupert said something to his mother and then pointed in his direction. When they drew level, Mrs Fonsworth asked him if he was taking part in Bob-a-Job-week. When Dennis told her he was, she explained that she had been on her way to see Akela about getting someone to clean her house windows, but if he wanted it, Dennis could have the job. Dennis could not believe his luck.

She wrote down her address and drew a little map and then explained that he should do the job on Saturday. The family were going away for the weekend, but she would leave a ladder and cleaning equipment by the front door. Rupert then whispered something in his mother's ear and she added "Rupert's kite got stuck somewhere on the roof, if you find that there's an extra sixpence for you," with that they walked off. Dennis ran home with a big smile on his face, thinking "That new badge is mine".

"Don't let people take advantage of you Dennis," his mother told him at dinner that night, "you know what happened last year with Mrs Goldsmith. You were building that house extension for several months, she only gave you a shilling."

"Don't worry about me, Mum," he told her, "I already have a nice easy window cleaning job organised, what could possibly go wrong?" His mother frowned but didn't say anything.

Dennis packed sandwiches, cake and a bottle of lemonade into his saddlebag, and set off on his bicycle. He wore his cubs' uniform; he was a bit concerned about damaging it whilst cleaning the windows, but felt that, as he was representing the cubs, it was important to be correctly dressed. He cycled towards Dudley Zoo, where his father had worked for the last year. His father always told him that he was the Head Zoo keeper, but knowing his dad was prone to exaggeration, Dennis had his doubts, and these had been confirmed when a lad at school had told him that actually *his* father was Head Zoo keeper and Dennis's father just cleaned the Elephant enclosure. This certainly explained why occasionally, his dad brought a large bag of Elephant poo home with him. He would put this around his roses, explaining that it aided the growth. Personally Dennis would have preferred smaller roses and less Elephant poo smell. He wasn't the only one not to appreciate the odour. Several neighbours had complained about his father bringing his work home with him.

Anyway, no time for that now, he thought, as he cycled past Dudley Castle and the houses slowly started to disappear. He stopped for a quick drink and studied the map Mrs Fonsworth had given him. "I must be nearly there now," he said to himself and then he spotted a narrow lane to the left and a small sign pointing to Valley View House. The hedgerow was very high and thick but all of a sudden he came to a gate and there was the house. Dennis's heart sank, it wasn't so much a house as a small castle. He closed the gate behind him and pushed his bike up the path towards the house. He started counting windows but soon gave up.

"I'm going to be here until midnight," he thought to himself. Next to the front door, a large extension ladder lay on the ground, next to it was a bucket containing various items of cleaning equipment and also a note saying "HAVE A NICE DAY," signed by Mrs Fonsworth, and underneath someone had added "AND DONT FORGET MY KITE".

It took all of Dennis's strength to lean the ladder against the house, and then pull the rope to extend it until it reached above one of the top windows. He had decided to do the top windows first whilst he was still full of energy. He carefully climbed the ladder, holding a bucket containing some water and a sponge in his one hand. It was only when he got near the top, that it suddenly dawned upon Dennis, that this was the highest he'd ever been. He started to get concerned, the ladder seemed a bit wobbly. He rested for a moment and then remembered the new badge that the cub who collected the most money would get, and that inspired him to carry on.

He reached the window, hung the bucket on a hook on the side of the ladder and commenced cleaning. After he'd finished he leaned his head back to appreciate his handiwork. "Not bad," he muttered, and then realised that if he climbed another couple of rungs, he could probably see over the guttering and onto the roof. That way he could check if there was any sign of Rupert's kite. Dennis slowly climbed, the ladder was certainly getting shakier. He put his hands on the gutter and raised his head above it. Amazingly, there was the kite, right in front of him but wrapped around a chimney pot, which stood halfway up the sloping roof.

Dennis slowly climbed back down the ladder. Initially he had decided that it was just too difficult to retrieve the kite. He would leave a note for the Fonsworths, explaining where it was. But he couldn't stop thinking about that extra sixpence and after eating a jam sandwich he gradually convinced himself that maybe it wasn't too difficult after all. Dennis pulled on the rope and managed to extend the ladder to its full height. It now leaned against the guttering, extending a couple of feet above it.

He carefully climbed the ladder, eventually reaching the gutter. The ladder wobbled a bit but it was much easier without having to carry the bucket. Once he had his head above the gutter, he hesitated; the roof sloping up to the chimney looked very steep, but the kite looked so close. He took a deep breath, climbed another couple of rungs and lifted his right foot off the ladder and onto the roof. It seemed pretty solid and he had a good grip, so he carefully lifted his left foot off the ladder. He leaned forward, so that he was on his hands and knees and slowly moved up the roof towards the chimney.

"Come on Dennis, nearly there," he muttered. It seemed to be going well, but then, just as he reached the chimney, he started sliding backwards…They say that your life flashes in front of you when death is imminent, and this is what happened to Dennis as he slid slowly down the roof, scraping the skin off his knees. He thought how he would never have a career, marriage, children, and most importantly, get his Basic Knot Tying Badge.

His feet hit the gutter and bounced past it into thin air, then just when all seemed lost, his cub's neckerchief tightened around his neck and he came to a sudden halt. Dennis slowly opened his eyes, he was facing the roof, but gradually looked up to his left and realised that his neckerchief had caught on a roofing nail which fortunately for Dennis had come loose. His legs from the knees down were sticking out over the edge of the roof. He slowly tried to draw his left leg back to the gutter but struck the side of the ladder, which slid along the gutter and disappeared; a second later there was a loud crash as it hit the ground.

The neckerchief appeared to be holding onto the nail but as he looked down he could see that his leather woggle which secured the neckerchief around his neck was starting to stretch. He took a deep breath and decided to review his situation.

He was lying on his stomach, on the roof of a two-storey house, with his feet dangling over the edge. His ladder had gone, and the only thing stopping him falling off the roof was a roofing nail, and a neckerchief which could rip at any moment. "Not only that," Dennis thought to himself, "I've lost my cap and elongated my woggle. Akela's not going to be happy about that."

He slowly tried to raise his left leg again and eventually got his foot into the gutter, then did the same with his other foot. The gutter seemed fairly secure. He looked up; "Just in the nick of time," he thought. His woggle had stretched so far, he felt that the leather must snap at any moment. He used the toes of his shoes to slowly push himself up the roof, unhooking his neckerchief from the nail as he passed it.

Eventually he reached the chimney, manoeuvred himself behind it, and for the first time since he had started slipping, felt fairly safe. He looked down at the view in front of him, and suddenly realised why the house was called Valley View House. He could see for miles. and the enormity of his predicament was obvious. He had no way down, no food or drink, the temperature was starting to drop, he hadn't told his parents whose windows he was cleaning, and the Fonsworths were not due back until tomorrow afternoon.

Dennis sat with his back against the chimney; he had no idea what the time was, but thought it must be mid-afternoon by now. He had noticed a hook sticking out of the side of the chimney, it was wedged between two bricks, probably left by the builders he thought, so he had removed his neckerchief and tied one end to his belt and the other to the hook, hoping that if he slipped this would stop him falling too far. He stared at the damaged woggle in his hand, and wondered if he had enough pocket money saved in his money box to buy a new one.

Just then he heard the sound of a vehicle in the distance. The hedgerow was so thick that he couldn't really see anything. A couple of times previously he had heard a similar sound, but whoever it was had driven straight passed, but now, as he listened carefully, he realised that this vehicle was slowing down and then coming to a halt. Dennis couldn't believe it when suddenly he saw that the gate was opening. Seconds later an old van slowly entered the property and came to a halt, an elderly man got out, closed the gate, got back in the van and continued towards the house.

Dennis carefully stood up behind the chimney and started shouting, "HELP! HELP! I'M STUCK!" the van stopped and the man got out. Dennis immediately recognised him as old Mr Bacon the plumber. Unfortunately, Dennis knew that Mr Bacon's hearing was so bad that he wore a hearing aid which he often neglected to switch on. He shouted as loud as he could but by now Mr Bacon had moved to the front door and Dennis couldn't see him anymore. Thinking quickly, He removed one of his shoes and flung it over the side of the roof, "HELP ME! I'M ON THE ROOF!" he screamed.

Below him, Mr Bacon was searching through his pockets for the door key Mr Fonsworth had left with him. He had to repair a leaky tap in a bathroom and had promised to have the job done before the Fonsworths returned from their trip. Just as he found the key in his trouser pocket, something hit the ground right next to him. When he turned he was shocked to see it was a shoe. At first he thought someone had dropped it from the top floor window, but as he looked up, he thought he could hear noise coming from the roof. He walked back away from the house to get a better view. At first he couldn't see anything but then was amazed to see a head sticking out of the chimney pot, someone was shouting but he couldn't make out what they were saying.

Dennis stood on his tiptoes looking over the top of the chimney. Suddenly Mr Bacon came back into view and stared up at him. Dennis shouted, "ITS ME DENNIS BISSKIT".

Mr Bacon tried to make out what the person was saying and why someone would be on the roof whilst the Fonsworths were away, suddenly he had a terrible thought.

"WHAT ARE YOU DOING UP THERE, ARE YOU A BURGLAR?" he shouted. Dennis couldn't believe it, Mr Bacon's eyes must be as bad as his ears, he thought. He waved his woggle and shouted as loudly as he could, "IT'S ME, DENNIS!"

Below him Mr Bacon saw the person on the roof raise his hand and point something at him.

"IS THAT A GUN?" he shouted, "DON'T SHOOT, I'M AN OLD MAN". He turned and ran for the protection of his van. Slowly raising his head above the vehicle roof, he shouted, "DON'T MOVE I'M GOING TO FETCH THE POLICE," then as he got into the van he had another thought and continued, "WAS IT YOU THAT STOLE MY UNDERPANTS OFF THE WASHING LINE?" He didn't hang around for a reply, but sped off, only remembering to stop and open the gate at the last second.

Dennis felt so frustrated that he was nearly in tears. Of all the people to turn up, why did it have to be Mr Bacon? The one bit of hope he had was that he thought he had heard the word "POLICE" mentioned. The only other word he had made out was "UNDERPANTS" and he couldn't really see the connection. He just hoped that Mr Bacon was sensible enough to report that there was someone stuck on a roof.

Thirty minutes later, just as he was losing hope, he heard a sound getting closer. He suddenly recognised it as a police siren. The sound immediately bought a smile to Dennis's face, although he did think it a bit unnecessary. The sound stopped, the gate opened, and three police cars swept dramatically into the property, spreading out as they approached. The cars skidded to a halt, doors flew open and several policemen jumped out and ran for cover, some behind their vehicles and some behind trees. Mr Bacon's van followed them through the gate, but stayed well back.

Dennis couldn't work out what they were doing, but waved his woggle and shouted "HELLO!"

Suddenly Dennis saw a megaphone appear above one of the cars and a booming voice said "PLACE THE GUN ON THE ROOF AND COME DOWN WITH YOUR HANDS UP!"

Dennis was in shock; he couldn't believe his ears. Then he heard a voice from behind Mr Bacon's van shout, "ASK HIM ABOUT MY UNDERPANTS!" followed by another voice urging the plumber to keep his head down. Dennis felt shaky, he gripped the chimney and thought, maybe it's all just a prank. Then, as he looked around, he spotted a policeman stick his head out from behind a tree, and immediately recognised it as belonging to P.C. Pratt, a neighbour and friend of his father's. He waved and shouted, "IT'S ME, DENNIS!" The voice behind the megaphone started up again, "PLACE THE GUN ON THE ROOF!" Dennis realised he still had his woggle in his hand; he immediately dropped it. P.C. Pratt emerged from behind the tree and shouted "IS THAT YOU DENNIS?" Dennis waved again, and replied that it was and he was stuck on the roof.

P.C. Pratt ran over to the central police car and spoke to the man holding the megaphone. A uniformed policeman with the three stripes of a sergeant, slowly emerged from behind the car, took a few paces towards the house, held up the megaphone and said "IS THAT YOU DENNIS BISSKIT, WHAT ARE YOU DOING ON THE ROOF?" Dennis explained how he'd been cleaning windows, climbed on the roof to rescue Rupert Fonsworth's kite and got stuck. The Sergeant asked, "DO YOU HAVE A GUN?" Dennis told him, the only gun he had was a toy cowboy gun that fired caps and that was at home. A voice came from behind the plumber's van, "ASK HIM ABOUT MY UNDERPANTS." The sergeant duly asked, "DENNIS BISSKIT, DID YOU, WITHOUT HIS EXPRESS PERMISSION, ON OR BEFORE THE 1st OF AUGUST 1955 REMOVE MR BACON'S UNDERPANTS FROM HIS WASHING LINE?" Dennis held his head in his hands for a moment and then shouted, "WHY WOULD ANYONE WANT MR BACON'S OLD UNDERPANTS?" P.C. Pratt looked at the Sergeant and said that this was indeed a very good point, who would want Mr Bacon's old underpants?

"I think it's all been a misunderstanding Sergeant, we'd better help Dennis down." Several of the policemen disappeared out of sight, then Dennis heard the sounds of the ladder being placed against the house. A few moments later the Sergeant's head appeared just above the gutter.

"Bad news Dennis," he said, "when the ladder fell, the top few rungs broke off, I'm afraid we can't reach you." He looked down and shouted, "We are going to need the Fire Brigade," then asked Dennis if he was okay.

"Not really," Dennis replied sadly, "I've severely damaged my woggle." The Sergeant gave a pained expression and shouted "Looks like we are going to need a doctor as well".

An hour later, Dennis stood on solid ground. A fireman had helped him down from the roof. He explained to them what had happened and thanked everyone for rescuing him. A reporter from the Dudley Times had followed the Fire Engine out from town, hoping for a scoop, and after writing down some notes asked Dennis to stand in front of the house, whilst he took some photographs. That was how Dennis came to appear on the front page of that week's edition, under the headline "BOB A JOB ENDS UP COSTING THE RATEPAYER A PRETTY PENNY", wearing one shoe, no cap, the tattered remnants of his neckerchief tied to his belt, chimney soot all over his face, and clutching the remains of his woggle in his hand. Akela would later describe it as the worst case of someone being improperly dressed she had seen in 20 years of service.

The only positive thing that had happened was when Mr Bacon approached him and said "It was you all along up there Dennis, why didn't you say?" and then he'd turned to P.C. Pratt and said, "I've just remembered, my underpants are still in the sink, I never hung them out in the first place".

Dennis spent the next few days in bed. He'd caught a bad cold, plus he didn't especially want to bump into anyone who'd heard about his misadventures. Wednesday evening though, was cubs' night and there was no avoiding it. He put on his uniform, including new cap, neckerchief and woggle and checked himself in the mirror. Not only had he used up his savings, but he'd needed an advance on future pocket money.

He made his way to the scout hall, and walked in hoping to keep a low profile, but as he entered, all activity ceased. One lad shouted "Bisskit's here, Akela," but she didn't need telling, she was already striding towards Dennis holding up the front page of The Dudley Times. She appeared to be foaming at the mouth.

After about ten minutes of explaining to Dennis that his actions had caused the end of civilisation as we know it. Akela calmed down and told everyone to gather around.

"Apart from one obvious exception," she told them, "I'd like to congratulate you all for your fine efforts in raising a record amount during Bob-a-Job Week. I'd especially like to congratulate Percy Higgins who raised the grand total of One pound five shillings and sixpence and he, of course will receive the special fund raising badge." Dennis was devastated, he had really wanted that badge. Suddenly Akela turned back to him and said "Now young Bisskit, you do not appear to have collected anything whatsoever."

Dennis quickly explained that he'd been in bed with a bad cold for most of the week, but Akela just tutted and said "And whilst you were cavorting around upon the roof, using your woggle as a plaything and then using up the valuable time of our emergency services, did you actually manage to clean any windows or retrieve Rupert Fonsworth's kite, which, let me remind you is the job that you were actually supposed to be doing." Dennis wished he was back on the roof, anywhere but here.

"In all the excitement, I'm afraid I forgot all about the kite, but I did clean one window," he told her, "she may pay me for that," he added.

"She may indeed," Akela told him, "in fact I can tell you now, that in what I consider to be an act of great generosity, Mrs Fonsworth has paid you sixpence for cleaning that one window," Dennis cheered up momentarily until Akela continued, "she has knocked that sixpence off the bill for five shillings and sixpence for repairs to her ladder which you managed to partly destroy. I, of course have apologised on behalf of this troop, the Wolf Cubs in general and Lord Baden Powell, the founder of the Wolf Cubs, who I know would be horrified if he heard about this." Dennis didn't feel the need to answer. Akela stood there for a moment and then said, "So, just so we get it straight, Dennis Bisskit raised the grand sum of minus five shillings, well done Bisskit, fine effort," She reached into her blouse pocket, pulled out a piece of paper and handed it to Dennis. It was a bill for five shillings for ladder repairs.

"See this is paid within the week lad," she told him and then sent them all off to practise some knots.

Dennis was feeling a bit despondent as he walked home that evening, but brightened up when his granddad told him he would lend Dennis the money to pay for the ladder. Now, as he lay in bed he tried to think of some way he could earn the money to repay him.

Amazingly, the next morning, his problems seemed to be solved. He was walking past the newspaper shop, when Mr Plum, the owner raced out and shouted, "It's the famous Dennis Bisskit." Dennis had no idea what he was referring to, until Mr Plum guided him into the shop and pointed at the wall behind the counter. Dennis was horrified to see the front page of the local paper with his photo on it wearing his tattered cubs' uniform, taped to the wall. He had been hoping that his picture would quickly fade into obscurity, but here it was for all to see.

"Oh, there's no need for that Mr Plum, I think you can take that down now," he said to the shopkeeper, but Mr Plum was having none of it.

"Nonsense," he told Dennis, "no need to be modest, it's not every day one of our own makes the front page." Dennis was about to beg him, but then noticed a small poster also attached to the wall.

NEWSPAPER DELIVERY BOY REQUIRED
MUST HAVE HIS OWN BIKE

Two days later at 6.30 in the morning, Dennis set off from the newsagents on his bicycle; he had a large sack of newspapers in a canvas bag around his neck and in the pocket of his duffel coat a list of addresses requiring newspapers.

He couldn't believe his luck; it was a beautiful sunny morning, Mr Plum had promised him two and sixpence a week, just to ride around delivering papers. He would pay his granddad back in a couple of weeks and then have money in his pocket. He whistled as he rode down the High Street. At last things were looking up, he thought, what could possibly go wrong?

Dennis pedalled to the end of the High Street, but slowed down as he noticed his shoelace had come undone. He slowly pulled up behind a parked delivery van, and dismounted from his bike. Taking the canvas bag full of papers from around his neck, he went to lay it on the ground so that he could retie his shoelace, but at the last second noticed the road was still wet and muddy from the previous day's showers. So instead he hung it from the rear door handle of the van, bent down and proceeded to tie his lace. Just as he straightened up, the van suddenly moved forward, taking his bag of newspapers with it. Dennis couldn't believe it and just stood there for a second or two, and then started waving his arms and shouted "STOP! STOP!" He then jumped onto his bicycle and pedalled after the van as quickly as his little legs could pedal. The road was quiet at that time of day so he moved into the right hand lane and waved his arms, hoping the van driver would see him in his mirror. A couple of early risers saw Dennis waving and waved back, shouting 'Good Morning Dennis''. Mr Thistle the Baker shouted, "Wake up Dennis, you're on the wrong side of the road," but Dennis was just concentrating on keeping the van in sight. He hoped that soon it would stop to make a delivery.

His legs were getting tired; the van disappeared around a corner, but amazingly, when he came around the bend, there it was, pulled up by the side of the road.

Dennis was so happy he laughed as he cycled closer to the van, but then, cruelly, just as he slowed up behind it, the van took off again. Laughter turned to tears, and once again Dennis waved his arms and screamed at the anonymous driver. He despondently started pedalling again, the van was heading for the big roundabout on the edge of town, where Dennis suspected it would carry on towards Birmingham. He was tempted to just give up, return to Mr Plum's shop and explain what had happened, but he thought he would keep going for a little longer. The road was still fairly quiet, and he could just make out the van slowing as it reached the roundabout. Amazingly he noticed the driver was indicating he was turning right. This gave Dennis a bit of hope, maybe he still had some deliveries to make in this area. When he reached the roundabout he was feeling exhausted; even though it was a cool early morning, sweat was dripping off his nose. As he braked, he glanced to his right, just in time to see the van signalling another right turn.

Dennis just put his head down and kept turning the pedals. Every now and again he glanced up; a couple of times the van was parked but took off again just as he neared it. He suddenly realised that they were heading back up Dudley High Street; he had followed the van on a big circle. He put his head down and had one last burst, then he knew he could go no further. He stopped pedalling and just rolled along, but when he looked up, there was the van, parked right outside the newsagents. He stopped behind it and quickly grabbed the sack of papers, got off his bike and fell to his knees on the pavement exhausted.

Just then Mr Plum walked out of the shop and towards the van with another man.

"See you next week George," he told him, then spotting Dennis kneeling on all fours, they stopped.

"Don't tell me you've finished already Dennis?" Mr Plum said incredulously. Dennis looked up, wiped the sweat from his forehead, took a deep breath and said "No, I haven't actually started yet Mr Plum, I was just admiring the footpath, it's some lovely workmanship." With that he put the sack around his neck, climbed back on his bicycle and slowly cycled down the street. Mr Plum and George watched his struggle for a while and then Mr Plum sighed and said, "I hope the lad's up to it, I didn't realise he was so unfit."

CHAPTER 3

The weeks went by, the summer holidays eventually came to an end and Dennis returned to school; not his favourite place but this term he felt more confident. So much had happened on his holidays that Dennis now felt more grown up, more capable of coping with school life. Also he was now in his final year at Primary School; next year he would move on to Secondary School, a new beginning and for some reason, he felt quietly confident that his life would improve. As it turned out, this was a false belief, but that was for the future.

After a few days of struggling. Dennis had finally got the hang of his paper round. It still meant an early start each day, especially now he was back at school, but he quite enjoyed being out and about before much traffic was on the road.

The days were starting to get a bit chillier, so this October morning Dennis had the hood of his Duffel Coat pulled down over his eyes as he mounted his trusty Raleigh bicycle. He adjusted the canvas bag of newspapers around his neck until he felt comfortable and then pushed away from the pavement in front of Mr Plum's newspaper shop. He suddenly braked as he felt a bit of give in his handlebars. He shook them from side to side and realised they were slightly loose. Dennis made a mental note to ask his granddad to check them out when he got back home. His granddad was never happier than when he was doing a bit of mechanical maintenance.

He delivered papers to the nearest houses first, and then started on those a bit further out of town. These were the ones he enjoyed the most, because he could get up a bit of speed. He felt so much fitter than when he'd first started and liked to imagine he was in a professional motorbike race.

Today there was a new house on the list, further out than he'd delivered before. He studied the map Mr Plum had drawn for him, then sped off as fast as he could down a long country lane. The road was deserted; Dennis imagined that crowds were cheering him on as he pedalled faster and faster. He had his head down so that his chin was almost touching his handlebars.

"Broom! broom!" he shouted, making engine noises, "the world champion Jack Smith is in the lead, surely no-one can catch him, but wait, who is this, I don't believe it, it's young Dennis Bisskit, coming up on the outside, I've never seen anything like it."

Dennis noticed a bend in the narrow lane coming up but decided to take it at top speed. He leaned his bike slightly over as he took the bend.

"Look at the way Bisskit took that bend, it's unbelievable," he shouted. As he rounded the bend he straightened up in his seat; as he did, the handlebars came away in his hands. For a second he didn't know what had happened, then he glanced down and realised that he had a slight problem: he was coming around the bend on a quiet country lane at top speed and he had no way of steering his bicycle, he was so shocked that he immediately dropped the handlebars, and they fell over the front of his bike, only the brake cable preventing them from falling to the road. Everything just happened in a blur, the bicycle drifted across the lane at high speed, with no way to slow it down or steer it.

"Oh no, Bisskit's going to crash!" were Dennis's last words before he veered to the side of the road, and shot down the grassy bank at the side of it. Halfway down, the front wheel hit a rock and stopped but Dennis continued over the top of where his handlebars should have been and sailed through the air. It could have been disastrous but luckily for Dennis, there was a fairly deep stream running alongside the lane and with a huge splash he landed in the middle of it.

A minute or so later Dennis slowly stood up in the stream; the water was above his knees. He dragged himself to dry land and sat down on the grass getting his breath back. Amazingly, apart from some scratches and scrapes he appeared to be in one piece. He noticed the canvas bag holding his last remaining newspaper floating past, so he dragged it out. Turning he looked for his bicycle and let out a groan when he saw the damage. He stood up to check it out but immediately let out a cry, as pain shot through his ankle.

Dennis sat down again and considered his situation. It was 7.30 now, surely cars used this road occasionally, he could just sit here and wait. He normally rushed home, got changed, grabbed a bite to eat and left for school. His mum would notice if he didn't come home, but now and again when he was running late, he just went straight to school, so she might assume that's what had happened. He saw a small straight tree branch nearby, so he grabbed it, and used it to stand up. Then he hobbled his way up the grassy bank and to the edge of the road. He looked left and right but saw nothing. He slowly walked along the road about ten yards, and looking through the trees to his left spotted a building down a track.

"Hello is anyone home?" Dennis shouted. No-one answered so he shouted a little louder. It had taken him ages to reach the front door of the old farmhouse and now he had the feeling that after all that effort no-one was home. He tried knocking at the door again and then pushed it and the door swung open a few inches. He opened it further and stuck his head in the opening.

"Hello, is anyone there?" Dennis threw his tree branch behind him and painfully entered the room. He was in a large kitchen. Immediately he felt warmer and noticed a fire burning under a large metal plate against the far wall, on top of the plate, water was boiling in a large jug.

Dennis looked about him, there were lots of pots and pans hanging from hooks and lots of ornaments on the shelves. On the wall next to him he saw two framed photographs hanging from nails. One was of an elderly man wearing a suit, the other one was a photograph of a young man looking very smart in his army uniform, he was smiling for the camera. Dennis leaned closer.

"Get away from that!" a voice screamed from behind him. Dennis nearly fell over from the shock, he turned around and an old woman with long, snowy white hair was pointing a shotgun at him.

"I'm s-s-s-s-sorry," Dennis stammered, "I shouted for help but no-one answered, the door was open. Don't shoot, I fell off my bike and injured my leg." The lady stared for a moment, lowered the shotgun and told him "I couldn't shoot you if I wanted to, it's not even loaded." She placed the gun on the table behind her and said, "You're dripping water all over my kitchen, sit there by the fire." She pointed at a small chair and Dennis hobbled over to it and sat down.

"Well you're in quite a state there," she said, "take off your shoe and I'll check the damage." Dennis slowly removed his shoe and took off his sock; water dripped onto the floor.

"I'm very sorry for messing up your floor," he told her. "My name's Dennis, Dennis Bisskit." She twisted his ankle from side to side, and felt all around it. Dennis cried out a couple of times.

"Well Dennis, it's not broken, but it's a bad sprain. You will live but you won't be doing a lot of running around for a few days." Then she held her hand out towards him and said "I'm Mrs Jenkins but you can call me Maud." Dennis shook her hand. She stood and said "Tea, that's what we need, tea always helps".

Dennis sat by the fire, not knowing what to say to this kindly stranger. Steam was coming off his clothing as it gradually dried. She dragged a small table closer to him, and then put a big mug of boiling tea on it along with a thick piece of bread and jam.

"Eat up, Dennis," she said "you look like you need building up," then she stared at him and said "haven't I seen your face somewhere?" Dennis sighed, and said "You may have seen me on the front page of the newspaper, the fire brigade had to rescue me off a rooftop." She nodded her head and said "You seem to be a little accident prone Dennis, my Rodney was just the same," she smiled at some distant memory and then quickly the smile disappeared.

Dennis hesitated before asking, "Is that Rodney in the photograph?" The lady took a deep breath and said "Yes, Rodney is my son, he went to war in 1940 and he never came back, he was just 19." Maud just stared into space and Dennis didn't know what to say; eventually he asked, "Who is that in the other photo?" She suddenly seemed to wake up and said "That was my husband Neville, he passed away in 1947, he was never the same after Rodney went." She shook her head and said,

"Anyway, that's enough about me, tell me about yourself, Dennis."

Dennis spoke to her for about an hour, he told her things he could never tell his parents. He told her he was born on the day the war ended, which should have been a good omen, but instead he seemed to move from one disaster to another. He told her about school and how he didn't like it much, he didn't make many friends, maybe because he was short and gingery. How he missed his grandmother, was close to his grandfather, but a lot of the time his mum and dad didn't seem to notice him much. She told him that she was sure they loved him but sometimes grown-ups are too tired and too busy and they forget to tell you. Then she looked away and said "And then before you know it, it's too late."

When Dennis was fully dried out, Maud helped him outside, and into her old car. On the way she stopped and put his damaged bicycle in the boot, and then threw the canvas newspaper sack on top of it. As they drove, Dennis was very quiet. Maud turned to him and said "You know Dennis, you can come and see me again if you want to, if you need to talk about anything." Dennis promised that he would, and he meant it. They approached his house and seeing his pinched face, she told him, "Don't worry about little things Dennis, there's more than enough important things to worry about,"

She parked in front of his house and told him to stay there whilst she got his mum. A harassed looking woman wearing a big apron opened the door, and Maud explained that she had an injured Dennis in her car. Mrs Bisskit sighed and said "What's he done this time?" They walked to the car but then Maud hesitated and said "I think he needs a hug, children aren't around for ever you know." They helped Dennis out of the car and sat him down on the front doorstep, retrieved his bicycle from the boot, and then Maud got into the car waved and drove off.

"She's a bit of a strange one," Mrs Bisskit said.

"No Mum," Dennis answered, "she's not strange, she's just sad." His mum helped him up and suddenly hugged him until Dennis got embarrassed in case someone saw them and pulled away.

"You must be more careful' she told him, "I don't know what I'd do if something happened to you."

The doctor came and bandaged up his ankle and told him to rest up for a couple of days. His mum brought him soup and his dad brought him comics to read; his granddad told him funny stories and even Gladys stuck her head around the door to see how he was going. He thought how lucky he was to have such a family.

When he eventually could walk without too much pain, his granddad took him into the shed and he was delighted to see he'd fixed his bike; it was as good as new.

A week later he cycled to Maud's house to thank her. He visited her every few weeks and had long chats and she gave him great advice, and then he missed a couple of months because he was busy with whatever keeps young boys busy; and then the next time he visited, a man in a suit opened the door and asked him what he wanted. When Dennis told him he was here to see Maud, the man gently explained that unfortunately Maud had passed away a few weeks ago.

"Luckily her brother was visiting from London at the time," the man told him, "the funeral was last week, only her brother was there, she kept to herself, didn't really have any friends."

"I was her friend," Dennis told him, and then cycled home with the tears running down his face.

The next Saturday Dennis and his mother walked to the Dudley Cemetery. The grave had no headstone but a man who worked there guided them to it, Dennis placed a small bunch of flowers on the recently disturbed earth and they both stood in awkward silence, until his mother said "I'll meet you by the gates son, you say a few words," with that she walked off. Eventually Dennis spoke in a low quiet voice. "Goodbye Maud, say hello to Ronald and Neville from me." He turned to walk away but then turned back and continued "I'm not going to worry about little things anymore."

They walked home with his mother tightly holding his hand, but just as they turned the corner into their street, Dennis spotted Stinky Blackshaw approaching. He quickly let go of his mum's hand but Stinky had seen it, he smirked and was about to say something when Mrs Bisskit gave him the look and he thought better of it.

CHRISTMAS 1955

Dennis opened the window and stuck his head out, the snow was still falling and it was bitterly cold. He quickly closed the window and walked into the front room. His mother was just placing the best cutlery on top of the best tablecloth. As far as Dennis could recall, the front room was only used for Christmas dinners or if someone visited whom his parents wanted to impress.

"Anything I can do to help, Mum?" he asked. His mum thought for a moment, and replied "It's all in hand Dennis, you can put some more coal on the fire; that will help. I've just got to check the sprouts." With that she left the room. Dennis gulped, he hated sprouts. Once he had mentioned it to his dad, who'd told him everyone hates sprouts and not to worry about it. When he'd asked, "Why do we eat them then?" his father had hesitated and then said "I've no idea, but for some reason women like to cook them and our job is to pretend we like them".

It had already been a great holiday, the previous night, Christmas Eve, the family had sat by the fire listening to music on the radio. Sometimes Grandpa would sing along, but after a couple of glasses of sherry, Mum had to tell him to calm down a bit or the neighbours would be complaining. They reminisced about the year, Dennis had learned something about life and death and not to worry too much. Also he had not only mastered the Bowline, but even Akela had commented upon his new confidence and attitude.

Maud's death seemed to have brought him and his mother a lot closer. His father was still working at the zoo and filling the garden with so much elephant poo that Granddad had searched through the shed until he found his old gas mask. He now wore it every time he visited the garden. Unfortunately, his granddad's budding relationship with Mrs Cruskett had come to nothing. They had joined forces for one Couples' Knobbly Knees Competition, which evidently had been a disaster. Granddad never explained what had happened but just told them that he and Mrs Cruskett got along a lot better when they were not getting along than when they were getting along.

The only person not in a good mood was Gladys, and she never seemed to be in a good mood lately. She had suddenly announced that she intended going to university one day and studying politics. Mum was amazed and told her she would never get a husband if she got too clever, but Gladys said she wasn't bothered and that one day she wanted to be Prime Minister. Laugh, Dennis thought they would never stop, especially when Granddad said, "I wouldn't hold my breath girl, man will walk on the moon before a woman becomes Prime Minister." And as it turned out he was right, by ten years, but that was all in the future.

The grown-ups moved into the lounge room and collapsed, full of turkey and plum pudding. Everyone complimented Mum on the sprouts. If the normal routine was followed, they would listen to the Queen's Speech and then fall asleep.

Dennis had considered building a snowman, but it was even too cold for him. He stood by the fire and told his granddad how on the radio they were already calling it the Big Freeze of 1955. His granddad slowly lit his pipe and then said "Big Freeze! They call this a big freeze; it was colder during the Great Chill of 1949." Dad put down his paper and piped in, "Must admit I felt colder during The Big Wind of 1937, that was really cold". Granddad nearly dropped his pipe in amazement, and spluttered "Big Wind, Big Wind! 1937, that was just a slight breeze compared to The Huge Blizzard of 1899."

Just then Mum raced out of the toilet coughing and shouted at Granddad, "Dad! I've told you before, when you use the toilet, please open the window, I was nearly gassed in there." Granddad looked momentarily guilty but then sarcastically told her, "Well I would, but since it's The Big Freeze of 1955, I didn't want us all to freeze to death." Mom finished coughing and said, "Well I think I'd sooner freeze to death than be gassed thank you very much." You could never win an argument with Granddad and after thinking for a few minutes he suddenly said "Gas! Gas! You call that gas? You should have been in the trenches in 1915…" but before he could say any more, the Queen's Speech started on the radio, and everyone told him to shut up.

Dennis left them to it, he always found the Queen's Speech fairly boring. Anyway he knew they would soon be falling asleep. He assumed Gladys was in her room, sulking and dreaming of becoming Prime Minister. He walked to his room; on the bed were his Christmas presents, a new Meccano Set, a Davy Crockett hat, some mandarins and his favourite, an Eagle Annual featuring Dan Dare. He lay on his bed, stuck his Davy Crockett hat upon his head and opened the book. Life doesn't get much better than this, he thought. He wondered what Secondary School would be like. He was short, ginger haired and had one ear bigger than the other, what could possibly go wrong.

THE SLIGHTLY LATER YEARS

CHAPTER 4

At 8.30 am, on the 1st of September 1956, Dennis Bisskit arrived for his first day at Dudley Secondary Modern School.

For some reason, Dennis had been strangely confident. He felt that he looked very smart in his new uniform. He'd bought himself a new jar of Brylcreem and used about half of it on his hair that morning. He felt that from a certain angle, to a person with really bad eyesight, he looked a bit like a young Cary Grant. He'd even managed to get his mum to not walk him all the way to the school gates, out of fear that she'd give him a good luck kiss in front of his new classmates. He had felt this was a new start, the start of the rest of his life, but his confidence had evaporated the moment he'd entered his new classroom. This was the moment when he realised that being a small, skinny boy, who wore glasses and had one ear bigger than the other, was totally unacceptable in modern society. Big boys would bully him, normal boys shun him, and other small, skinny, bespectacled boys were just happy that someone had finally come along who took the pressure off them, someone who not only looked as unacceptable to modern society as they did, but also had the misfortune to have one ear bigger than the other. They would join in the cruel taunts of "Big Ear", whenever he walked past. That didn't last long though, because apart from everything else Dennis had ginger hair, so of course, once his new teacher Miss Dobson did the roll call, and shouted out "Bisskit", his incredulous classmates could not believe their luck… "Ginger Bisskit," they screamed as one. And so that was it, Ginger Bisskit, for the rest of his school life, apart from the school intellectuals who still called him "Big Ear."

This humiliation continued for some time, until one wonderful day, a new boy started school. A boy who also was small, skinny, wore thick glasses and had one ear bigger than the other, but also, joy of joys, he had a big nose.

It's great to be part of the in crowd, thought Dennis, as he stood amongst his peers and shouted "Big Nose," at the new boy. The new boy's name turned out to be Colin Flounder, and it was possibly the finest moment of Dennis's young life, when one morning, whilst the class was unusually quiet, he suddenly came out with the classic line, he had spent all morning rehearsing, "There's something fishy about Flounder," he blurted out. Dennis had never felt so proud, as he heard the laughter and shouts of "nice one Ginger," and "that's a classic, Ginge."

Of course it couldn't last and unfortunately Flounder turned out to be the best fighter at school, and soon took great pleasure in returning Dennis to his usual position, outside of the in crowd.

It took a total accident to get Dennis accepted by his classmates again. It happened one morning during Mr Dingleberry's geography class. Mr. Dingleberry was an unusual teacher, he rarely spoke, in fact he showed very little interest in teaching at all. He would walk into the classroom, tell everyone to shut up, and proceed to write on the blackboard for about ten minutes, then he would sit down and read the paper, and then at the end of the lesson, he would stand up, point at the blackboard and say, "I'll be asking questions about that next week." Luckily he never did, because apart from the few who were actually interested in geography, most of the others in the class either caught up on some sleep or took advantage of a teacher having their back turned, to fool around.

On this particular morning, a couple of the usual offenders, Stinky Blackshaw and Tommy Atkins, had brought a tennis ball into the class, and proceeded to throw it across the classroom to each other whilst Mr Dingleberry had his back turned. After a while they started getting more daring and bouncing the ball off the walls. Suddenly the ball shot off a wall and headed straight for Dennis. Wow, thought Dennis, this is my big chance at getting back in with the lads. I will do a tremendous catch and flick the ball back to Stinky all in one movement. Unfortunately, Dennis's hand to eye coordination was on a par with the average tree stump and what actually happened was, the tennis ball went straight through his hands, hit him on the forehead and shot into the air towards Mr Dingleberry's back. The whole class held their breath especially Dennis, who had no idea that what would happen next would catapult him into legend status amongst his classmates.

It all seemed to happen in slow motion. The ball headed towards Mr Dingleberry; at the last moment he suddenly decided he had written enough for one day. He turned and saw something headed towards his head. Now, what the class didn't know was that Mr Dingleberry was still suffering the effects of World War Two. If they had known, they probably wouldn't have been so surprised when he shouted, "Grenade, down, down, down", and dived over the top of his desk, knocking himself out when his head hit the floor.

There was complete silence for a moment as everyone stared at their teacher lying prostrate on the floor. Dennis just sat still with his mouth gaping, hoping it was all a nightmare that he would wake from. Then there were whispers of "You've killed him Bisskit", and "You're in big trouble now", mixed with "You're a legend Ginge", "Best thing I've ever seen." No-one knew what to do, but then they heard the lunch bell ringing, so an instant decision seemed to be reached by everyone at the same time. Just carry on and pretend it never happened. They all rushed from the classroom and proceeded to the canteen.

Dennis was in shock, but cheered up slightly when Stinky and some others insisted that he sat and ate lunch with them; he was back in the in-crowd.

There was no sign of Mr Dingleberry when they walked past his room after lunch, and no sign for several days after that. Dennis was beginning to slowly relax and think maybe it would just all be forgotten about. In fact, he was just thinking that at the moment Miss Dobson interrupted his thoughts with the most feared words a schoolboy can ever hear: "Bisskit, report to the headmaster's office".

As soon as Dennis left his classroom, his stomach started playing up, as it always did lately in times of stress. He raced as quickly as he could to the toilet and sat in nervous contemplation. Obviously the game was up, Mr Dingleberry had returned to work, and would be in the headmaster's office, debating just how many strokes of the cane Dennis should receive. So far in his school life Dennis had managed to avoid a caning, but had heard enough tales from others who'd not been so lucky, to know that it was something to be avoided. Evidently Mr Walpole the headmaster relished the opportunity to wield his cane at the slightest excuse. Just last week, Lofty Jennings had received six of the best for breaking wind in the music class and when he'd returned from his thrashing he could barely walk.

Despite his churning stomach, Dennis knew he could put it off no longer, but as he opened the toilet door, he suddenly had an idea. He could see no way of avoiding the cane but at least there was a way of lessoning the pain. He left the toilet and stuck his head in the sports changing rooms and just as he'd hoped, there were the usual amount of forgotten football shorts lying around. He quickly removed his trousers and pulled on as many pairs of shorts as he could find, one on top of the other, then after a great deal of effort he managed to pull his trousers back up. He glanced in the mirror: not too bad, he thought, although it did look like he'd stacked on a bit of weight in the last few minutes. As he turned, he noticed that the cleaner's door had been left open, and there on the table was a copy of the Sunday paper. Even better he thought, as with great difficulty, he managed to wedge the paper down the back of his pants.

It took Dennis a long time to reach the headmaster's office, partly because of fear but mainly because it is difficult to walk wearing five pairs of shorts and a Sunday newspaper under your trousers. Eventually though, after staring at the door for five minutes, he plucked up the courage and knocked.

"Enter!" said a booming voice. Dennis entered. "Bisskit, about time, I was wondering where you'd got to." Dennis who had decided to get his excuses in as soon as possible, shouted "It was a complete accident sir". Mr Walpole looked a bit bemused; "What are you talking about boy?"

"Mr Dingleberry, it was an accident sir," Dennis tried to explain, but the headmaster just waved his hand and said, "Well of course it was, he's told me all about it; he slipped on some water and banged his head, poor man's taken some leave".

Dennis immediately realised what had happened, Mr Dingleberry must have been too embarrassed to say what really happened and had concocted a far less embarrassing story. Dennis had never felt so relieved until he suddenly remembered that he'd still been ordered to see the headmaster.

"I was told you wanted to see me sir," he muttered.

"Yes, quite my boy; I've just got two words to say to you, Bismarck and Monty." The headmaster stared at Dennis, who just stared back completely baffled by this sudden turn of conversation. Dennis also noted that technically Bismarck and Monty were three words, but felt that now was not the time to mention it. Mr Walpole continued "Bisskit Dog Walking Service," and pointed at Dennis, who suddenly realised what he was referring to. He had lately been trying to find an easier way of making a bit of extra pocket money and had thought dog walking might be the answer. He had, a couple of days earlier put a sign advertising his services in the window of the greengrocers.

"Are you saying you want me to walk your dog sir?" he asked. "Well obviously boy, are you deaf?" answered the headmaster, who by now was wondering if it was such a good idea, especially as young Bisskit had seemed to struggle to even walk into his office, so he wasn't sure if he was up to dog walking.

"Actually my wife's dogs, Bismarck and Monty. She's overseas for a few weeks visiting her sister, and I'm far too busy to walk them, so the job could be yours boy. Obviously as your headmaster I would expect a discount."

"Obviously sir," said Dennis, which seemed the correct answer.

Dennis left the headmaster's office and proceeded back towards his classroom. Stinky Blackshaw was the first to spot him and couldn't help but notice how badly Dennis was hobbling.

"Wow, Ginge, that must have been some thrashing, you can hardly walk," he cried in admiration.

"Oh that's just the News of the World, I've got stuffed down my underpants, not to mention the five pairs of shorts," replied Dennis, "anyway I didn't get the cane; in fact he's going to pay me to walk his dogs."

Stinky could not believe it. "Wow, no cane and you're getting money off old Tadpole, I've said it before and I'll say it again Ginge, you are an absolute legend."

CHAPTER 5

ONE MONTH LATER

Dennis turned the knob on his father's radiogram, tuned it to the Light Programme and settled into his armchair. A couple of moments later the unmistakable sounds of the Victor Sylvester orchestra filled the room. "Brilliant", said Dennis to himself, "you can't beat a bit of Victor." He tapped his feet as he admired the gleaming radiogram, it was his father's pride and joy. On many Sundays, his father would gather the family together in the dining room, and put on his long playing record of Sir Winston Churchill's greatest war speeches. Sometimes he would have tears in his eyes as he stood at the end of the record and saluted, muttering "For the dead". He would then rub the brown ale bottle scar on his forehead and add, "And those who suffered."

Dennis was suddenly reminded of a strange incident that had happened a couple of weeks earlier. He had been sitting in this same spot, when his elder sister Gladys had slowly entered the room with her hands behind her back. She had glanced furtively around and then asked if the house was empty. When Dennis had replied in the affirmative, she had said, "You must listen to this" and produced a record from behind her back. As she placed it on the player, she explained that it was some Yankee chap, Elvis Parsley or something and evidently all the young kids were listening to him. Dennis had explained that he was young and he'd never heard of him, and then this terrible noise had come from father's radiogram.

"For God sake get that off" he'd shouted, "if father came home and heard that noise coming from the same speaker that Sir Winston comes out of, he'd never forgive you. It's terrible," he'd added. Gladys had just stared at him and shaken her head and then had the audacity to accuse him of knowing nothing about music. "May I remind you", he had reminded her, "I was a founding member of the Billy Cotton Band Show fan club, and I think I can say with great confidence that six months from now, no-one will have heard of this Elvis chap."

Dennis still couldn't believe it; fancy accusing me, of all people, of knowing nothing about music. Anyway, time to walk some dogs he thought as he glanced at the old grandfather clock in the hallway.

Dennis gave a low whistle; the headmaster's two dogs obediently trotted alongside him as he opened the garden gate and stepped out onto the pavement. A tall man wearing a heavy raincoat and carrying a suitcase approached him.

"Excuse me," the stranger asked, "do you know the way to Millington Street?" Dennis shook his head, "Sorry I've no idea," he replied. The tall man pointed down the road and told him "If you go down there about half a mile, turn left and then first right, it's the first road on your left." Dennis thanked him and the man walked off. Dennis watched him for a while, thinking how strange it was, wearing a heavy raincoat on a nice day like this.

His mother had come up with the idea, she'd said it was a good way to make some pocket money and she'd been correct. He'd always loved dogs and if people were willing to pay him to walk them, so much the better. The headmaster's dogs were very well behaved, even if they did make a strange sight. On the end of the leash in Dennis's left hand was the greatest Great Dane he had ever seen, Monty was nearly as tall as he was. Although to be honest, Dennis was never going to get a game in a basketball team. On the end of the leash in his right hand was a miniature dachshund called Bismarck. It was not much bigger than a cat.

He stopped at the base of a tall tree. Bismarck lifted his back leg and a small puddle appeared on the ground. Monty trotted alongside his little friend, raised his own leg and a puddle appeared on Bismarck's head.

They walked to the park. The warm sun was making Dennis a bit tired, so he found a park bench, tied the dogs securely to the back of it and sat down to enjoy the tranquillity. An old man slowly hobbled past him, his walking stick tapping the ground. Watching him reminded Dennis of his own sore back, he felt embarrassed even thinking about it.

Dennis had always been a bit on the short side. Whenever he complained, his mother would remind him that good things come in little packages, but this did little to impress Dennis, and he spent most of his time trying to make himself appear taller. At the moment he was wearing shoes with six-inch extensions glued to the bottom. His granddad, who was very clever with his hands, in fact occasionally a lot cleverer with his hands than he was with his head, had made them for Dennis. He had glued some thick rubber to the base of the shoes, it worked quite well, although Dennis was careful not to break into a trot whilst wearing them because of a tendency to start bouncing. He wore a pair of baggy trousers, several sizes too large with his shoes, that way, the trousers practically reached the ground and at first glance he looked like an average-sized lad. The only problem was that he tended to walk in a bit of an unusual bouncy manner.

Dennis, ruefully rubbed his back, which was still sore after his latest attempt to gain height. For some time now, he had taken to hanging from tree branches as often as he could. He had read somewhere that doing this for as long as you could, with your arms outstretched and your feet not touching the ground, would stretch the spine and gradually increase your height.

One evening after his father had gone off to the pub with granddad, and his mother had gone to Bingo, Dennis suddenly had a brainwave. All this hanging from a tree branch did not seem to be having the desired effect; obviously what was missing was a bit of weight attached to the ankles, this would almost certainly stretch the spine. His father had been busy building a retaining wall in the back garden, in fact he'd been busy building it for about the last decade, he didn't like to rush into these things. Dennis carried four house bricks into the lounge, then found a couple of his mother's carrier bags and put two bricks into each bag. All I have to do is tie a bag to each ankle and we're laughing, he thought.

Of course the next problem was the lack of a tree branch in the house, to hang from. As he looked about him, he suddenly looked up and spotted the trapdoor into the attic. He dragged a table across the room until it was underneath the trapdoor, placed a chair in the middle of the table, and climbed on to it. Reaching up he pushed the trapdoor open a few inches and wedged a book under one corner, then gripping the edge of the opening with his outstretched hands, he lifted his feet off the chair to test it out. Perfect, he thought, now let's add a bit of weight. He dropped down to the floor, and lifted the bags onto the table, then he climbed back up, sat on the wobbly chair and, using some rope, tied a bag to each ankle. He stood and slowly turned to face the chair. With great difficulty, he lifted his right leg and bag up onto the chair, then with all his strength, he pushed up, lifting his left leg and attached bag, and slowly stood up to his full height. By now the chair was shaking about violently on the wobbly table. He slid his fingers over the edge of the attic entrance, got a good grip with both hands, took a deep breath and lifted his feet off the chair.

"Aagh!" screamed Dennis, as the pain shot up his body from his toes to his scalp. "I must be about a foot longer already," he muttered between clenched teeth. He held on for several minutes but could take the pain no longer and was just about to lower himself to the chair, when all of a sudden there was a loud crash from above. As if he wasn't already in enough pain, he suddenly felt great pain in his hands. He glanced up and realised the trapdoor had fallen, trapping his hands. As he lashed out with his feet, one of the bags struck the chair sending it flying across the room. His baggy pants fell down to his ankles, revealing his Victor Sylvester Midlands Tour of 1956 souvenir Y-fronts.

The pain was so intense that Dennis started to feel faint. His last thought was how unusual it would be for him to be found dead, seven feet long with a bag of house bricks attached to each leg. Then everything went black.

The next thing he remembered was waking up in his bed, in great pain. Dr Jackson was asking Dennis's mother, if he did this sort of thing very often.

If the pain was great, the humiliation was even greater. Only extreme good fortune had saved Dennis from being stretched to death.

His mother had, as usual, gone to Bingo with her friends, Doris and Bert Longbottom. Unfortunately for them, they had been forced to return home, when they discovered that the Bingo Hall, had been converted into a Lebanese restaurant since they had been there a week earlier. Luckily, Dennis's mother had invited her friends in for a cuppa, and as they opened the front door, they were immediately met by the most bloodcurdling scream they had ever heard. They followed the direction of the sound, and entered the lounge. The sight that confronted them was so shocking that Mrs Longbottom had immediately fainted. She was placed in an armchair, whilst Mr Longbottom and Dennis's mother had somehow managed to get Dennis down onto the floor. It was going to take a very long time to live this down, in fact his mother, just that morning had mentioned that even now Mrs Longbottom had to turn the radio off every time Victor Sylvester came on.

"Your little dog just ran off with my dog." Dennis's daydreaming was interrupted by a strange voice. He looked up to see a hugely overweight man, with a knotted handkerchief on his head. He was carrying two bags of shopping and was dripping with sweat.

"You there, your dog just ran off with Custer." Dennis suddenly realised the man was talking to him, he looked behind him and on the end of the one dog leash, a Great Dane was happily snoring away, and on the end of the other leash was…nothing.

"Aagh!" screamed Dennis for the second time in recent days. They looked anxiously about the park; about 50 yards away from them, there was a sudden commotion in the bushes. A black Labrador shot out of a bush as if fired from a cannon.

"Custer," yelled the large man and ran off, great waves of fat vibrating up and down his wobbling body.

As he disappeared over the horizon, he was clutching his chest and sweat was flying off him in all directions. Dennis would have raced off after him, but Monty had decided he was very happy where he was and if a Great Dane is happy where he is, then there is no moving him. Dennis carefully checked to see that Monty was very securely tied to the bench, and only then took off to join the dog hunt.

It took Dennis twenty minutes of searching before he spotted young Bismarck. In the middle of the park was a lake, and in the middle of the lake was a small island and in the middle of the island sat a small, bedraggled dachshund. The only way to reach the island was across several strategically placed stepping stones.

With great difficulty, Dennis made his way across the stones. With his built-up shoes and baggy pants, he nearly slipped on several occasions. Eventually he made it safely to the island. Bismarck trotted over, he looked a bit the worse for wear and waited for Dennis to pick him up, so that he could show his appreciation by slobbering all over his face.

Crossing back was even more difficult as he now had his hands full with the bedraggled dog, and the stepping stones were quite slippery. About halfway across he misjudged a step and his right leg went into the water, which came up past his knee. He tried to pull his leg out but his foot was stuck fast in the thick mud at the bottom of the lake.

"Great, that's just great" muttered Dennis to no one in particular. He pulled with all his might and suddenly his leg came free. As he struggled to maintain his balance, he realised to his horror that his shoe was missing. He bent down and felt around in the dirty water, but eventually was forced to admit defeat and continued hobbling across the stepping stones. This was not easy, with one leg six inches shorter than the other leg. As he stood on dry land, wishing he'd just stayed in bed that day, a black Labrador trotted past him followed a few moments later by the overweight man who looked close to death.

Dennis was close to tears.

"Look at that," he said, pointing at his remaining shoe. "I had it especially constructed, they are very hard to get," he continued. "Is that why you only bought the one?" spluttered the man as he staggered past.

Dennis's mother was just pouring Mr and Mrs Longbottom a cup of tea when he burst into the room. Mrs Longbottom immediately grabbed the crucifix around her neck and made the sign of the cross.

"Never again," shouted Dennis, "you see this," he held up a shoe with a six-inch rubber sole. "There's another one just like it at the bottom of the lake."

"Yes, it's amazing what you can find in the lake" answered Mr Longbottom over the top of his cup. Dennis stormed out of the room, slamming the door behind him.

"Are you sure Dr Jackson said he's okay?" asked Mrs L, "They can do great things with electric shock treatment nowadays."

"Oh no, no, no," said Dennis's mother, "he's just at that funny age. Another scone, anybody?"

CHAPTER 6

For some reason, especially on his birthday, or if they had visitors or even if she could drag some passer-by in off the street, Dennis's mother loved to get the photographs out. His father was an avid photographer, never without his trusty Kodak Brownie 127 camera. Unfortunately for Dennis, his father always seemed to be there at the wrong moment. On many occasions Dennis would enter the room just in time to see his mother showing some total stranger a photograph and saying, "This is when Dennis accidentally sat on some nettles, that's my hand applying some lotion to his bum," or "that's his first day at school, look at the huge boil that came up on his nose." As if all that wasn't bad enough, she would next proudly show them Dennis on the front page of the newspaper having been rescued from a roof by the fire brigade. His now best friend Stinky Blackshaw told him that this was perfectly normal, his mother was just the same and he felt that humiliating their children was just something that mothers enjoyed doing. Dennis managed to avoid photos and any embarrassing situations for some time until one day in 1958 he managed to outdo himself. An event occurred that put all the previous embarrassing situations in the shade. For many years afterwards his mother didn't need to get the humiliating photographs out, she would just have to say. "Did you hear about..."

AUGUST 1958...

Dennis read the story again just to be certain he hadn't misunderstood. But no! It was all there in black and white.

"I don't believe it," he muttered. His mother looked up from her ironing and said, "What Dennis, what don't you believe?", but Dennis just shook his head and dropped the newspaper on the floor.

"How could it possibly happen," he said. Mrs Bisskit put down the iron and turned to Dennis, "What Dennis, what are you talking about?" but Dennis was already striding out of the room.

"Oh no, I'm not putting up with this, this just isn't good enough, I'm going to have to see Stinky about this," was all Mrs Bisskit heard before the front door slammed and Dennis was gone. Mrs B looked at the iron, shook her head and said "I'll never understand that boy." The iron made no comment.

Stinky slurped down his milkshake, placed the empty glass upon the table, looked up at Dennis, and said "Yes, I'm sure it's all very sad Ginge, but what can we do about it?" Dennis sighed, sometimes it concerned him that other people didn't seem as patriotic as he was. The country was changing. Only the other day he'd had an argument with Shorty Pankhurst at school about this new American, so-called Rocking Roll music. Evidently Victor Sylvester and the old big bands were finished and this new Rocking Roll music was taking over. Well, "Not in my house Shorty", Dennis had told him. "I shall remain loyal whatever happens." He wiped some chocolate milk from his chin and explained to Stinky.

"In 1954, you will recall that Roger Bannister, in a great day for the nation, did the impossible and broke the four-minute mile." Stinky interrupted him, "Well obviously it couldn't have been impossible if he did it," Dennis shook his head, and said, "Okay but the point is, it was thought to be impossible, but he did it Stinky, and do you remember what joy it bought to the nation?" Stinky actually couldn't but knew that once Dennis was off on one of his rants it was best just to let him get on with it.

"And then," Dennis continued, "you will recall the terrible sadness that overcame the nation when that colonial bloke from Australia did an even better time." Stinky could recall no such thing but nodded his head in agreement and said

"It was terrible Ginge, I could not sleep for days; I was so overcome with sadness."

"As were we all," Dennis told him, "and then remember the sheer joy when that great runner Derek Ibbotson took the record back; Britain ruled the waves again Stinky." Stinky nodded and said "Who could forget the joy?" hoping that Dennis would hurry up and get to the point. Dennis held up the newspaper and said, "Now they have done it again, another colonial, Herb Elliot has broken the record, something has got to be done." Stinky frowned and muttered, "I don't know how these Australians do it. If you look at a globe, they're at the bottom of the world. How come they don't fall off?" Dennis was quiet for a moment and then replied, "That's a good point Stinky. Maybe that's why they run so quickly, it stops them falling off the planet. Anyway, the point is, we have to get that record back for the sake of the country."

"Well I can't see what we can do," Stinky told him. "I'm a hopeless runner and you're even worse than me."

Dennis started to say something but Stinky continued, "I'm sorry Ginge, but you just have no coordination, I've seen you try and head the ball and it's hit your knee. No offence."

"None taken," Dennis assured him, "training, that's what it's all about. I am going to train every day for a month, that should be more than enough time, and then I am going to get that record back for Great Britain, what do you think of that Stinky?" Stinky did not know what to think, but was more concerned about what his part in the scheme was.

"Sounds like a good plan Ginge, but what do I have to do?" he reluctantly asked.

"Well obviously you're my trainer Stinky, you have to hold the stopwatch," Dennis replied. A greatly relieved Stinky smiled and said "Sounds difficult but I think I can manage that,"

The following evening after school, Dennis changed into his shorts and plimsolls and met Stinky on the sports field. Dennis handed Stinky his father's old stopwatch, it had been lying in the bottom of a wardrobe for years but still appeared to be in working order.

"Okay," he said to his friend, "One circuit of the sports field is 400 yards, so four times around is the mile." Dennis took a couple of deep breaths, as he'd seen Roger Bannister do prior to races and then continued, "It's my first training run, so I'll be happy with any time under five minutes, no doubt I will gradually improve as we go along."

Stinky, didn't bother replying as he had grave doubts about Dennis even being able to run 400 yards but didn't want to dampen his friend's enthusiasm. He set the stop watch to zero, counted down 3…2…1 and in the absence of a starting pistol, shouted "BANG!" at the same time pressing the start button on the watch. To Stinky's surprise Dennis set off at quite a good pace, his spindly, white legs almost a blur as he raced off around the track, but after about 200 yards, he started to slow down; as he reached the 300-yard bend he was almost walking and Stinky could hear his gasps for breath even from where he stood at the 400-yard line. As he got closer, Dennis stopped to a slow shuffle and as he reached Stinky he collapsed in a heap onto the field. Stinky pressed the stop button on the watch. It took Dennis several minutes before he could speak, then he gasped "t.t.t...time Stinky, what t-t-t-time did I d-d-d-d do?" Stinky checked the watch and told him, "Three minutes, 52 seconds Ginge." Dennis couldn't believe his ears.

"Three minutes, 52 seconds," he repeated, "You mean I've broke the world record on my first training run?" For a second, Dennis was disappointed that no one had been here to congratulate him, but then Stinky said, "No, that's not the mile time, that's the 400-yard time, so, let's see," Stinky counted on his fingers, muttering to himself for a few minutes before continuing, "I think that would be just over fifteen and a half minutes for the mile." Dennis rolled over onto his back and said "Well, that can't be right, the watch must be broke."

"I certainly hope so," said Stinky, "my tortoise Apollo could probably run a mile quicker than that." Dennis slowly climbed to his feet.

"The main thing is," he gasped, "that's very impressive for a first attempt." He limped off rubbing the back of his leg and then turned and shouted, "Same time tomorrow Stinky." Stinky smiled, that was one of the things he liked best about Ginge, nothing ever got him down, he always assumed that things would be better next time.

By the end of the week, Dennis had completed his first mile, in 13 minutes and 35 seconds.

"Not bad," Stinky told him, "knock another nine and a half minutes off that and you'll be getting close," he added sarcastically. But sarcasm was wasted on Dennis.

"The point is Stinky, as I'm sure you will agree. I work best when the pressure is on. I will be happy if I can get under ten minutes in training, because I know that on the day, with the eyes of the world upon me, and the hopes of the nation pushing me along, I will beat that world record and put the Great back into Great Britain," Dennis actually stood to attention as he made this speech and even Stinky felt mildly inspired.

"Well my old mate, I'll assist you in any way I can," he told Dennis, who smiled and said, "I know I can always depend on you Stinky."

After three weeks of training Dennis was running the mile in under eleven minutes and feeling much fitter. Until the race was run and the world record back where it belonged, Dennis had decided to make the supreme sacrifice and give up all lollies, even sherbet dips, which were his favourite. After some early scepticism, his family had agreed to be there at the finishing line to cheer him on, except for Gladys who told him she had better things to do with her life than watch him make a fool of himself. Dennis got in touch with Mr Dimple, the reporter at the local newspaper. He was the chap who had written the article about the Fire Brigade having to rescue Dennis from the rooftop some years earlier and sensing another humiliating headline, he immediately agreed to be there with his camera.

"You will not want to miss this historic event," Dennis told him, and he agreed that he definitely wouldn't. When Dennis came home and mentioned that a reporter would be there with his camera on the big day, Gladys immediately said nothing would stop her being there to support her beloved brother, just as long as she could get her hair done the day before he ran.

Dennis stared at the calendar on the back of the door. He had drawn a big circle around September the 10th. Only five days to go, he thought. The evening before had been a turning point. Out of the blue, he had run a mile in under ten minutes, only by a few seconds, but still it had filled Dennis with great confidence. His mother walked past and Dennis said "Just think Mum, five days from now you will be the mother of a world record holder." Mrs B smiled and said "I'm sure you will do your best, son, but don't get too disappointed if you miss out." Dennis looked surprised, "Well," he told her, "with the amount of training and planning I've done I can't see how anything can possibly go wrong Mum,", but she seemed to recall hearing that comment several times over the years, usually prior to something going very wrong.

On Thursday September the 8th, Stinky was at school kicking a ball against a wall during morning break, when he suddenly spotted Dennis striding towards him, not looking too happy.

"Disaster, Stinky." he said, "There's been an absolute disaster." He proceeded to explain that he'd been ordered to report to Mr Divitt the Sports Master, who'd told him that unfortunately the sports field could not be used this weekend as new turf was being laid. Stinky groaned and said "Did you explain about the world record and the eyes of the world being upon you?"

"Of course I did," Dennis replied, "he told me to go away before he hit me with a plimsoll."

"Well that's it then," said Stinky, "you'll have to call the run off," but Dennis was adamant that the run had to take place as scheduled.

"It's the training," he told Stinky, "all my training has been planned to peak this Saturday; anyway Mr Dimple from The Dudley News is going on his holidays next Monday." He thought for a moment and then said, "Don't worry Stinky, I will just sort something out." He turned and walked off, as usual leaving Stinky admiring his optimism.

FRIDAY 9th.

Stinky was lost for words for some time but finally said "It seems a bit vague Ginge, are you sure The World Athletic Association will recognise it?" Dennis just nodded and said, "Well, I can't see any reason why not, a mile is a mile, surely it doesn't matter where you run it." Stinky was quiet for a moment and then asked Dennis to run the route past him again.

"From my front gate, up Castle Street, across the road to the zoo grounds, follow the track that runs next to the zoo for about half a mile, turn right, down a little lane about 100 yards and then turn right and back into town along Trindle Road, behind the bus station and back to my front gate."

"Yes," Stinky said, "but how do you know it's exactly a mile?" Dennis smiled and told him, "Granddad and I measured the route last night in his van; of course we couldn't take his van on the zoo grounds so we measured that part with Mum's tape measure; it was hard work, Granddad's still got a bad back this morning."

"Well they can't argue with that," Stinky replied, "as long as you got your measurements right."

"No problems there." Dennis told him, "In fact to be exact it's one mile and two inches to the front gate so if I only equal the world record, I will be able to say that I ran an extra couple of inches." As usual Stinky looked troubled but before he could say anything Dennis told him confidently "We are all set, Stinky, the world record awaits. I will see you in the morning, don't forget the stopwatch."

THE BIG DAY… 9.55am SATURDAY 10th.

Dennis stood by the starting line, a line of chalk on the pavement next to his front gate. He was wearing a white school vest, his blue football shorts and plimsolls. Mr Dimple lifted the large camera and shouted, "Smile Dennis". Dennis not only gave a big smile but stuck his two fingers up in a confident victory salute. At the last second a recently coiffured Gladys, wearing a new dress, stepped behind Dennis, ensuring that she would also be in the photograph when it appeared in the Dudley Times. She would later come to regret this, nearly as much as Dennis, but obviously not as much as he regretted the other photograph that would appear next to it.

Stinky stood next to the starting line with the stopwatch poised in his hand, nearby were The Bisskits, Mr Dimple and even a couple of neighbours who had come out to see what all the fuss was about. Dennis took a deep breath and shivered in the cold morning air. Mrs Bisskit turned to her father-in-law and said "How can a boy that eats so much be so skinny?"

"He's got lucky legs," Granddad told her.

"Do you think so?" said Mrs B.

"Yes," Granddad answered.

"Lucky they don't snap off at the knees," Stinky said, "good luck Ginge, get that world record for Great Britain," and then, in the absence of a starting pistol, shouted, "3…2…1…GO!" at the same time pushing the start button on the watch.

Everyone cheered as Dennis took off at tremendous speed.

"Wow," Stinky shouted, "I've never seen him run so fast." They watched him disappear up Castle Street until he went out of sight.

Some runners start off steadily to conserve their energy, but Dennis had decided the only way to beat the record was just to blank everything else out of his mind and run as quickly as he could from start to finish. Thankfully, Castle St. was fairly quiet, but then a car slowed down beside him and Mr Turret from the greengrocers shouted, "Where are you running Dennis, did you need a lift?" Dennis didn't even glance at him, he just waved him away. A bit further along, an elderly lady came out of her house carrying two large boxes, one on top of the other. Just as Dennis neared her, the top box started to slide off.

"Can you help me lad?" she shouted but Dennis never faltered, he just raced past her, hearing a large crash seconds later. As he neared the end of the street, he was pleased to see PC Pratt, his father's friend, standing near the road as he'd promised. As he saw Dennis approaching, he stepped into the middle of the road and held up his hand, stopping a car, and waving Dennis through.

"Good luck Dennis," he shouted, but Dennis completely ignored him, nothing would distract him from his mission.

Dennis raced along the track next to the zoo grounds, a few people passed by and said "Good Morning" to him, but he barely noticed, "Keep going, keep going," he muttered to himself. He came to the gap in the trees and turned right, he knew that this was nearly halfway on his run. He deliberately hadn't worn his watch because he thought it may distract him, but he estimated that he'd been running about one and a half minutes and was well inside World Record time.

Stinky was getting a stiff neck from looking up the street and then down at the stopwatch. He looked up again but there was no sign of his friend. "Three minutes, 55 seconds," he shouted, "56, 57, 58, 59, four minutes, I'm afraid he never made it."

"Well that was a waste of four minutes of my life," shouted Gladys as she turned and marched back into the house. Mrs Bisskit tutted and said "We better wait for him; he'll be disappointed."

Dennis sprinted down the narrow lane about one hundred yards and then turned right onto Trindle Road; he ran past the packed houses, someone waved but he ignored them, "Keep going, keep going," he gasped, now feeling a little bit tired. Suddenly he spotted someone in the middle of the road about fifty yards in front of him. As he got closer he saw a workman holding up a sign, beyond him he could see more men dragging barriers across the road. He could now see water shooting high into the air, then he saw what was written on the sign the man was holding "ROAD CLOSED".

Dennis kept running at top speed and as he got close to the man, he shouted "I'm trying for the World Record, let me through," but the man held up his hand and said "I don't care what you're doing, we have a burst water main, you will...," but by then Dennis had raced past him. He ran towards the barriers but another burly workman walked towards him and shouted, "You can't come through, go back." Dennis was devastated but at the last second spotted a narrow alleyway between the houses on his left. Without slowing he raced down the alleyway, he desperately looked about him, hoping to spot some way of getting back onto Trindle Road, this would cost him a few seconds, so he hoped he was still on World Record time.

"Eight minutes," Stinky muttered, "I really thought he would do better than this." The neighbours had already gone home. Mr Dimple yawned and said "Well, that was fun but I must get back to work." Mr and Mrs Bisskit turned and looked at Granddad and Mrs B said "Time for a nice cup of tea." They wandered off into the house. Stinky suddenly realised he was alone and said "Well, I'll just stay here on my own then," to no one in particular.

Dennis couldn't believe it, he had run several hundred yards and could find no way to get back towards town, in fact the lane he had got onto seemed to be curving away from town. He started to slow down, eventually to a jog and then a walk and finally he stood still in the middle of the lane, he leaned down with his hands on his knees gasping for air. It slowly dawned upon him that the record attempt was a failure. He straightened up with sweat dripping off the end of his nose. Then it started to pour down with rain. Dennis looked up at the sky with his hands on his hips and said "Oh that's just great, wonderful, thank you very much for that, that's just all I needed."

Stinky looked at the stopwatch, fifteen minutes had passed, he pushed the stop button, thinking whenever Dennis finally got home he's not going to be too interested in his time. He walked into the Bisskits' house, they were drinking mugs of tea and eating cake.
"Here's your stopwatch Mr Bisskit," he said, "I don't think we will be needing it anymore." Mr Bisskit

thanked him and took the watch. Nobody spoke and then Mrs Bisskit noticed Stinky staring at her fruit cake. "Would you be interested in a piece of cake, Jack?" she asked. She was the only person he knew who refused to call him Stinky.

"Oh, I would love a piece Mrs B." he replied with a big smile on his face.

Dennis slowly walked down the road. He had no idea where he was, but felt that he must reach a main road soon. The rain still came down, his vest and shorts were dripping wet and he was starting to feel very cold and miserable. Just then he heard a sound behind him and a small car approached moving very slowly. It pulled up alongside him and he saw that an elderly lady wearing glasses sat in the driver's seat. He waved and after a few seconds, the window wound down a couple of inches.

The lady leaned towards the window and in a stern voice said "You, boy, what are you doing walking in the rain in your underwear?" Dennis sighed and replied, "I was trying for the World record, I'm afraid I failed," The lady just stared for a moment and then said, "I didn't even know there was a World Record for walking in the rain in your underwear."

Dennis tried to raise enough energy to explain but before he could she told him he had better get in the car before he caught his death of cold. Dennis tried to shake as much excess water off himself as he could before he climbed into the passenger seat. He immediately felt a bit warmer. The lady stared at him in fascination as if he'd come from another planet, so he held out his hand and said "This is very kind of you, my name's Dennis, Dennis Bisskit." She looked at his wet hand and just shook the tip of one of his fingers and said "Doris Darcy-Mandeville," and then added, "You may know the name". Dennis shook his head. "The Sutton Coldfield Darcy-Mandevilles." Dennis shook his head again.

"Purveyors of the finest cheeses." Dennis again shook his head, she looked surprised that there was someone on the planet who didn't know her family name but reached behind her and pulled out a blanket.

"You'd better wrap this around yourself," she told him, and then explained that she was driving into town if he wanted a lift. Dennis thanked her and said that would be wonderful.

After Stinky picked up his third slice of cake and quickly began devouring it, Mrs Bisskit picked up what was left on the plate and took it away. Stinky stood up and said "Well, I'll be off." Then he stopped and added, "Where do you think Dennis has got to?"

"Oh you know what he's like," Granddad said, "He probably got halfway, stopped to chat to someone and forgot all about the run." They all laughed and Stinky walked off home, kicking a stone along the road.

Dennis listened to Mrs Darcy-Mandeville humming a tuneless tune. He pulled the blanket over his head, it smelt doggy. He suddenly realised how tired he was; his legs were aching. The warmth of the car made him feel sleepy, he closed his eyes. It only felt like seconds later that he opened them again and had to think where he was for a moment. He peeled the blanket back from his eyes, he was on a busy road, looking around he noticed how many houses there were. He suddenly recognised where they were.

"This is Birmingham!" he shouted. Mrs Darcy-Mandeville nodded and said "Well, of course it is, where did you think it would be, New York?" Dennis couldn't believe it, "But you said you were going into town, I

88

assumed you meant Dudley." She looked surprised and said "Dudley, why would anyone go to Dudley?" Dennis felt like crying.

"But Birmingham's not even a town, it's a city," he told her, but she just smiled and said "I've lived here for over 70 years, it will always be a town to me."

Mrs Bisskit peeled the potatoes; every now and again she looked over her shoulder and could see the two men shuffling around and glancing at the clock. Eventually she decided to put them out of their misery. She wiped her hands on the towel, turned and said "Well, I suppose you two will want to get down the pub." They gave her a surprised look as if it was the last thing on their mind and then Granddad said "Oh! I suppose we could pop down for a half," They quickly left before she changed her mind.

"And make sure it is just a half," Mrs B shouted after them.

Dennis waited near the Birmingham Railway Station ticket office as she went to buy him a ticket back to Dudley. Mrs Darcy-Mandeville had turned out to be a saint. As soon as she saw how upset he was, she had immediately told him that she would lend him the money to get the train back home. Not only that but when she saw him shivering on getting out of her car, she had opened the car boot and bought out a brown work jacket of her husband's.

"He's got plenty," she had told him, "he won't miss this one for a few days." It was a brown jacket with DARCY-NEVILLE FINEST MAD CHEESES printed on the pocket, evidently due to a printing error. It was several sizes too large for Dennis and came down to his knees covering his shorts, so that it looked like he was just wearing a huge jacket and plimsolls. Still at least he was warm now. She passed him the ticket and said "Platform 2 in 10 minutes," "You're a lifesaver Doris," he said, "I'll post the jacket and the money back as soon as I get home," She hesitated then gave him an embarrassing hug and left.

Birmingham Station was the biggest railway station Dennis had ever been to. He walked down a tunnel and then spotted a sign pointing left to Platform 1 and right to Platform 2.

"What platform did she say?" Dennis muttered, then he heard a train arriving on Platform 1. "That will be it," he said and ran down the tunnel to Platform 1.

"I think we have time for another quick one," said Granddad to his son, and then added, "I wonder if Dennis has finally finished his mile yet." They both chuckled.

Stinky lay on his bed reading a comic. He looked up at the clock and thought, "I suppose Dennis will be at home feeling a bit upset about not beating the record. I won't disturb him."

Mrs B put down her knitting and glanced at her watch.

"I suppose Dennis has gone around to Stinky's house to discuss where they went wrong," she said to herself, and then suddenly realised she had called him Stinky. After sitting next to him whilst he was eating cake she now knew where he'd got the nickname.

Dennis raced down the tunnel and onto the platform; the train had come to a standstill. Several people were already climbing on board, so he followed, found himself somewhere quiet to sit and collapsed into his seat. After a few minutes a whistle blew and the train pulled slowly out of the station. He couldn't wait to get back home and put this day behind him, he never wanted to hear about the world record again. He felt bad that no doubt everyone was still standing by the finishing line waiting for him to appear. Looking up he noticed that several people were staring at him, he self-consciously pulled the jacket down over his knees and then decided to pretend he was sleeping, he leaned back against the seat and closed his eyes and before long he didn't have to pretend.

Mrs Bisskit stood with her hands on her hips waiting for her husband George to speak. As soon as they had staggered in, Granddad had raced to the toilet. George wobbled slightly and said, "Dad bought me a half, and we drank that and I said we must go home and he agreed that we must," he paused for a moment and then continued, "then just as we were leaving, I suddenly thought, it's just not fair, Dad's bought me a half, so really I should buy him a half, so we discussed it and I bought us another half, I think you would agree I did the right thing there Edith.," Mrs B didn't seem to be agreeing so he continued, "Then, just as we were leaving again Piggy Jenkinson walked in and he looked upset so I said 'What's wrong Piggy?' and he said 'My Aunty May in New Zealand has passed away,' and he looked so upset that we thought we better have a drink with him." He sat down in the armchair and said "I think you will agree I did the right thing."

Mrs Bisskit thought about it but before she could answer he was snoring. As she stood there, Granddad slowly entered the room, saw George sleeping and started giggling. He pointed at him and said "He, he, he, him there, did he tell you about Piggy Jenkinson?" She sighed and said "I've heard all about it, his Aunty died."

Granddad looked surprised and said "Did she, that's strange, Piggy never mentioned it in the pub when he was buying us pints from his big win in the betting shop." Mrs B just shook her head and told him to go and have a lie down. She looked at the clock again and thought, I'll give it another half an hour and then I better go around to Stinky's house to see if Dennis has recovered from his run.

Dennis sprinted down Castle Street, it seemed as if the entire population of Dudley had come out to support him, the crowds cheered wildly as he approached the finishing line. Stinky held up the stopwatch and shouted, "Come on Ginge, come on." He crossed the line and his family all hugged him.

"I can't believe it," Stinky said, "52 seconds for the mile, you've beaten the world record by over three minutes. The crowd started chanting "Bisskit! Bisskit," but then it seemed to change to "Ticket! Ticket!" Dennis opened his eyes, a huge red-faced man in uniform was staring down at him.

"Come on lad, I haven't got all day, where's your ticket?" he demanded. Dennis reached into the jacket pocket and brought out his crumpled ticket. The man stared at it and then said "What's this?" Dennis wasn't sure if it was a trick question, so said "It's a train ticket."

The man looked him up and down and said "Where's your trousers?" Dennis lifted the bottom of the jacket to show he was wearing shorts. The man grunted and said "You might think you're clever wearing your beatnik clothing and your ticket to Dudley but as it happens this train is going to Coventry; I'm going to need your name and address," Dennis couldn't believe it, he must have got on the wrong train; now what was he going to do? The ticket collector wrote down his details and said "Just sit there and you can get off in Coventry, but any more of your hooligan behaviour and I will stop the train and kick you off." Dennis wanted to protest but everyone was staring at him so he closed his eyes again and hoped that when he opened them he would find it was just a nightmare.

George woke up with a throbbing head, got himself a cup of water and then asked, "Any sign of Dennis yet?"

"No," replied his wife, "I'm getting a bit worried. What if he's been kidnapped?" Gladys walked in and said "If he has been kidnapped, can I have his room? It's better than mine." Granddad had walked in behind her and added "Maybe the Russians have kidnapped him, you know what them Communists are like, they do strange experiments. I was reading where they taught a monkey how to ride a bicycle." George laughed and said "That's ridiculous Dad, anyway what would be the point? Dennis can already ride a bicycle." He could see that his wife was still concerned so added "You know what him and Stinky are like, they lose track of time. One thing's for sure, he'll be home in an hour, he never misses his tea".

Dennis sat on a park bench outside Coventry Railway Station. He had only been to Coventry once in his life, all he could remember about it was it had a big cathedral and was about 35 miles from Dudley. It's amazing, he thought, I started out to run a mile and now I've travelled 35 miles. He looked around, it was quiet now, Saturday afternoon so the shops were closed and people had gone home. There were no more trains to Birmingham or Dudley until tomorrow morning, not that he had any money to get a ticket. Also his legs were cold and he was hungry and thirsty. He felt despondent; this is the worst day of my life, he muttered. Then he stood up and walked down the road, hoping to come up with some sort of plan.

After walking for about ten minutes, he came to a crossroad; he looked up and saw a road sign, BIRMINGHAM 20 MILES. He stood for a moment and then made up his mind and strode off towards Birmingham. After walking about a mile, he found he was in an industrial area. Up ahead of him he saw a large van parked by the side of the road; one of its rear doors was open. As he got closer a man came out of a nearby building grabbed a box from the back of the van and then carried it back to the building.

Dennis nearly burst out laughing when he saw what was written on the van door. DUDLEY TRACTORS, he knew it well, it was a big business on the edge of town that sold farming equipment. He ran towards the van, sure that the man would give him a lift back to Dudley, but as he ran he suddenly thought, what if the man says "Sorry son, I'm not allowed to give lifts". The door of the building the man had entered started to open. Dennis made a split second decision; he ran and leapt into the back of the van, ducking down behind a large wooden crate. Seconds later the other door slammed shut and shortly after, the engine started and the van moved off. Dennis slowly got his breath back and thought to himself, "Once we get to Dudley and the man starts to unload his van, I'll wait until the coast is clear, then it's a ten-minute walk home." He was exhausted but smiled as he thought what a great story this would be to tell Stinky, he felt much happier now. Of course, he wouldn't have felt quite as happy if he'd been standing outside when the van driver had closed the other door, and seen what was actually written there: DUDLEY ARMSTRONG... TRACTORS REPAIRED... NORTHAMPTON.

Mrs Bisskit looked at the clock and said "Right, that's it, I'm going around to Stinky's house".

Granddad said, "Maybe he's got that ammonia and forgotten where he lives".

Mr. Bisskit said, "I think you'll find you mean amnesia Dad".

Gladys said, "If he's got amnesia he won't remember which room he's got anyway, so I may as well have his".

Dennis held on to the side of the van as it careered around bends; the driver seemed in a rush to get home.

"Suits me," he thought, "I should imagine everyone's starting to wonder where I've got to by now." After what felt like hours, the van started to slow down, then come to a halt. He heard the driver get out and then the sound of large metal gates being opened. Next minute the van took off again and shortly after came to another halt.

Dennis made sure he was well hidden behind a crate. He had worked out a cunning plan just in case the man climbed inside and spotted him. It mainly involved crying and pretending that he was mad. The doors suddenly opened and through a small gap Dennis watched as the driver started to climb in, but just at that moment someone shouted, and he climbed back down before walking off.

Dennis wasted no time, he leapt out from his hiding place, jumped down onto the ground and ran for the gates. As he got close he risked a quick glance over his shoulder and saw two men talking near a shed; luckily they had their backs to him. He burst out laughing as he stepped out through the gate and into the street.

"Home sweet home," he muttered but suddenly stopped and looked about him, up and down the road. He was obviously in an industrial area of town; he didn't recognise it. In the distance he could see lots of houses, one thing he knew for sure, wherever he was, he wasn't in Dudley. He started walking in the direction of the houses, eventually coming to a sign reading WELCOME TO NORTHAMPTON.

Dennis couldn't believe it, how could he possibly be in Northampton, the more he travelled, the further away from Dudley he seemed to be getting. He sat down by the side of the road, now starting to feel a little scared. The sun had gone down and his bare legs were feeling the cold, also he knew it must be around tea time as he was feeling hungry. His mum always told him, "Whatever you're doing, be home for tea." He knew she would get worried if he was late. He tried to think what to do, he had no money and he was miles away from home in Northampton. NORTHAMPTON! He suddenly shouted it out and started laughing.

"Why didn't I think earlier," he said to himself. Northampton! His mum's sister, Aunty Beryl lived in Northampton, he had visited a couple of times; not only that but he remembered her address, 8 George Street. His birthday was on the 8th and his dad's name was George. He stood up, suddenly feeling much better.

"She will help me," he muttered. The only problem was, he had no idea which direction George Street was in, so he just carried on straight ahead. After walking for about fifteen minutes, he spotted a man walking a dog, the man reluctantly stopped and gave him directions. Luckily it was less than a mile away.

Stinky was shocked, he stared at Mrs Bisskit and said "What! Do you mean he hasn't been home all day?" She told him that she had thought he was with Stinky.

"Don't worry Mrs B," he told her, "maybe he called in to see one of our other friends. You go home and have

*a cup of tea and I'll check around. You know what
Dennis is like, he's probably just lost track of time." He
tried to sound confident but for some reason didn't feel
it.*

Dennis knocked on the front door once again and
then hearing nothing from inside the house, he tried
opening the door but found it was locked. Dennis was
amazed.

"Who locks their front door?" he muttered. His
Aunty Beryl lived on her own, her husband had died
many years ago, leaving her "very comfortable,"
according to his mum. Dennis walked down a
passageway at the side of the house and opened a gate
into the small rear garden. He looked around, there was a
small coal shed, a scruffy looking lawn with a deckchair
sitting in the centre of it, some colourful flowers near the
back fence and a washing line with a pink flannelette
nightgown hanging from it. There was a tap with a
hosepipe attached to it on the side of the house, and
Dennis carefully turned the tap, held the hose to his
mouth and greedily gulped down some water.

"Maybe she's popped out somewhere" he thought
and sat down on the deckchair.

*When Stinky called around to the Bisskits' house to
let them know that none of his friends had seen Dennis,
he found Dennis's father and granddad just leaving the
house.*

*"We are going to drive around just in case there is
any sign," Mr B. told him, "he may have injured himself
and just not be able to walk." Then when he was sure his
wife couldn't hear, he told Stinky they would also check
at the Dudley Hospital. Stinky entered the house. Mrs
Bisskit was sitting on the sofa looking close to tears.*

"I'll make you a cup of tea Mrs B." he said, and then added, "And maybe there's some of that cake left." He noticed that Gladys was busy moving some of her clothes into Dennis's bedroom.

Dennis drew his legs up on the deckchair and rested his chin on his knees. He pulled the large jacket down as far as it would go but his legs still felt cold. As he rubbed them he looked up, saw the nightgown and had an idea. He removed the jacket, reached up and took the nightgown off the washing line and pulled it over his head. Aunty Beryl was only a short lady, so the nightgown was only a little bit long on Dennis; he put the jacket back on over the gown.

"That's better," he thought, and then as he turned, he noticed that one of the windows on the side of the house was slightly open.

FIVE MINUTES LATER

Dennis gently picked himself up off the floor. He'd managed to climb in through the kitchen window but had got tangled up in his nightgown, tripped over the sink and landed on the ground with a thud.

"Hello," he shouted "Aunty Beryl, are you there?" It had suddenly occurred to him that she might be asleep in bed, but the house was silent. He walked from room to room, everywhere looked a bit untidy which was most unlike his aunt. He walked back into the kitchen, suddenly realising how hungry he was. Opening the pantry door, he spotted; bread, butter and cheese and commenced making himself a huge sandwich. Before he had a chance to start eating it, he heard a loud knock on the front door. He put down the sandwich, walked to the door and opened it. Standing on the doorstep was a

Police Constable. He looked Dennis up and down and then said "Do you mind telling me your name sir?"

"D-D-Dennis B-Bisskit," he stammered. The policeman looked him up and down again and then said "Bisskit! That's an unusual name."

"Not really," Dennis told him, "I'm one of the Dudley Bisskits." The policeman then asked Dennis if this was his house. Dennis said no but before he could explain, the policeman pushed him back into the house and into the kitchen. He pointed at a chair and said "Sit down there and do not move." Dennis sat, and started shivering. The policeman quickly moved from room to room, shouting "Is anyone there?"

"It's my Aunt Beryl's house but she's not here, I don't know where she is," Dennis told him when he walked back into the kitchen.

"And she doesn't mind you being here?"

"No, of course not, she's my aunty," Dennis replied. "Well a neighbour reported a strange person climbing in through a window," the P.C. continued, 'was that you?" Dennis told him it was but before he could say anything else, the policeman said "There's something not right here lad, I think you better accompany me down to the station to have a word with my sergeant, it's only a five-minute walk."

As they left the house a man and a woman stood and watched from out front of the house next door. The woman held her head in her hands and then asked, "What's he done to poor Beryl?" The policeman told them to go indoors, and that investigations were ongoing. They turned, but not before the man had shaken his fist at Dennis and shouted "You swine". Dennis was devastated, he looked down and realised he was still wearing a ladies' pink nightgown, no wonder he'd got some funny looks.

"This isn't my nightgown, it's Aunty Beryl's," he quickly said. The P.C. stared at him for a moment, noticing the size of the jacket. "What about that jacket, is that yours?" he enquired. Dennis chuckled and said "Oh no this belongs to Mr Darcy-Mandeville". The policeman just stared at him, so Dennis continued, "Purveyor of the Finest Cheeses," and pointed at the writing on his jacket. He still didn't say anything; Dennis was secretly pleased that he wasn't the only person who hadn't heard of Mr Darcy-Mandeville. The P.C. put one hand on his truncheon, he wasn't sure if the lad next to him was insane or a master criminal but he wasn't taking any chances.

The door opened and George and Granddad walked in. Mrs Bisskit and Stinky immediately stood up but before they could speak, Mr Bisskit shook his head.
"We've been everywhere, I called in to Peter's house to tell him; he's gone into the station to put the word around, he says not to worry, everything will be fine," but Mrs Bisskit was worried, and she knew George must be as well if he'd got his friend P.C. Peter Pratt involved.

The policeman marched Dennis into the station, then into a small room and told him to sit down, then he left him alone. Dennis heard words being spoken in the corridor, the door opened and a large Police Sergeant entered, followed by the man who'd escorted Dennis to the Police Station. The Sergeant sat down in his chair, whilst the other man stood behind Dennis. The Sergeant shuffled some papers and then looked over at the young lad in front of him. He noticed that the lad was wearing a long brown jacket several sizes too big, a ladies' pink nightgown and muddy plimsolls, but he never mentioned this, instead asking Dennis his name.

"Dennis Bisskit, sir," said Dennis quietly.

"Are you sure lad?" the Sergeant said, "It wouldn't do to be telling lies." Dennis felt tears in his eyes and said "I never tell lies sir, my name is Dennis and my mother's Edith Bisskit and my father's George Bisskit, he's a war hero sir, injured during a secret mission." He never mentioned the beer bottle, but added, "My Granddad Bill was also injured in the trenches sir." He never mentioned that the injury had occurred in a trench in Dudley whilst Granddad was installing the plumbing.

The Sergeant stared again and then said, "Have you ever been in trouble with the police before lad?" Dennis said "Not really sergeant, although, they were called out when I was stuck on a roof and a man thought I was a burglar, but it was all a misunderstanding." The two policemen looked at one another, then the sergeant said "Okay let's start at the beginning, tell me in your own words what happened."

Dennis thought back over his day and started, "Well, Sergeant, I left my front door to try and regain the World Record back for Great Britain, but then I got lost and a lady accidentally took me to Birmingham, and then I got the wrong train and ended up in Coventry." He had thought about what to say next, so chose his words carefully.

"I managed to get a lift to Dudley but instead it went to Northampton....," at this point the Sergeant stood up and banged his fist on the table.

"I've never heard such a preposterous story lad, I think we will see if you've changed your story after some time in a cell, take him away, P.C. Rogers."

There was a knock on the door and when George opened it, his friend Peter Pratt entered; everyone stared at him. "I won't give you any false hope," he said, "I've checked all around, I've asked all the bobbies who've been on duty today, I've checked several hospitals. Nothing, it's as if he's disappeared off the face of the planet."

"Do you mean aliens have taken him," asked Granddad. Then they heard a crash and cry for help, Gladys's mattress had fallen on her as she tried to move it into Dennis's bedroom.

Dennis had sat in the small cell for a long time, wondering if his life would ever get back to normal. Maybe this is it, he thought, maybe I'll just spend the rest of my life in this cell. My family will just forget about me. He was still feeling sorry for himself when suddenly the cell door opened. P.C. Rogers walked in and said "Right lad, I hope you've learned your lesson, follow me and no more of your silly stories,"

Dennis told him that everything he'd said was the truth, although he may have exaggerated about his father's war record, and then followed him back into the room he'd been in earlier and sat down. The Police Sergeant looked down at some files on his desk, not speaking. Dennis looked at the clock on the wall and couldn't believe it was 8.30; through the window he could see it was getting dark. It seemed like a lifetime ago that he was running up Castle Street with his family and Stinky shouting encouragement behind him, even PC Pratt, there to hold up the traffic so he could get across the busy street. Wait, PC Pratt. That was it, why hadn't he thought sooner?

"Excuse me Sergeant, my dad is a friend of PC Pratt in Dudley, he can vouch for me." The sergeant looked up, then PC Rogers coughed and said "Excuse me Sarge, I did a course with a PC Pratt from Dudley Station, he was an idiot." Dennis smiled and said "Yes, that's him."

The Sergeant thought for a moment, looked at the constable and said "Give Dudley nick a call, see what you can find out."

Shortly after nine o'clock in the evening, there was a knock on the door, PC Pratt came in with a smile on his face.

"He's okay, I've just had a call from Northampton Police Station. They are holding him there." Everyone looked at one another and at the same time said "Northampton! Who goes to Northampton?" then Mrs Bisskit added "Maybe he decided to visit his Aunt Beryl".

"It does seem a bit strange though," said Stinky, "you get halfway through a World Record Mile attempt and then suddenly decide to visit a relative in Northampton," It was too late for them to get fuel for the car now, so it was arranged that Dennis would spend the night in a cell and they would set off in the morning.

The next morning as they drove through town on their way to Northampton, Mrs B spotted Stinky walking out of the corner shop and told him they would be back with Dennis in about three hours if he wanted to be there to greet him. As Stinky walked home he bumped into Mr Dimple from the Dudley News and told him what had happened. Sensing a story Mr Dimple told him that he too would be there to meet Dennis.

At midday, Stinky was standing by the finishing line, still drawn on the footpath in front of the Bisskits' house, alongside him stood Mr Dimple. As the car pulled up and Dennis emerged from it, Stinky looked at his watch and said "26 hours and two minutes, not bad Ginge, it's not the World Record but a good effort none the less." Mr Dimple stepped forward and shouted "SMILE," and took a photo of Dennis looking bedraggled in his muddy footwear, big brown jacket and long pink ladies' nightgown. This photo appeared on the front page of that week's Dudley News, alongside the one taken the previous day of Dennis looking very smart and confident in his vest and shorts. A sort of 'Before and After'. Above the photos was the headline, WORLD RECORD and underneath in smaller writing it asked, "Could this be the world record for the slowest mile attempt ever?"

A few days later Dennis and Stinky sat in the café, drinking lemonade.

"Turns out Aunt Beryl had gone up to Glasgow to visit an old friend," Dennis said, then added "I asked her why she'd locked the door and she said she'd accidentally overslept in the morning and hadn't had time to clean up. She was afraid that her neighbour might come in, see the state of the place and mention it at Bingo. Next thing she said, it would have been all around town and she wouldn't have been able to show her face because of the disgrace."

"Wow," Stinky said, "I had no idea it's so complicated being a grown-up."

"Oh yes," Dennis told him, "they really worry about that sort of thing." A man entered the café, saw Dennis and said "I saw you in the paper, nice nightgown," Dennis thanked him and wondered how long he'd have to put up with this. He held up the paper and sighed.

"The point is Ginge, you said you would try and beat the World Record and it looks like you did. Just not the record that you wanted, that's all." Dennis thought for a while and then said "You know, you're right Stinky, and I'll tell you one thing, anyone can run the fastest mile, but it's really difficult to run the slowest." They both laughed and finished their drinks.

CHAPTER 7

1960

Dennis listened intently; History was his favourite subject at school, especially as it was taught by the delightful Miss Bevin. According to Stinky, Dennis was Miss Bevin's "blue-eyed boy". It was always, "Well done Dennis," or "Excellent answer Dennis".

"No need to be jealous, I can't help it if I'm good at the subject," he'd told his friend "anyway you're normally asleep," he'd added.

"Well history is so boring," Stinky told him "it's all about old stuff."

On this particular morning Miss Bevin was telling them the history of Dudley Castle.

"The original castle was built in 1086," she told them. Dennis stuck his hand in the air, shouting "Miss, Miss, do you know it's mentioned in the Doomsday Book?" Miss Bevin congratulated him and told him she did.

"Miss, Miss, do you know Queen Elizabeth the First visited the castle?" he enquired.

"I do Dennis, well done," she said. A balled-up piece of paper hit Dennis in the back of the head and a voice sounding not unlike Stinky's whispered "Crawler," but Dennis ignored it. Miss Bevin told them a story of King Henry the Eighth visiting the castle for a jousting tournament in 1534. She went on to tell them that evidently his favourite jousting helmet had gone missing after the tournament and there was a rumour that it was buried somewhere near the castle.

"Miss, Miss, would it be worth much, if someone found it?" Miss Bevin said "It would be priceless Dennis".

The following Saturday they walked to Benton's farm, carrying a shovel, sandwiches and a bottle of lemonade. Stinky wasn't certain that digging a hole in a field was the ideal way to spend a pleasant Saturday morning.

"You heard what Miss Bevin said," Dennis told his friend, "priceless, and that's just the helmet. Remember last week she said that you can dig practically anywhere and find old Roman coins. And it's not just that, if we find that helmet we will be world famous, like that man who found that old tomb in Egypt, people never forget his name."

"What man?" Stinky asked.

"I don't know I can't remember his name," Dennis told him. Stinky still wasn't convinced, "What makes you think that old Henry's jousting helmet is in Benton's field?" Dennis stopped and took a swig from the bottle of lemonade before passing it to Stinky.

"Well, obviously it could be anywhere but this field is near the castle and Mr Benton gave me permission to dig in his field, just as long as we fill the holes in." They climbed over the gate and jumped down onto the grass. Dennis looked around him and eventually walked about ten yards onto the field before announcing "This is the spot, let's dig here, I have a good feeling about it." Dennis rolled up his sleeves and picked up the shovel.

"Are you sure you don't want me to do the digging?" Stinky asked.

"No, stand back my friend, this is delicate work, leave it to me," Dennis told him.

"Suits me," said Stinky. He lay back on the grass, closed his eyes and relaxed in the sunshine, all he could hear was the buzzing of insects and after a few minutes the puffing and panting of Dennis. Eventually he opened his eyes. Dennis had managed to dig a hole about the size of a plant pot. Sweat was dripping off him.

"This is worse than the world mile attempt," he said. Stinky stood and removed his shirt, took the shovel off him and said "Move over, you may be good at history but I am good at digging." Dennis crawled away and collapsed onto the grass; after a few minutes he moved further away because soil started to land on his head. He glanced over and Stinky was just a blur of arms, slowly disappearing into the ground.

Ten minutes later Dennis heard a shout. He leapt up, there were piles of soil everywhere. He could just see Stinky's head above the hole. He ran over.

"Wow, nice hole," he said but Stinky had got down on all fours and was scratching in the soil. Suddenly he stood up in triumph and said "Look at this." He passed a lump of hard soil up to Dennis; sticking out of it was a coin. Dennis carefully pulled the soil away from it. Stinky was jumping up and down telling him to hurry,

"Is it Roman, Ginge?" he asked. Dennis read the date on the coin; "Only if the Romans were still here in 1948," he told his friend. But Stinky was not disheartened, he got back to shovelling. Dennis stepped back to avoid the flying soil. He listened to the sound of singing coming from the hole, but suddenly it stopped. He walked back to the, by now, nearly grave-sized hole and once again Stinky was on his hands and knees.

"What's the matter," he asked, but there was no reply. Then Stinky said in a trembling voice, "You better get down here." With difficulty Dennis climbed down into the hole and got on his knees next to his friend. Sticking up out of the soil was the unmistakable shape of a helmet. It was rusty and damaged. Dennis got a stick and carefully dug around it; eventually he could pry it out of the ground. Neither of them could speak. Eventually Dennis said "I think this is it." They placed it on the side of the hole and managed to climb out. They just stared at it for several minutes and then Dennis turned to his friend and solemnly shook his hand.

"Well, it looks like we are about to become world famous and make a lot of money Stinky, people all over the world will know our name."

"Like the man in Egypt?" his friend asked; "Yes… him… that person." Dennis said and then added, "We better fill the hole in and get straight round to the museum. They close at midday." Stinky immediately got to work with the shovel. Dennis had never seen anyone work so quickly. After about fifteen minutes the hole was half full but there was no soil left.

"That's an amazing thing," Stinky shouted "whenever you dig a hole and then fill it back in there is never enough soil."

"That is very true," Dennis replied, "Although, in this case it could be explained by the fact that you threw most of your soil into the field next door. Anyway, no time for that now, let's be on our way. World fame, here we come."

Stinky carried the shovel and Dennis carried Henry the Eighth's jousting helmet wrapped up in his woolly jumper for safe keeping.

"What are you going to do with your share of the money Ginge?" Stinky asked. Dennis thought and said "I might get a new bike and something for Mum and Dad and Granddad, but firstly I am going to take Miss Bevin a bunch of flowers on Monday, because it was she that inspired us Stinky, and I don't expect to hear cries of "crawler," coming from behind me." His friend laughed and said, "You know something I can't understand is, how come all these Roman coins are scattered all around Great Britain? The Romans must have had really bad pockets in their trousers."

"Oh well that was the problem," Dennis replied, "they didn't wear trousers, they used to wear a little skirt." Stinky tried to imagine this for a moment and suggested that maybe they carried their loose change in a handbag.

"Well, it would have made sense," Dennis told him, "but in all the pictures I've seen of Roman soldiers fighting in battle, I must say I've never seen one carrying a handbag. Anyway you never said what you would do with your share of the money."

"Oh that's easy," Stinky said "I'm going straight to the baker's and I'm buying twenty jam doughnuts, I love them."

They walked as quickly as they could but when they reached Dudley Museum, it appeared to be closed. They banged on the front door for several minutes but got no reply.

"Let's try around the back," Stinky shouted. They walked around the side of the building and found another door. Just as they approached it, the door opened and an elderly man wearing a flat cap walked out.

"Excuse me sir," Dennis said to him, unwrapping the helmet, "we think we have found Henry the Eighth's jousting helmet." The man stopped and hesitated.

"Well you will need to see Mr Preston, come back on Monday morning." He turned to walk off but Dennis chased after him.

"Please sir, can you not look at it, we are at school on Monday and I really don't want to carry it around in case I damage it." The man took the helmet off Dennis and held it up to the light.

"Henry the Eighth you say, well it certainly looks like it's from the right period." He turned it this way and that and said "You know, I do believe you may be onto something, I'll tell you what, I'll put it on Mr Preston's desk and leave him a note explaining what it is, come in and see him after school Monday."

He shook hands and told them his name was Charlie. They thanked him and walked home. Dennis could hardly contain his excitement for the rest of the weekend, he told his parents and granddad all about it. At first they were sceptical but when he told them that an expert at the museum also thought it was Henry's helmet, they started to share his enthusiasm.

On Monday morning Dennis and Stinky made their way to History class, they had never felt so proud. Dennis carried a large bunch of daffodils in his hand. There were a few jeers and shouts of "Bisskit's a crawler," and "Bisskit loves Miss Bevin," when they entered the classroom, but Stinky shushed them. Miss Bevin looked shocked and slightly embarrassed when Dennis handed her the flowers, but he quickly told her that they were to thank her for inspiring him and Stinky to search for King Henry's jousting helmet. She smiled but looked doubtful when he told her they had actually found it.

"Are you sure it wasn't just some old scrap metal Dennis?" she asked. But Dennis explained to her that they had taken it to Dudley museum already for confirmation.

"We saw Charlie," Stinky added, "He's one of their top experts, and he's almost certain it's genuine."

"Well this is very exciting boys," Miss Bevin told them, and then got the class to give them a round of applause.

"Of course, if it turns out to be King Henry's helmet," she added "you will be world famous, everyone will know your name."

"Just like that explorer in Egypt who found the tomb," Stinky shouted.

"Exactly," Miss Bevin said.

"What was his name again Miss?" Stinky asked; she thought for a moment and said she could never remember, "Any idea?" she asked the class but they just shook their heads.

"Anyway, the point is you'll be remembered in Dudley, they will probably put a plaque on the wall of the Town Hall." she said.

The rest of the day dragged, they couldn't wait to see Mr Preston.

"I wonder if they will give us our money straight away," Stinky asked, "I'm dying for some jam doughnuts." Dennis told him he thought they may have to wait a day or so until it was all confirmed. Stinky looked disappointed.

As soon as the school bell sounded to signal the end of the day, the two friends raced out of the door and as quickly as they could, made their way to Dudley Museum. They asked the lady at the reception desk if they could see Mr Preston. She pointed them down a corridor and told them "Third door on the right." They knocked and a gruff voice said "Enter." A chubby man wearing a bow tie sat at a large untidy desk, he was studying something under a microscope. He ignored them for several minutes and then suddenly looked up, snapped his fingers and said "Well, well, I haven't got all day."

Dennis stepped forward, and said "Excuse me sir, I'm Dennis and this is Stinky, we brought the historic jousting helmet in on Saturday afternoon." Mr Preston looked confused.

"We gave it to the other gentleman, Charlie," Dennis told him. Mr Preston suddenly understood and pointed to a bench in the corner, "Oh you mean that piece of junk," they looked over and there sat the helmet of top of a pile of what looked like scrap metal.

"I don't understand," said Dennis, "Did it not belong to Henry the Eighth?"

"I very much doubt it," Mr Preston told them, "It's a racing car driver's helmet, looks like a Bell design, I'd say about five years old, and judging by the scratches it looks like it was ploughed into a field." The lads couldn't believe it.

"So it's not Henry the Eighth's jousting helmet," Stinky muttered.

"Why would it be?" Mr Preston asked, and then added sarcastically, "in thirty years of studying mediaeval history, I have yet to discover any concrete proof that Henry the Eighth even owned a racing car," and then he pointed at the door and said "close it on your way out." They slowly walked across the room, but then Dennis turned and said "Your other expert Charlie was convinced it was genuine." Mr Preston laughed and said "Charlie, an expert! He cleans the toilets and he's not even an expert at that".

The boys dejectedly walked home.

"You do realise we can never tell anyone about this?" Dennis asked his friend, adding, "If anyone asks, we just say experts are still looking into it." Stinky had never felt so disappointed.

"I just wanted to be famous like that man in Egypt. His name's Carter by the way, I looked it up." Dennis was already starting to regain his normal optimism and said "Well, there you go then, it's early days for us my friend. It's just a matter of time before we are as famous as your man Mr Cooper."

"Carter," Stinky corrected him.

"Him as well," said Dennis.

CHAPTER 8

A FEW WEEKS LATER

All in all, things were going fairly well for Dennis, he was now quite popular at school and rarely got teased about his appearance. Other, younger children had come along to take his place, especially Billy Flynn, who was not only hugely overweight but was also cross-eyed. Dennis, remembering his own unfortunate start to school life, went out of his way to be nice to Billy and very rarely referred to him as Fatty Flynn, like the other lads did.

At this particular moment Billy was occupying Dennis's thoughts, because on top of school not being so bad now, Dennis had also risen to the dizzy heights of Patrol Leader of Raven Troop in the Dudley Boy Scouts, and Billy Flynn was a member of Dennis's troop. It was lunch-time and whilst the other lads were discussing what it would be like if aliens invaded, Dennis was busy planning this coming weekend's camping trip. It was a great responsibility, as he would be solely in charge of his six-man troop and as usual the weak link was Billy.

The big day of the camping trip arrived with bad news. Badger Grimshaw's mother had called around to let him know that Badger would not be going, as he'd come down with the mumps. Dennis suspected that it was just an excuse. Badger always used it to get out of things. Dennis could recall at least six occasions already this year that he'd had the mumps, no-one could be that unlucky.

Anyway no matter, thought Dennis as he inspected the rest of Raven Troop. His best pal Stinky was second in command, then there was Jimmy Smith (whose family owned Smiths the Greengrocers, so Jimmy could always be relied upon for some apples. Lofty Jackson (who was actually shorter than Dennis), Billy "Fatty" Flynn (who as usual looked like he'd spent the night sleeping in a ditch, and was still eating the remains of his breakfast) and bringing up the rear was Horace Barnstaple, the Professor, or the Prof as they affectionately called him.

Horace was called the Professor because he was the most intelligent person any of them had ever known, more intelligent than the teachers even. He was always coming out with amazing facts and information. Sometimes Dennis suspected that he made it up. Only yesterday during lunch break, the Prof had suddenly told them that if every person in China suddenly shouted "Good Morning", they would hear it in Dudley. Stinky had correctly pointed out that this was unlikely to happen because most of them probably spoke Chinese, but you could rarely get the better of the Prof and he came back with "Obviously, they would say "zao shang hao," but I wasn't sure if you could understand Chinese"; he actually said it with a Chinese accent. He then tried to explain how there were many different dialects in China, but they made excuses and left, sometimes the Prof could go on a bit. Still, all in all they were a fine body of men and Dennis was proud to be their Patrol leader.

Dennis produced a small map he had made and placed it on the ground.

"OK lads, we will march down the high street, and I'd like us to look smart. You never know who's watching. Billy, try not to start eating anything until we are out of town. Once we reach the end of Grommet Street, we can cut across Benton's farm, he said it was ok, then into the woods and on to the camp site near the river. I'd say about two hours, including a halfway snack break."

Billy was sweating already and they hadn't moved yet.

"It seems a long walk, lads. Couldn't your dad give us a lift Dennis?" he asked.

"No way," replied Dennis, "he's already dropped off the tents and other stuff, by the river. We only have to carry our essentials. Anyway you're missing the whole point Billy, being in the scouts is all about comradeship and having adventures together. That's what this camping trip is all about; Raven Troop, all for one and one for all, like The Three Musketeers, except there's six of us." The troop gave Dennis's rousing speech a little cheer, all except Billy who didn't seem convinced. He muttered "Didn't The Three Musketeers have horses?" But when he looked up the rest had started marching so Billy trotted after them.

Dennis was proud to see how smartly his troop marched through town, even Billy made a bit of effort, though he was obviously struggling. Unfortunately, someone else was struggling, Dennis. They had only gone a short distance when he realised his mistake. Ever since the lake incident, he had given up on his platform boots, not that they would have been much use for hiking anyway. For his 15th birthday his parents had bought him a new pair of walking boots, but foolishly Dennis had forgotten to wear them in and already he could feel blisters developing on his feet. He had packed his comfortable school plimsolls in amongst his tent and sleeping bag, but those were now waiting for him at the camping site. As they finally reached the gate to Mr Benton's farm, Dennis could stand the pain no longer.

He called the troop to a halt.

"Lads I'm afraid I've let you all down badly, I can't go any further in these boots." Billy immediately turned and started back home.

"Where are you going Billy?" shouted Dennis, "I don't mean the trip's off, it's just that I'll have to walk barefoot for a while. It won't be easy but a great leader has to lead by example." He removed his boots and socks, stuck them in his pack and climbed over the farm gate, "Follow me men," he beckoned.

The field had recently been ploughed over, so the soil was quite soft under Dennis's sore feet.

"Watch out over there," Dennis pointed to a hole in the ground.

"Wow," said Billy, "is that where you found Henry the Eighth's jousting helmet? I hear old man Benton is going to start charging the public to come and look into it. He already has his son Colin making little souvenir helmets out of balsa wood, he reckons he's going to make a fortune."

Dennis and Stinky tried to change the subject but then Billy asked the question they always tried to avoid.

"What's happened about that, have you heard anything?" Dennis gave the standard answer they had rehearsed many times, "Experts are still studying it, it could take ages; you know what experts are like." They all nodded as if they did indeed know what experts are like, but then for some unknown reason, Stinky felt compelled to add, "Yes, they have now sent it to America, so that one of their experts can have a look." Everyone turned and looked at him, especially Dennis.

"That's strange," Billy said "What would a Yank know about Henry the Eighth?"

"Yes what would he know, Stinky?" Dennis said "I'm intrigued to know myself." Stinky never answered for a moment and then shrugged his shoulders and said "Well, that's what experts do, they talk about stuff to other experts, they know things that we don't know and that's why they are called experts." With that he took off across the field and after a moment the rest followed him.

Dennis always liked to discuss some random subject when he was out with the troop. He felt it increased the comradeship and also he was keen to change the subject.

"What are we going to discuss today lads?'

"I'll get things going," said Lofty, "we are now in the 60s so what is your big prediction for the decade?"

Dennis without hesitation said "I am very confident in predicting that before the end of the decade the Davy Crockett hat will replace the Trilby as the best-selling hat in England." The lads agreed and there were cries of "Nice one Dennis', "Good prediction".

The Prof then stated, "Okay, I predict that by the end of the 1960s, man will walk on the moon." The entire troop came to a standstill.

"Are you mad?" blurted Stinky, "Everyone knows it can't be done. How would you get there? We went to Blackpool last Bank Holiday and it took us all day to get there; even if you could get there, you would die of old age before you got there."

"You would need a very big spaceship to carry enough food for the journey," a worried Billy added to the conversation.

"Especially if you were on board Billy' said Stinky.

Everyone, even Billy fell about laughing, but their joy ended when Dennis suddenly let out a loud scream "aagh!"

The lads turned as they heard Dennis's plaintive cry, "Help me lads, help me". He had a look of terror on his face and was staring down at his bare right foot.

"Is it a landmine, Dennis?" shouted Jimmy as he dived to the ground.

"Worse, much worse," muttered Dennis.

The lads slowly moved towards their leader. Stinky was the first to reach him. "My god, Dennis, I see what you mean, that's the biggest cow pat I've ever seen and your foot is stuck in the middle of it."

"That's not a cow pat, that's an elephant pat," suggested Billy, "there's no cows in the field, maybe a bird did it." The Prof, who had finally joined the others, immediately started to explain that the only bird capable would be the pterodactyl and since they had been extinct for approximately 150 million years it was unlikely, on the other hand…

"ENOUGH! Prof", screamed Dennis, "this is not the time, find me a stick to clean it off my foot." The troop were only too happy to go off looking for a stick, as the smell was getting a bit much to take.

Unfortunately, with the field being recently ploughed, there was nothing useful lying around.

"You will just have to walk downwind of us until we reach the river, Dennis," suggested Lofty.

There was a large sucking sound as Dennis pulled his foot from the middle of the cow pat; he flicked his foot about but most of the cow poo stuck to his foot like glue. "I can't walk like this," Dennis replied, "and it's still a long way to the river, I'll see if I have anything in my pack." Dennis knelt down, keeping the offending foot as far away as possible. He opened his pack, and stuck his hand inside.

"Can't use those" he said, holding up his spare socks, "or this spare vest". He pulled out the last item of clothing and stared at it, until a look of resignation came to his face. Stinky immediately realised what it was and cried "No Dennis, you can't do it", then Billy saw what Dennis held in his shaking hand.

"No, not your Victor Sylvester Midlands Tour of 1958 souvenir y-fronts."

"A great leader has to make tough decisions," Dennis told them, "anyway my mum's repaired them twice, their time has come," he added. Lofty, who rarely spoke, said "To be honest Dennis, he is a bit old-fashioned now anyway," Dennis could not believe his ears.

"I'll tell you one thing," he said, "something I can predict for the 1960s, whatever music appears, there will be nothing as good as the Victor Sylvester Orchestra, I think I can say that with great confidence."

With that the lads moved away and left Dennis to clean his foot, because at a time like that a chap needs to be on his own, plus the smell was getting worse.

Dennis finished as best he could, then dropped his all-time favourite underpants to the ground. "Wait a minute," said Stinky, "they deserve better than that." He scraped a small hole in the field, kicked the underpants into it and covered them over.

"Would you like me to say a few words, Dennis?" Dennis had tears in his eyes and looked at Stinky with new respect, "Thank you Stinky, that would mean a lot," The troop gathered around and lowered their heads, Stinky thought for several moments and then said

"Farewell underpants, you served Dennis well." The lads moved away again, because at a time like this a chap needs to grieve alone, also despite the cleaning, the smell was still not the best.

Dennis grieved for a few moments, then turned and said, "Okay lads, onwards and upwards". He immediately tripped over Billy who had taken advantage of the break, to catch up on some sleep. The amazing thing about Billy, apart from his eating abilities, was his ability to fall asleep anywhere, at any time. After sorting themselves out, the troop carried on their journey in silence, apart from the odd "ouch!" from Dennis as he stood on a sharp stone. They left the fields and entered the woods, walking along the narrow track until they came to the clearing near the river. Dennis immediately sat on the riverbank and stuck his aching feet into the cool water.

"Good idea," shouted Stinky, "give that foot a good wash, you've attracted every fly in the region."

After a soak, Dennis got up and walked to the big oak tree at the edge of the clearing. Looking behind it, he was pleased to see a large tarpaulin covering several bags.

"Excellent," he shouted to the others, "I was worried Dad would forget to drop our gear off." Everyone ran over and started sorting through the bags. Tents, sleeping bags, rope, a small axe, tins of baked beans and other essential items were uncovered, including, much to Dennis's relief, his comfortable plimsolls. Billy grabbed the axe and said "I'll look after this," but Dennis quickly took it off him and explained that as Patrol Leader he should be in command of the axe and proceeded to use the little piece of string on the end of the axe handle to tie it to his belt.

The next hour was spent erecting the three tents the lads would sleep in that night.

"Gather around lads," ordered Dennis, "remember, this isn't a holiday, we are here to learn how to survive in the outdoors. The first thing you always need is fire, and I'm going to teach you how to light a fire using two sticks." Stinky inwardly groaned, he had watched Dennis's futile attempts to do this many times, so some time later when he could see their leader getting a bit frustrated and everyone else yawning, he produced a box of matches from his pocket and said, "Would these help Dennis?" Dennis hesitated for a moment, wiped the sweat from his face and said, "I could make fire at any moment lads, but just this once we will use matches to save time."

"Lofty, open some baked beans and someone go and wake Billy up, he won't want to miss lunch." The Prof suddenly burst into song and they all joined in, "I'm riding along on the crest of a wave", it was a favourite of Scouts worldwide, "What could be better than this?" shouted Dennis, and the rest of the lads agreed that nothing could be better.

They ate their lunch and sang more songs, and told stories and jokes, and then Dennis showed them a new knot he'd learned, and then they woke Billy up because they knew he wouldn't want to miss the cleaning up. Then in the distance they heard a vehicle crashing and bashing its way through the woods.

"That should be Dad," shouted Dennis, "bringing some other stuff." It suddenly occurred to him just how much his father did to help. His dad sometimes embarrassed him, but he was always the first person to help him out.

The battered old Bedford van suddenly appeared through the trees and Mr Bisskit jumped out.

"Howdy lads, how's the camping trip going?" He was his usual jolly self.

Now that his hair had receded to the back of his head, the old beer bottle scar seemed to stand out more than ever. Every morning he spent about half an hour, plastering his few remaining hairs to his head, but now, in the breeze they were blowing around behind him. From a distance it looked as if he were getting attacked by a swarm of bees.

"The old war wound is looking a bit sore Mr B," suggested Lofty. Mr Bisskit rubbed the scar and said, "I can't complain, there's plenty suffered more than me". Dennis quickly changed the subject; "Did you notice the Union Jack flying from my tent, Dad?" he asked. His father turned, saw the flag and immediately snapped his feet together and saluted. The lads were so impressed, they followed suit. As Dennis snapped his still bare feet together, the string snapped on the axe, which was still attached to his belt. It fell down on his big toe and Dennis let out a cry and hopped all around the camp site, whilst everyone, even his father fell about laughing.

The lads cleaned up from lunch, whilst Dennis and his father unloaded the van. Mr Bisskit drove off and the lads were surprised to see what he had brought them. Four large tins with lids, and several planks of wood. The tins were marked 'Cooking Oil"; Billy asked hopefully "are we doing some chips?"

"No", Dennis explained, "those tins are empty, we are going to make a raft and sail it on the river." Billy did not seem happy. "Are you sure, Dennis, I'm not much of a swimmer."

"Don't worry" Dennis told him, "we will look after you, this is all part of our scouts' training and will go in the report." The lads glanced at each other. Dennis took his position as Patrol Leader very seriously and wrote a report after every meeting, even if nothing had happened.

It was mid-afternoon by the time they had finished building their raft and they all agreed it looked rather impressive. There was a tin at each corner with planks attached by rope.

"I'm not sure it will carry six of us," Dennis said, "so Stinky, Billy, the Professor and myself will go first and then we can swap and let Lofty and Jimmy have a go." Lofty and Jimmy quickly agreed to this, "Good idea" said Jimmy, "you test it out and if you don't die, we will have a go."

"It could get pretty wet", added Dennis, "best to just wear shorts and vest." Billy looked unhappy again.

"I haven't got any shorts," he told them, "they are hard to get in my size."

"Well just wear your underpants" answered Dennis, "you can soon dry them off on the fire", then he quickly walked away before Billy could think of any other complaints. The lads got changed and left their clothes on the grassy bank for when they returned.

They then carried the raft to the river's edge, stepped into the shallows and as gently as they could, lowered it onto the surface of the river. They were pleased to see that it floated and didn't sink. Jimmy and Lofty held onto the attached rope whilst the others climbed aboard.

"Billy, I want you to stay in the centre, don't go near the edge of the raft, then you won't get wet," ordered Dennis. Actually he was more concerned that if Billy went to the edge of the raft, it would tip up, but he knew that Billy was very sensitive about his weight.

"Okay lads, let go of the rope, ship ahoy!" shouted Dennis and the raft slowly started drifting towards the centre of the river. They had no oars but each had a tree branch, whilst Stinky had a cricket bat he'd found abandoned at the camping site. They tried to row but for some reason the raft just went around in circles as it slowly drifted down river.

"Maybe if I move to one side it will go in a straight line," suggested Billy, and before anyone could stop him, he clambered to the edge of the raft, which immediately tipped up throwing them all into the river.

When Dennis surfaced, he looked around and spotted Stinky and the Prof treading water, but Billy was nowhere to be seen. He turned his head and could make out the raft floating off down the river.

"Billy!" They shouted; suddenly he shot to the surface, coughing and gulping for air'

"Help me!" he spluttered. Dennis was the first to reach him, just as he was starting to sink beneath the surface again. He grabbed Billy's nearest arm and hung onto him until Stinky and the Prof swam over. Between them they managed to drag Billy and themselves back to the river's edge, where Jimmy and Lofty jumped into the water to help.

They lay on the grassy bank getting their breath back for several minutes, Billy kept apologising between coughing up water. Then he turned to Dennis and said "I suppose this will have to go in the report Dennis," Before Dennis could answer, Stinky said "Well at least we can say we have done our lifesaving training."

Billy lay back on the ground in his soggy underpants, he looked close to tears and was just muttering about this being the worst day of his life, when a black Labrador suddenly dashed out of the woods, grabbed Billy's trousers from where he'd left them and ran off, wagging his tail.

"Quick, he's got my pants," he yelled. Jimmy chased after the dog and a few minutes later came back carrying a trouser pocket.

"This is all I could find, sorry Billy," said Jimmy.

"Is there a cheese sandwich in it," asked Billy hopefully, but Jimmy sadly shook his head.

"Well, that's just great", said Billy slowly getting to his feet, "I've got nothing to wear, none of your shorts would fit me, I've sunk the raft, I'm going to be mentioned in the report, I've lost my cheese sandwich". He slowly walked to his tent, lifted the flap and climbed in letting the flap fall behind him.

"Best to just leave him alone for a while, lads," said Dennis, "meanwhile let's get a fire going, at least he can dry his underpants. Just this once to save time we will use your matches Stinky."

Twenty minutes later the lads sat drying around a fire, the Prof was toasting some bread on the end of a thin stick, whilst Jimmy opened a couple of cans of baked beans.

"I'm not sure Billy should have any more beans" he said, "remember I have to share a tent with him." Billy had still not emerged from his tent, although a few moments earlier, there had been a bit of noise and muttering from inside the tent, shortly followed by the flap opening and Billy's soggy underpants flying through the air towards them.

"He'll be fine soon," Dennis assured them.

And sure enough, not long afterwards, Billy emerged from the tent, although at first they thought it was a fat green caterpillar. Billy had cut a hole in the bottom of his old green sleeping bag, so his feet could stick out, then zipped himself into it up to the neck; he had also cut a couple of holes in the side of the bag, to put his arms through. He had buckled his scout belt around his waist and his tin mug dangled from it. The lads tried their best, but were soon falling about laughing. After a few seconds, even Billy joined in.

"It was all I could think of," he told them. Dennis stood up and said,

"I will have to mention this in my report." Billy looked glum, until Dennis continued "Billy showed exceptional improvisation, in the face of adversity." Billy had never felt so proud, "This calls for baked beans," he announced.

They had eaten their food and now sat relaxing. Billy had attached some rope to two branches either side of the fire and hung his underpants over it to dry; steam was coming off them. Stinky yawned and asked, "What are you going to do when you leave school Dennis?"

Dennis surprised them by saying he'd always wanted to work in a big department store.

"I'd like to work my way up to be manager," he'd added.

"You'd make a good manager Dennis, you're always honest and reliable," Stinky told him.

Dennis thought about this and felt guilty. He suddenly came to a decision and stood up.

"I have something I have to tell you lads, but you must promise me that you never reveal what I tell you to anyone else."

They looked at each other and instantly agreed.

"What I have to tell you is a family secret, but hearing Stinky call me honest, I knew I could not keep it to myself any longer." He took a deep breath and said "It's about my father's war wound." He looked around him and noticed the lads looking disappointed.

"You mean the beer bottle scar?" asked Billy. "Is that all, I thought you were going to say you robbed a bank or something exciting."

Dennis couldn't believe it. "You mean; you knew?" he asked Billy.

"We all knew that ages ago, Lofty's Aunty Gladys was the nurse that stitched him up, during the war," Billy explained.

Dennis couldn't speak for several moments and then asked "Why didn't any of you ever say anything?" Stinky, answered for the rest of them, "We didn't want to embarrass you Dennis, you're our friend. Anyway, not everyone could be off fighting. Mr B still did important work."

"The main thing is he's a good man," added Billy, "he's never been unkind to me."

Dennis sat down again, he couldn't believe it, all this time he'd felt slightly ashamed of his father, but Billy was right, he was a good man, that was the main thing.

The silence was broken by a whooshing sound and they all looked up to see Billy's underpants burst into flames.

"It's been a really bad trip for underpants," the Prof said solemnly.

They sat around the campfire and spoke for hours, mainly about their hopes and fears for the future. Normally they would joke and fool around, but it seemed they all realised that it was the end of an era. This could be the last time they were all together like this. Some would be finishing school soon and entering the workforce; others, like the Professor were hoping to go on to university. Work, marriage, children, Dennis for one just couldn't imagine it. Eventually exhausted from a long day, they all said their "good nights," and wandered off to their tents.

Dennis was sharing a tent with Stinky who immediately complained that Dennis's foot still smelt of cow poo. So eventually, Dennis agreed to open the tent flap a few inches and stick the offending foot outside.

"If my foot gets frostbite and falls off it will be your fault," he told Stinky. They lay back in their sleeping bags and there was quiet for several moments before Stinky suddenly spoke.

"That was very honest of you to tell us about your father," he said in a low voice.

"Bit pointless though really," replied Dennis, "since everyone in Great Britain appears to know already." Stinky continued as if he hadn't heard, "Now I need to tell you a secret, you remember the other week when you wanted me to go to the cinema to see The Sword of Sherwood Forest with you," Dennis yawned and said, "Yes, it's a pity you were busy, I've heard it's brilliant".

"I wasn't really busy," whispered Stinky, "it's just that I'd seen it the night before with Brenda Rumble."

Dennis fumbled around until he found the torch, turned it on and shone it in Stinky's face. "I don't believe it," he said "you saw The Sword of Sherwood Forest with Brenda Rumble, but she's...well... she's a girl."

"I'm well aware of that Dennis, it's just that I've always liked her, and she asked me and I couldn't say no. Anyway, she's in the Girl Guides, so we have something in common," he explained. Dennis couldn't believe his ears, "Something in common, what could we possibly have in common, we are highly trained Scouts, prepared for anything, and they do", he thought for a moment and said "whatever it is they do."

No words were spoken for some time and then Dennis asked "Did you have a good time?"

"I had a great time," replied Stinky, "she's funny and nice looking, but it's not just that, she's good at other things as well, for example she beats me every time we play conkers."

"Well let's face it," Dennis said, "you've never been very good at conkers. Still, I'm pleased for you Stinky. I suppose I will get a girlfriend myself one day." He thought for a moment and then continued, "She would have to like dogs, and of course share my taste in music." Stinky suspected it was highly unlikely that Dennis could find anyone who shared his taste in music, but kept it to himself, and after a while they dozed off to sleep.

Sometime later Stinky was awoken by Dennis shouting, "Is that you licking my foot Stinky?" closely followed by the torch light coming on and Dennis frantically ripping open the tent flap. In the torch beam they could see a black Labrador, wagging his tail as he licked Dennis's toes. He climbed into the tent, dragging what appeared to be the remains of Billy's trousers with him and happily went to sleep between them.

At the end of the school term, they all promised to keep in touch, but Stinky and Billy were the only two whom Dennis saw regularly over the next few years. One day when they were catching up for a coffee they bumped into the Professor. He told them about an invention he was working on, and explained that one day everyone would have a small portable telephone, you just carried it in your pocket and could call from anywhere. He told them to keep it to themselves so that no-one else would steal the idea. They said their goodbyes and watched him walk away.

"Well, I'll definitely be keeping it to myself," said Stinky, 'I wouldn't want anyone to think I'm as mad as the Professor." They fell about laughing and then walked off.

THE EVEN LATER THAN THAT YEARS

CHAPTER 9

Summer 1961…It all just fell into place. Dennis was 16, he had recently finished school and managed to obtain the highly sought after Junior Tea Boy job at Fosdyke's Department Store. He had a spare couple of weeks' break before he started work and was just wondering what to do when his granddad came up with an amazing idea.

"France!" Dennis was stunned, "France, but that's abroad."

"I realise that Dennis," said Granddad, "I spent a long time up to my knees in mud over there, getting shot at. I realise exactly where it is," Dennis had rarely seen his granddad so worked up.

"I'm nearly 65," he continued, "I'll be retiring in another month, this will probably be my last chance." Granddad hadn't worked for several years so Dennis didn't really see what difference retirement would make but obviously he would never say that to his granddad, so instead he told him, "Well, I've got a spare few days and some money saved, let's do it, let's go to France."

It was an idea that had been building in Granddad's mind for a while now. For many decades he'd deliberately not given France a thought, nor his old friend Percy Dorsey. Those memories were too sad; it was best not to think about it. But for some reason, maybe it was just his impending retirement, he had suddenly known that he had to return one more time, he had to say his goodbyes properly.

"France!" George and Edith Bisskit said it simultaneously as if joined at the mouth, "France, but that's abroad".

"Don't worry," Dennis told them, "I'll look after Granddad." this did not fill them with confidence, and after a few moments a stunned looking Mrs B. said "I bet they don't even speak English, how would you ask for a cup of tea?" Dennis laughed, "Of course they'll speak English Mum; just about everyone speaks English. Anyway, I'm sure Granddad picked up a few words when he was there." Just then Granddad walked in and shouted "Oui!" Mrs Bisskit looked up and said "You don't need to tell us Dad, just put the toilet seat back down".

"No," Granddad explained "Oui. That means yes in French."

"There you go then," Dennis exclaimed, "we can practically speak the language."

"Well, to be honest," Granddad added, "that's the only French word I remember, I mean I was surrounded by Birmingham lads, so we didn't speak a lot of French".

"Don't worry about that," Dennis reassured him, "I know the very person to see. By the time we leave I should be fluent."

A few days later Dennis sat in the back garden with his old school friend Horace or the Professor as he was affectionately known. The Professor had easily been the most intelligent lad at school, although obviously he'd deferred to Dennis in the Scouting department. Unlike most of the other lads Dennis knew, the Prof wasn't entering the work force. Instead he'd been accepted at Oxford University.

"I'm glad we could catch up," Dennis told him, "I was worried you might have moved to Oxford by now."

"I was there last week to have a look around and meet people," Horace told him, "just back home for a week and then I'll be off to study physics." Dennis didn't really know what physics was, so he asked Horace what it was he was actually studying.

"It involves the study of matter and its motion through space and time," the Prof told him, but Dennis was none the wiser.

"Sounds a bit strange," he told Horace, "I didn't even know that was a job, can you make any money out of it?" Horace laughed and said, "I suppose eventually, but you don't really study physics to make money Dennis."

"Well, you'll probably be amazed to hear that I've just secured the highly sought after Junior Tea Boy's job at Fosdyke's," Dennis told him proudly, and then added "Two pound a week, with the possibility of rising to four pound a week eventually, when I get the Senior Tea Boy position." Then he felt like he was bragging, so he quickly told Horace that if things didn't work out with this physics thing he would use his influence to get him a position at Fosdyke's.

"Let's face it," he told him, "someone with a knowledge of physics could probably even get a job in the wages department." Horace laughed and said he would keep that in mind if things didn't work out. Dennis felt quite sorry for him.

"Must be strange going to some new school Prof," he said, "having to make new friends."

"Oh it will be okay," Horace answered, "in fact I met a nice chap last week, Stephen Hawking; he'll be in the same class as me. We got on fine, we have very similar interests. In fact we are both convinced that man will walk on the moon by the end of the decade."

"Wow, he sounds as crazy as you Prof," Dennis laughed, then added "still, I don't suppose you can have an intellectual conversation around the campfire with him like we used to have. Did you tell him about your idea for little telephones that people could carry around in their pockets?" Horace smiled and said "He thought it was a very interesting idea Dennis, mark my words, someday everyone will have one." They both laughed and then Dennis said, "Anyway, to more important things, I need to pick your brain Horace."

He told him about the coming visit to France with his granddad and how they needed to learn some French words before the end of the week.

"I remember you telling me that you visited Paris with your parents last year, is there anything important I need to know?" Horace was surprised.

"Well, it's very different from Dudley." he told Dennis, "They certainly eat some strange food; snails, frogs' legs, that sort of thing." Dennis couldn't believe his ears; "That's terrible," he told Horace, "Can't they afford proper food?" The Prof laughed again and said, "I'm sure they can, they just eat different things to us. For example, for breakfast they like these little pastries, they are called croissants." Dennis was aghast, "Oh no, no, no, that won't do," he told Horace, "Granddad likes his bacon and eggs, and so do I, I'm certainly not eating pudding for breakfast and I definitely won't be eating any slugs, frogs, toads or anything like that!"

Horace told him that he couldn't stay long so he would write a few French words down for him. Dennis got a pen and exercise book and gave it to him. He thought for a moment and said "Look Dennis, really all you need to know are Bonjour, which means Good Morning and Merci, that's Thank You," he wrote them down and added "just say that and then you can bluff your way through, that's what I did." They said their goodbyes, Dennis wished him well and said "Watch out for that Hawking lad, he sounds a bit strange." After he left Dennis chuckled to himself and muttered "Portable telephones, men walking on the moon, crazy."

Later Dennis told his granddad the French words. He thought for a moment and then asked, "What about if it's night time, do we still say Good Morning?" Dennis felt bad, he hadn't thought to ask Horace that.

"I think they just say Bonjour whatever time of day it is, Granddad", then added "the main thing is, be very careful what they offer you for lunch, especially if it looks like they've just been in the garden."

His mother hugged him so hard that he struggled to breathe, tears ran down her cheeks as she urged him to be careful and not talk to strangers, especially foreign strangers. He tried to explain to her that they were only going away for three days. But she just sobbed a long list of instructions into his ear.

"Do this! Do that, don't touch those, and especially avoid that!" her final instructions were to always wear clean underpants and avoid getting abducted by white slavers. He wasn't sure whether there was some connection. White slavers only abducted people with clean underpants, but didn't say anything, as his mouth was full of his mother's hair.

They had decided to catch a ferry in the early hours, so that they would be in Calais for breakfast and get a full day's sightseeing in. The ferry pulled away from the dock in Dover, there was still a full moon, and Dennis and his granddad watched England gradually disappear from view. His granddad was unusually quiet now that the journey had begun. Dennis looked up at him and said "Thank you for inviting me Granddad, this is the most exciting thing I've ever done". His granddad smiled in the moonlight and told him he was glad to have him by his side.

"Let's face it," he said "if you're off on an adventure, who better to have by your side than Dennis Bisskit," but Dennis wasn't listening any more, he was suddenly feeling a bit queasy.

"I don't know whether it's the moonlight," Granddad told him, "but you appear to be turning green." Dennis suddenly turned and bolted for the toilets.

Granddad stared over the side of the ferry at the water, the moon was so bright it appeared as if there were a giant floodlight above them. Seeing Dennis run off had brought back memories of the last time he'd made this trip, long ago. He remembered a group of new friends, laughing and joking, unaware of what the future held. They had all volunteered together and were known as the Birmingham Pals. Most of them had met for the first time on that chilly morning in Birmingham when they had been so quick to sign their names on a piece of paper. He recalled standing on a deck much like this as his best mate Percy, just like Dennis, was suddenly overcome with seasickness. He had thrown up over the side of the boat, but had made the mistake of facing into the wind and most of it had blown back over him. Everyone had rolled about laughing, even Percy had joined. "Strange," he thought, "I can't remember us laughing much after that."

After about fifteen minutes, Dennis slowly staggered towards him. He pulled a handkerchief out of his pocket to wipe his face, and as he did, he failed to notice a piece of paper fall from his pocket, dance in the breeze for a second and then disappear back in the direction they had sailed from.

"Do you fancy some of that cake your mother packed?" Granddad asked. Dennis immediately turned and ran off towards the toilets again.

As the coast of France came into view Dennis emerged from the toilet, looking a lot better than when he'd run off. Granddad pointed and said, "Not long now."

"I think they should build a big tunnel under the English Channel," Dennis said, "Then you could just drive across, it would save a lot of messing about." Granddad chuckled, it was good to see his grandson back to his old self.

"A tunnel between England and France, you're starting to sound as mad as your friend the Professor," They both laughed. Not long after, they docked at Calais, got off the ferry, stretched their legs, exchanged some money and set off on their adventures.

They walked the short distance from the dock into Calais town centre, Granddad carried his small suitcase and Dennis wore his backpack, the same one he'd used on many Scouting weekends away.

"Doesn't look very impressive so far," he said.

"Early days," said Granddad, "at least the sun is shining; first thing is some breakfast I think." Dennis was gradually feeling better now he was back on dry land.

"Good idea Granddad," he told him, "a nice cup of tea to start the day." He reached into his trouser pocket and then felt into his other pockets.

"Oh no! I've lost the piece of paper with the French words on," he cried.

"Well I remember *Thank You* was *Mercy*," Granddad told him.

"That's right," Dennis replied, "oh yes, and, *Good Morning* is *Bongers,* phew! Lucky we remembered or we would have been in big trouble."

Just as they entered the town centre a couple walked towards them. Dennis looked over and in a loud voice said "Bongers," the couple looked at him and carried on.

"Well that's rude," he said "in England if you say Good Morning to someone they say Good Morning back," They stood in what looked like a town square. It was not long after 7.00 am but there was already some activity. Down a small alleyway they noticed a sign LE CHAT NOIR CAFE; a man in a white apron was placing small round tables and chairs outside on the pavement. They headed towards it. They noticed that above the writing was a picture of a black cat.

"The Professor told me they eat frogs and snails," Dennis said to his granddad, "but he never said anything about cats;" he pushed open the door and added, "you grab one of those tables Granddad, you better leave this to me." Granddad put his suitcase down, looked at the man in the white apron and said "Bongers," the man just shook his head and followed Dennis into the café.

Granddad pulled back a chair, sat down and yawned loudly. He could see Dennis through the window having some sort of animated conversation with the man in the white apron and an elderly lady, well it wasn't really a conversation, Dennis was doing all the talking and they were just staring at him with baffled expressions on their faces. The door was only half closed and Granddad distinctly heard the words "That's a proper Full English Breakfast, none of yer cats and dogs, and a pot of tea for two." He smiled and closed his eyes.

Five minutes later he awoke with a start. For a second he wondered where he was, then he heard a strange grunting sound coming from inside the café. Looking through the window, he saw Dennis was down on his hands and knees grunting like a pig "Bacon! Pig!" he heard him shouting. The man and the lady were just staring at him, shaking their heads and looking completely confused. Granddad smiled and closed his eyes again. When he next opened them and checked, Dennis was hopping around the café making a pecking gesture with his finger and clucking like a chicken, "Eggs! Quack; quack eggs!"

A few minutes later Dennis emerged from the café. He was struggling for breath and sweat was dripping off his nose.

"All sorted Dennis?" his granddad asked. "Oh yes," Dennis replied, "I think I've sorted it, although it was a bit tricky, I just decided upon bacon and eggs, I didn't even bother attempting black pudding."

"Probably a wise move," Granddad told him.

Ten minutes later, the man in the white apron emerged from the café carrying a large tray. He placed a pot of tea and cups and saucers on the table and then a plate in front of Dennis and his granddad, on which was a slice of ham with an uncooked egg still in its shell balanced on top. Dennis said "Bongers, Mercy very much," and the man walked back into the café. They stared at their breakfast and then Dennis looked through the window and saw the man and lady laughing hysterically, the man was bent over with his hands on his knees.

"I see," said Dennis, "so that's the way they want to play it," he rolled up his piece of ham and chewed it slowly; "absolutely delicious," he said loudly, "just the way I ordered it," then he picked up his egg and carefully placed it in his trouser pocket, saying in an even louder voice, "Mmmm! I'm so full of ham, I'm going to save my egg for later." Granddad barely noticed he was busy spitting out a mouthful of tea onto the pavement.

They stood up and Dennis said 'I'll get this, Granddad, I have some of that funny French money we got at the exchange." He stood up and shoved his hand into his pocket breaking the egg.

"Brilliant, just brilliant," he muttered. He entered the café whilst Granddad waited by the door and without speaking handed the lady some French francs; she gave him some coins in return. Dennis turned to leave but then stopped and said "My granddad is a war hero, if it wasn't for him and his friends, you would probably be eating German sausages now instead of frogs and cats." With that he turned and strode out with as much dignity as you can when you have egg yolk running down your leg. Granddad ruffled Dennis's hair and said "Thank you for that Dennis." Dennis didn't reply. Granddad noticed that he was walking a bit strangely and kept shaking his leg, after a while he said "I'll tell you one thing Granddad, I'm starving, I wouldn't mind a German sausage right now."

They had a quick look around Calais but soon got bored and made their way to the bus station. Before they had left England, Granddad had explained that they would be heading to the town of Albert, but to break up the journey, tonight they were staying in Lille. Luckily, the surprisingly friendly lady in the ticket office could speak fairly good English and told them that the next bus to Lille would be in nearly two hours. They put their bags down in the waiting room and settled down on a bench. Granddad soon began to nod off but not before

Dennis had said to him. "Lill and Albert, they have some funny town names over here."

"Oh, I don't know," Granddad replied, "I suppose they would think some of our names were a bit unusual. Remember last year we drove through that village Goldfish Bottom, and in Dorset there's even a place called Scratchy Bottom." Dennis laughed and said "I suppose you're right Granddad, I'm glad we don't live there and I had to explain that to a French person, I'd probably get into even more trouble than I did with the bacon and eggs."

They closed their eyes and seemingly seconds later, the nice ticket lady was shaking them awake, and telling them that the bus was due in five minutes. They stood up and stretched and took it in turns to go to the toilet whilst the other watched their bags. As they waited Dennis asked his granddad if he'd been to Lille during the Great War.

"Certainly did," he told him, "in fact it's one of my few good memories, I helped to liberate it in 1918." Dennis couldn't believe it.

"You did Granddad?" he asked.

"Well, not me on my own," Granddad explained, "I was one of thousands. The local people lined the streets. They were so happy to see us; they had suffered badly. The town was just about destroyed last time I saw it, so I'm hoping it looks a bit better now."

And it certainly did, many of the old buildings had been restored to their former glory.

"You wouldn't know it was the same place," Granddad told Dennis as they walked the streets enjoying the afternoon sunshine.

They had decided to stay at a good hotel that night and after wandering the streets for some time they came across a distinguished looking building with a sign on the front advertising the HOTEL DE LA LIBERTE.

"I remember that word," Granddad told Dennis, "Liberté. That means Freedom, sounds just the place for a couple of wild lads like us on their holidays." The man on the reception desk was fairly unfriendly to Dennis when he enquired about a room, but as soon as he heard Granddad comment about how much the town had changed since 1918, his attitude suddenly changed. He shook his hand and told them they could have his finest room at a greatly reduced price.

A severe looking woman in a starched uniform showed them to their room and left them to it. It certainly was a grand room with two large beds, a sofa and a table with chairs in the corner. There was even a television set on a small table, but Dennis was disappointed to find only one channel and that was in French. They had eaten sandwiches from a shop as soon as they arrived in Lille. Dennis wasn't sure what was in them, but just to be on the safe side he had checked before biting into it, just to make certain he could find no sign of whiskers. It had actually tasted quite nice but now he was starting to feel a bit queasy again. He rushed to the bathroom, telling Granddad he may be gone for a while. As he flung the door open and raced into the room, he got a glimpse of a small bath in the corner, tiled walls, a large sink and incredibly, two toilets side by side, he didn't have time to think about this so just chose the one on the left. After about ten minutes his churning stomach started to calm down and he looked at the toilet next to him. Dennis couldn't make sense of this; he couldn't think of any situation where he would want to sit on the toilet with someone sitting alongside him on another toilet.

"I'll never understand the French," he muttered to himself. He looked around, there was no paper next to his toilet, so he had to lean over and grab some from the adjoining one. Eventually he felt a bit better, He stood and turned to flush the toilet; there was no chain to pull, like at home. Instead there was a metal button above the toilet so he pushed this and water shot up about two feet into the air splashing on to his trousers. Dennis was distraught, he couldn't believe he'd made such an elementary mistake. He felt embarrassed to face his granddad, but after a while he opened the door. Granddad was sitting on the sofa, staring out of the window. Dennis couldn't look him in the face.

"Granddad," he said quietly, "I've made a terrible mistake, I went to the toilet in the Water Fountain." His granddad looked shocked, so Dennis quickly added, "but in my defence, it's a really, really stupid place to put a Water Fountain, right next to the toilet, I mean who is going to want to stand next to the toilet having a drink of water?"

Granddad stood up and walked across the room, opened the bathroom door and glanced in. He smiled before saying, "It's okay Dennis, I think I made the same mistake myself fifty years ago." Granddad went on to explain to his grandson what a bidet was. Dennis just stared at him for several moments and then said "We can never bring Mum to France, Granddad, if she found out about that I could never look her in the face again."

That evening as they walked around town they came across a nice little family restaurant and decided to give it a try.

"I think this time I'll do the ordering," Granddad said. As luck would have it, the owner spoke English very well and Granddad did not have to impersonate fish and chips. They sat at a corner table and a young girl brought Dennis a glass of lemonade and a small jug containing wine for Granddad.

"It's red wine," Granddad said in answer to Dennis's inquiry. "Even young people drink it in France, here, have a sip," he passed his glass to Dennis, who sniffed it, took a small sip and grimaced.

"How do people drink that?" he asked, "it's like a punishment." Granddad smiled, "It's an acquired taste," he told him. The young girl brought their fish and chips, Dennis said "Bongers, mercy very much," and she smiled as she walked away.

"I think they really appreciate it, when you make a bit of effort with the language," he told Granddad, who replied "I think she was smiling because she likes you". Dennis blushed and said "I'm not very good with girls, I never know what to talk about with them". He ate a chip and asked "How did you meet Granny Winifred?" Granddad ate a mouthful and nodded in appreciation, "This is good fish," he said, and then lay his fork down on his plate and said "Well it wasn't difficult to meet your gran, I just looked over the fence one day and there she was. Her family moved next door when I was about five, and if I looked over the other fence, there was my best friend Percy Dorsey." Granddad ate a bit more and then continued, "We grew up together, played together, went to school together; I asked her to marry me when we were twelve, but obviously we had to wait, I wanted to get in early before Percy asked her," he smiled at the memories and then carried on, "I think she loved us both but of course she chose me."

"How come she chose you, Granddad?" Dennis asked him. Granddad turned his head and looked up and said "Just look at this profile, who wouldn't want to marry me?" Dennis laughed and said "Good point, granddad". They quietly finished their meal and when the owner came over to collect the plates, Granddad told him it was the best meal they'd eaten in France. They sat quietly for a moment and then Dennis asked him to finish his story.

"Well, I left school in 1911 when I was 15, got a job down the coal mines."

"For three days," Dennis interrupted.

"Yes, for three days," Granddad continued, "decided breathing coal fumes wasn't for me, so I got a job in a grocery shop, then in 1913, your grandmother and I got married. Percy was our best man." Now Granddad paused, Dennis just stared at him and waited. Eventually he said, "And then came 1914 and the war and life was never the same again. I didn't see Winny for 18 months until I got three days' leave, I think I'd changed a bit by then." Dennis thought about this for a while and then asked "Were you not scared to go back after your leave?"

"Of course I was," Granddad told him, "but my friends were all still over here. I would have been even more scared of letting them down if I hadn't come back."

"Do you still see any of them, Granddad?" Dennis asked.

"One or two," Granddad told him, but then he stared out of the window and added, "most of them are still over here." He didn't seem to want to talk any more but Dennis asked one last question.

"You've never told me, Granddad, what happened to Percy." He didn't answer for some time and then said "Maybe tomorrow." They walked back to the hotel, yawning as they went.

"I'll sleep well tonight, I can barely keep my eyes open," Dennis muttered as they entered their room. He sat on his bed and bounced up and down a few times, then noticed the large heavy curtains on the far wall; they were almost floor to ceiling height. He walked over to them, reached up and pulled them apart. He was surprised to see that behind them was a very solid looking wooden shutter which ran from the floor up to the ceiling.

"That's strange," he thought. He pulled a couple of the thick wooden slats apart about an inch and peeked through. Behind it was a balcony and he could see the street lights beyond.

"Excellent," he shouted as his granddad walked out of the bathroom, "we have a balcony, I'm going to get up early and sit in the sunshine." He walked towards the bathroom and Granddad said "Now be sure you don't go in the Water Fountain." Dennis shook his head and said "Ha ha! Very amusing Granddad." When he came back out five minutes later, all he could hear was loud snoring.

Dennis slept like a log but awoke early and lay there for a while thinking about the day to come. He had a feeling it wouldn't be an easy one for his granddad. He looked at his watch, 6.20 am. He knew there was no chance he'd get back to sleep and suddenly remembering the balcony, he decided to get up and watch the sun rise. He quietly climbed out of bed, looking resplendent in his Dan Dare pyjamas. Pulling back the heavy curtains, he looked for a cord to lift up the shutter, but couldn't see anything. Puzzled, he thought maybe he could lift them up, so he bent his knees, put both hands under the bottom wooden slat and lifted with all his strength. The shutter hardly budged.

"This is strange," he muttered to himself, and then realised he only needed to lift it about 12 inches and he'd be able to crawl underneath. So he bent down, placed his hands underneath and tried again. He strained so hard that veins were standing out on his neck, sweat dripped off his nose, but the shutter never moved.

Dennis sat down for a moment exhausted; "Stupid French design," he muttered, but by now he was more determined than ever to open it, so he had another look around. He pulled the curtain back at the end of the shutter and noticed a thick chain running from the floor to the ceiling, it was like a bicycle chain only much bigger and thicker; it ran around a cog wheel at the top and bottom. Dennis couldn't believe his eyes; "Why do they make everything so difficult?" he thought to himself. He put both hands around the chain and pulled down; the shutter rose about an inch.

"Now we are getting somewhere," he said, but when he took his hands off the chain he noticed they were covered in thick brown grease. Dennis sighed, but was determined that this time he would open the shutter far enough to climb under. He clasped the greasy chain with both hands. Getting a firm grip, he lifted both his feet off the ground and let the chain take his weight. The shutter lifted slightly but all of a sudden a large lump of plaster came away from the wall at the top of the shutter, bounced off his head and crashed onto the floor. Dennis fell to the ground his face covered in grey plaster, there were lumps all over the room. His granddad went quiet for a moment and Dennis thought he would wake up, so he quickly pulled the curtain across a bit to hide the damaged section of wall. Before long granddad recommenced snoring.

"Why does it always happen to me?" he murmured, brushing some plaster from his face. He picked up the largest lumps of plaster and put them under his bed, then he got a towel out of the bathroom and used it to sweep the floor as best he could. By now he felt worn out so he sat upon his bed, then when he stood up again, he realised he'd left brown greasy stains all over the white bed sheets.

At that moment there was a loud knocking at the door. Dennis nearly had a heart attack and then raced to answer the door before his granddad awoke. At the last second he remembered the dirty hotel towel in his hand and threw it behind the sofa. When he opened the door, the severe looking woman who'd shown them to their room the previous day was standing there. She stared at him, noticing he was not only wearing strange pyjamas, but was covered in grey dust and had streaks of something brown on his face. She barged past him into the room, then turned and said "Complaints... noise... you have party," it was obvious that English wasn't her first language.

"No party here," he told her, "it's all very peaceful." She stared at him and he suddenly remembered that he was the paying guest here, so he put on an annoyed voice, pointed at the shutter and said, "Rubbish, absolute rubbish, doesn't even open, I demand a refund." She looked at him as if he was an idiot for a moment, then turned to the wall next to her and pushed a button alongside the light switch. A motor started up, somewhere behind the shutter and it slowly rose until you could walk underneath it through onto the balcony. They stared at each other for a moment and then Dennis said "Well obviously I know that, but I'm not happy with all this dust on the floor, it's just not good enough, I may have to have a word with the owner." With that he gestured towards the door as if to let her know she could leave the room. She shook her head but as she turned to go she noticed the brown stains all over his white bed sheets. She pointed, stamped one of her feet and shouted "disgusting," slamming the door behind her.

"It's not what you think," Dennis shouted, trying to come up with a logical excuse. Eventually he opened the door just in time to see her disappearing around the end of the corridor.

"It was Granddad," he shouted, "it's not his fault, he's a very old man." As he walked back into the room, Granddad shot up in bed, yawned and said "Bongers, Dennis, everything okay?"

"Fine," Dennis told him, "I thought I might just go and sit on the balcony."

"Good idea," Granddad replied, and then added, "that shutter is motorised you know, the button is up on the wall there." Dennis gave a little chuckle and said "Obviously, I'm not an idiot, mercy very much."

Granddad seemed to get quieter the closer they got to Albert. Apart from commenting that the miserable woman who worked at the HOTEL DE LA LIBERTE had given him a very funny look when they left.

"That's strange," Dennis had commented.

"It was a bit," Granddad said, "and then she spat on the floor and said, 'I suppose you want me to clean up your disgusting mess!'" Dennis told him that maybe she was just having a bad day and then quickly tried to change the subject, but Granddad's mind seemed elsewhere.

The bus pulled up in the smallish town; they grabbed their bags and stepped out into the warm morning air. Dennis looked around.

"Albert looks quite nice, Granddad, who is it named after?"

"It's changed a lot since I was last here," Granddad muttered, and then turning to Dennis said "I have no idea." Dennis thought for a moment and said "I wonder if it's Albert Higginbottom, you know, the mechanic at

150

the Dudley Garage." Granddad smiled, "I wouldn't have thought so," he replied, "let's see if we can find a half decent cup of tea."

They walked up the main street and Granddad suddenly stopped and dropped his suitcase.

"I don't believe it, the old girl's still standing," he shouted and pointed into the distance. Dennis looked up and in front of him was a magnificent church with a high tower, and perched on top of the tower was a statue of a woman and child.

"Mary and Jesus," Granddad told him, "until I saw that it all felt like, maybe I'd imagined it all." He rubbed his eyes and said "Let's get that cuppa".

They sat at a table outside a small café, took a sip of their tea, looked at each other, pulled a face and shook their heads.

"They just can't seem to get the hang of it," Dennis said, "I don't think they are letting it stew in the pot long enough."

Across the street from them was the entrance to a large cemetery, surrounded by white fences and trees, but Granddad avoided looking at it, instead staring down the road at the church.

"You see that statue up there," Granddad said pointing, "the last time I saw that it was lying down, somehow balancing on top of that tower. Lots of shells landed nearby but it just refused to fall down. It became a symbol; we thought if it ever fell down, one way or another, that was the end of the war." Dennis stared up at the statue and finally said "It outlasted everybody Granddad".

They left most of their tea and went off in search of a taxi. Dennis asked where were they going, but got no answer. They finally spotted a taxi sitting under a tree. Granddad spoke to the driver for a moment and then indicated for Dennis to get in. The driver threw his cigarette out of the window and took off as if he were driving a getaway car.

"Bongers, mercy very much," Dennis said but the driver never spoke until they were out of town and then looked at Granddad through the rear view mirror and finally said, "You were here, sir?"

"1916" Granddad replied in a quiet voice. The man just nodded. They only drove south of the town for a few minutes and the car slowed down next to some fields and pulled into a small car park. Granddad reached into his pocket, but the driver held up his hand and said "No sir, there is no cost, I will return for you in an hour".

There was a large sign with a map and writing on it, but as Dennis walked towards it he realised Granddad was walking across the field. Dennis followed him. They stood on a hill looking across fields and small areas of woods. At first Dennis thought they were just normal fields but he suddenly noticed all the ditches, now covered in grass. In some areas they were filled in but you could still make out that at some time in the past, vast trenches had covered these green fields.

"Is this where you were, Granddad?" he asked. Granddad stared into the distance and then said "Apparently so, although I don't remember it looking anything like this, the place I remember was covered in mud, and barbed wire, and noise." Dennis couldn't make any sense of it and told his granddad, "I don't understand it, what is so special about these fields?" The old man shook his head and answered, "The only thing that makes these fields special is that thousands of men died here". He pointed to his left and said "That's where we were," and then pointed further across the fields, and added, "And that's where the Germans were."

Dennis thought for a moment and said "You know what you should have done, Granddad, you should all have sneaked out of the trench in the middle of the night and gone back home. The enemy would have been waiting for weeks before they realised you'd gone." Granddad smiled and said "Now that, my lad, is an excellent plan, and a far, far, better plan than the one the generals came up with, which was to climb out of our perfectly good trench and walk towards the enemy's trench."

After a while Dennis asked the question he'd been putting off.

"Is this where your friend Percy died, Granddad?" Granddad pointed into the distance and answered his grandson, "Somewhere over there. We were side by side as always, bullets flying all around us. Percy got stuck in some barbed wire for a minute but I got him free, then we came under heavy fire and I saw a large crater just in front of us, so we ran and jumped in." He was quiet for a moment and then continued, "I didn't even realise he'd been shot for a while, it must have happened as we jumped into the crater. I could hear fighting going on for hours but I just sat with him. Then it started to get dark and the shooting died down. Eventually I managed to get him out of the crater, put him over my shoulder and carry him back to our lines. I nearly got shot by my own mates, I had to shout out "It's me, Billy Bisskit!" Dennis looked across at him and said "Billy Bisskit?"

"Yes, I do have a proper name Dennis, I'm not actually called Granddad," Billy Bisskit told him, and then added, "actually I was Young Billy, there was a lad two days older than me and he was Old Billy."

They stared across the fields for some time, both with their own thoughts and then Dennis asked, "So what became of Percy, do you know where he is?"

Granddad turned to him and said "Of course I know where he is; why do you think we came here? He's buried in that cemetery in town and I'm going to say goodbye to him".

They booked into a small hotel for the night, and after a rest, walked down the road to the cemetery. Granddad went and had a word with a man who seemed to be working there and got some directions. Dennis couldn't believe it, white gravestones and crosses as far as the eye could see. As they searched he noticed the ages of the dead, and suddenly realised most of them were not much older than he was. Running along the path they were walking down was a long trench about thirty feet long and three feet deep. The soil was piled up next to it.

"Is that a grave?" Dennis asked quietly. Granddad looked and said "Well, if it is, the deceased was a very strange shape. I think you will find they are putting some pipes down, Dennis." Then he suddenly stopped, looked down at a cross and said "Hello Percy, it's me Billy." Dennis read the simple words written on the cross. PERCY DORSEY, ROYAL WARWICKSHIRE REGIMENT, 1897-1916.

Dennis remembered when he'd visited Maud in the Dudley Cemetery after she had passed away, and how he'd needed some time alone, so he said to his granddad, "I'll go for a walk, Granddad, you can say what you need to say." He slowly walked around the cemetery looking at the names. It was so peaceful; it was easy to forget where you were. After about fifteen minutes, he walked back and Granddad was waiting for him.

"Have you said your goodbyes?" he asked.

"No," Granddad replied, "no goodbyes. I told him what I'd been up to for the last, nearly fifty years, and said, until we meet again."

"Well that's nice," Dennis told him, "but I'm sure you won't meet again for a very long time, in fact I'm expecting you to get a telegram from the Queen." With that Dennis turned around, tripped over the pile of soil and fell head first into the ditch.

They sat on a nearby bench. Granddad tried to keep a straight face but every now and again he would burst out laughing. Meanwhile Dennis tried to remove the muddy soil from his clothes.

"You never fail to cheer me up, Dennis", Granddad said, "I think I could even hear Percy laughing, he used to love stuff like that." Dennis didn't speak, he just pulled a pebble out of his ear. Granddad helped him up and said "Let's go and get cleaned up, I don't know about you but I'm ready to go home".

Two days later, they sat at the kitchen table as Mrs Bisskit poured them a cup of strong, hot tea. Dennis took a sip and purred.

"Beautiful Mum, best cuppa we have had since we left".

"I don't think I could ever go to a place that doesn't make a good pot of tea," Mrs B. told them, and then asked, "What was it like, apart from the tea?"

"Well, we met some strange people," Dennis told her.

"And they eat some very strange things," Granddad added.

"And don't even ask me about the Water Fountain in the bathrooms," Dennis said.

"It sounds as if you didn't enjoy it much," Mrs Bisskit said. Dennis put down his cup, "Now that's where you would be wrong, Mum. It was the best thing I've ever done." He looked at Granddad and added "I will never forget it as long as I live," then he stood up and told them, "I better go and report in to Stinky." He opened the front door but then turned and said "Oh, there was just one thing, Mum. If you get a letter from the Hotel de la Liberté, mentioning some minor structural damage done to walls and bed sheets, just pretend you don't know me."

Mrs Bisskit slammed her tea cup onto the table and stood to say something, but when she looked up, Dennis Bisskit had left the building.

CHAPTER 10

A WEEK LATER

The Number 41 bus came to a shuddering halt and Dennis Bisskit stepped down onto the pavement. He looked across the road at the huge building. Fosdyke's Department Store, the biggest store in Wolverhampton. It was 1961 and Dennis was about to start his first day at work. He crossed the street and stopped to check out his reflection in the store window. He had wanted to make a big impression on his first day, so he had borrowed his dad's best suit. Now looking at himself staring back, he wished he hadn't bothered. His father was taller than he was, in fact most people were taller than he was, and he now realised that the rolled up sleeves and trouser legs were not a good look. Still, too late now, he thought, and at least there was some good news. He had always had one ear smaller than the other, but it appeared that they had now gradually caught up with each other. Apart from now having two big ears, Dennis, was still small and skinny. Still, all in all not too bad, he said to himself, and slowly walked nervously towards the store entrance.

It had been a red letter day when Dennis had been told he had his first full time job. Of course the lady had explained he would be on probation at first, but if he worked diligently as Junior Tea Boy for five years, he could very well be promoted to Senior Tea Boy, which would not only mean a pay rise but also allow him to wear the coveted brown jacket. He took one last look at his reflection, pity about the suit he thought, but at least I have the Junior Tea Boy job sewn up. He climbed the steps and entered the store.

As Dennis entered his new workplace, his confidence suddenly evaporated and a churning sensation started in his bowels. He instantly felt the same as he had done some years earlier when he was walking towards the headmaster's office at school. It stopped him in his tracks for a moment, but then he thought to himself, "I'm a young man, an ex-Scout Patrol Leader, I have my whole life ahead of me, I've already achieved something by getting the highly coveted Junior Tea Boy position, what could possibly go wrong?" And with that he confidently strode into the store. Unfortunately, as was usual for Dennis, there was a dark cloud on the horizon. This time it was in the form of Mrs Ricketts who ran the store canteen as if she were in charge of a prison chain gang. Now, everyone has a perfect right to be ugly, but Mrs Ricketts completely abused the privilege. She had a face that even scared her mother, but not only was she a bit scary in the face department, she also had the personality of an extremely bad-tempered Doberman who'd had his favourite bone stolen by the next door neighbour's cat.

Of course this could all have been okay, but for some reason she seemed to take an instant dislike to Dennis. After Mrs Ricketts had shown Dennis around, she introduced him to Mr Pike, the Senior Tea Boy. He was wearing a faded brown jacket, which didn't look quite as impressive as Dennis had imagined, he also had a stoop, which Dennis found out later was caused by decades of pushing the tea trolley around. He looked as if he should have retired years ago and sensing a threat to his privileged position, immediately joined Mrs Ricketts in disliking Dennis. "This is Mr Pike", Mrs Ricketts told him, "he's worked for Fosdyke's for nearly 50 years, man and boy, never taken a day off sick, don't know how the store would run without him, follow his every command, Basket, no one knows more about a tea trolley." Dennis had noticed that Mrs R. seemed incapable of remembering his name. He tried to remind her once again.

"Bisskit, Mrs Ricketts."

"There will be time for biscuits at lunchtime, boy, just pay attention," she told him, then continued "and never interrupt me, boy, interruptions cost Fosdyke's valuable money." With that she turned and left him to Mr Pike, who reluctantly set him to work polishing the tea trolley, but only after informing him that the tea trolley had to be immaculate at all times as it was the Queen Elizabeth the Second Memorial Tea Trolley, especially commissioned for Her Majesty's historic 1955 visit to the store. Mr Pike stood to attention as he told Dennis this just to emphasise the point.

Over the next few days it appeared that polishing the tea trolley was Dennis's sole occupation. Occasionally the boredom was relieved by having to deliver the odd message to different departments, but mainly he would polish, and then Mr Pike would come and stare at it for several minutes, grunt and say, 'I suppose that will have to do lad."

At 9.55 each morning Mr Pike would inspect the trolley, take off his faded brown jacket, replace it with a brand new, immaculately ironed one, place a silver tray containing tea, milk and biscuits on top of the trolley, push it into the lift, and deliver morning tea to Mr Fosdyke on the fourth floor. Dennis had never seen Mr Fosdyke, in fact it turned out that he rarely left his office.

Mr Pike had told him that only he was allowed to deliver the tea, it was a great privilege.

"Maybe when you've been here a few years and proved yourself, one day a week, I may let you do it," he had said, as if he was going to let Dennis take the controls of a fighter plane. Dennis tried not to feel too excited.

A week or two went by and Dennis spent most of his time trying to look busy and avoid Mrs Ricketts and for once in his life he seemed to be managing to avoid trouble. But of course it couldn't last and one Wednesday morning everything went disastrously wrong. As he'd entered the store that morning, an agitated Mrs Ricketts was there to meet him. "Quick, Brisket, there's been a disaster. Mr Pike's haemorrhoids have flared up; a team of surgeons are attempting to get to the bottom of it. This is your big moment Basket, seize the day." Dennis was somewhat confused until Mrs R, explained to him that for the next few days until Mr Pike was back on his feet, he, Dennis Winston Bisskit, was acting Senior Tea Boy.

"Does this mean I get to wear the brown jacket?" he asked hopefully.

"Absolutely not Breadboard," she told him, "but it's at times like this, careers are made, the brave come to the fore, just like your father did. I understand he was a war hero boy, now it's your turn to show what you're made of at Fosdyke's time of crisis. Are you ready for the battle young Bandstand?" Dennis assured her that he was and polished the trolley with new-found vigour.

After several minutes of polishing, Dennis suddenly realised that he was acting Senior Tea Boy and therefore, his own boss, so he immediately gave himself some time off to wander around the store. It was a very large store and he'd been looking around for about half an hour, when he found himself in the Household Medicines and Fancy dress section. Just as he was admiring a new batch of false legs on the Surgical Appliances counter, he suddenly became aware of a sound that was slowly building up like an approaching storm. People appeared to be disappearing before his eyes to avoid whatever was approaching, then a terrifying voice screamed... "Birdseed, has anyone seen young Birdseed?" He quickly ducked down behind the Non-Prescription Household Medicines display, but it was too late and around the corner strode a grim-faced Mrs Ricketts. Dennis immediately felt a familiar churning sensation in his bowels and his ears began to twitch uncontrollably. He had noticed this reaction whenever Mrs Ricketts was nearby and was beginning to think it was more than just coincidence.

"Ah! Birdseed, where have you been hiding, boy? I wasted five valuable minutes looking for you, that's five minutes when Fosdyke's have had to manage without me. I'm a very busy person, Birdseed, every minute is accounted for and yet that is five minutes of my life that can never be regained." She rarely paused long enough to actually answer any of her questions, so Dennis butted in at the first opportunity, "Sorry", he stammered. "But it's Bisskit, not Birdseed."

"I don't care what it is, so long as when I shout its name it comes running," screamed Mrs R. "Yes, sorry," continued Dennis, "I was just helping Mr Trump with his haemorrhoid cream." Mrs Ricketts looked shocked and said, "Well, I think Mr Trump is quite capable of applying his own haemorrhoid cream without your assistance, boy."

Dennis quickly explained that he meant he'd been helping him stack the cream on the shelf but as usual when Mrs R. was in full flight she just ignored him.

"Forget all that young Brisket, I wish to inspect you, now stand to attention." He stood as still as his shaking body would allow, his ears were practically rotating. Mrs Ricketts looked at him with disgust.

"What's the matter with those ears boy, any more of it and I'll have to pin them to your head. I don't like that tie, I don't like that tie and I don't like those ears. The tie we can do something about; I suppose the ears will have to stay. Now listen and listen carefully, in Mr Pike's absence, you will have the great honour of taking Mr Fosdyke his morning tea. Normally I would do it but I'm too busy, especially as I've wasted," She glanced at her watch… "eight minutes and 42 seconds talking to you…now report to Mr Fish in Menswear and Chainsaws and he will sort you out a proper tie. Have the trolley gleaming and I shall inspect you at 9.45.

With that she turned and stormed off, people suddenly appeared from behind counters again and everything returned to normal. Dennis walked to Menswear and Chainsaws and explained to Mr Fish that he needed advice on a new tie.

"I'm so glad you came to see me," Mr Fish told him, as he measured Dennis's inside leg, "Correct measurements are essential for a good tie fitting." Dennis couldn't quite see the reasoning, but he assumed Mr Fish must know what he was doing.

"Now," he said, "you're a strangely attractive young man, so we must find something that compliments those ears." Mr Fish was very keen for Dennis to join him later for morning tea but he managed to get away after explaining how busy he was, and at precisely 9.44 he stood next to the gleaming tea trolley wearing his smart new tie. Not surprisingly, at precisely 9.45 the formidable Mrs Ricketts strode around the corner. She looked him up and down as he stood to attention.

"Mmmm!" she muttered," I suppose it will have to do. Is that the tie Mr Fish chose? It's a little flamboyant for my liking." Dennis told her that Mr Fish had found him strangely attractive and that this tie complimented his ears.

"Mmmm!" she continued, "there's nothing that could compliment those ears, and a word of advice Bumfluff, Mr Fish knows his Menswear but if I was you, I would avoid him at all times. Now let's get the tea and biscuits loaded on the trolley, then it's your big moment, my boy,"

At precisely 9.55 Dennis started pushing the loaded and gleaming tea trolley towards the lift. He was shaking with nerves. It all seemed simple enough but he knew from experience that if something could go wrong it would. Dennis reached the exclusive lift to the fourth floor. It had old wooden doors and looked well past its use by date but he took a deep breath, adjusted his new tie, and pushed the button next to the lift. The doors creaked, opened a few inches, closed again and then very slowly opened all the way, making a loud whining noise as if something needed a good oiling.

Dennis pushed the tea trolley towards the lift but when he reached it, he noticed that the lift actually stopped about two inches above the floor. He tried pushing the down button again but the lift just shuddered a bit and then stopped in the same spot. Dennis decided that the best way was for him to get in first and then lift his end of the trolley and pull it in behind him. Disaster struck when the trolley was halfway through the doors.

All of a sudden they closed, trapping it half in and half out of the lift. Tea and biscuits shot into the air and crashed to the floor.

Dennis looked at his watch, it was 9.59. This can't be good he thought, but then things went from bad to worse. The lift suddenly shot eight feet into the air and then came to a shuddering halt. Cups and saucers slid backwards and then fell down to the floor below. Someone shouted up to him, "Everything okay up there?" Dennis tried to sound as confident as he could.

"F-f-f-f-fine, yes, all under c-c-c-control." He pushed the DOWN button but nothing happened, and then saw the notice on the wall explaining that the lift would not work until the doors were closed. He realised that he would have to press the OPEN button and quickly pull the trolley into the lift. The only trouble was, he couldn't reach the buttons and hold on to the trolley. I'm going to have to move quickly, he thought.

He pressed the OPEN button and as the doors started to open he leapt towards the trolley, but before he could even reach it, the doors had opened a few inches and then slammed shut with such force that the trolley buckled in the middle. Seconds later there was a loud crash as the Queen Elizabeth the Second Memorial Tea Trolley plaque snapped off and fell to the ground below.

Dennis glanced at his watch, it was 10.03; no doubt Mr Fosdyke was looking at his clock now and wondering where morning tea was. Next thing he'd be ringing Mrs Ricketts and asking what the delay was, and then all hell would break loose. Dennis tried to think how a Scout Patrol Leader would solve the problem and a few moments later he had his new tie attached to the trolley handle, and his hands holding onto the tie whilst reaching out with his right foot towards the OPEN button. Not for the first time he wished he was a bit taller, but then, just as he was losing hope, his shaking foot reached the button and jabbed it.

Once again the doors began to open. Unfortunately, the trolley rolled out of the doors, and Dennis, still holding on to it and being off balance, followed it. Just as he was halfway out, the doors suddenly closed. Having nothing better to do, Dennis reviewed his situation. He was hanging halfway out of a lift, the floor was eight feet below him and he had a once valuable tea trolley attached to his new tie dangling below him. He wondered if things could possibly get any worse and then he heard a, by now familiar voice.

"Barnstable, you idiot, what do you think you are playing at?" Then she obviously noticed the damage, and raised her voice even louder, "You've killed the Queen Elizabeth the Second Memorial Tea Trolley! Mr Pike could very well have a relapse with his haemorrhoids when word gets back to him." Mrs Ricketts stood with her hands on her hips, took a couple of deep breaths and seemed to get herself back under control.

"Well, don't just hang there sightseeing, young Bumble, get down immediately whilst I explain this unmitigated disaster to Mr Fosdyke. He may well require hospital treatment through lack of morning tea by now boy, and if he does, it will be you who has to face him when he regains consciousness." With that she turned and stormed off leaving Dennis to enjoy his upside down view.

A couple of weeks later, Dennis sat opposite his best friend Stinky in The Copper Kettle Café. Stinky listened open-mouthed as Dennis bought him up to date on his latest disasters.

"That's amazing Ginge, so did you get the sack?" he asked.

"No, far from it," Dennis laughed and went on to explain to his friend what had happened. As he hung upside down from the broken lift, wondering what to do next, he suddenly heard a commanding voice shouting instructions. Next thing he knew, people were taking the trolley from him and lowering it to the ground, then ladders appeared either side of him and two large men pulled the doors open and helped him down. A man in a suit who seemed to be giving the orders helped him to his feet and introduced himself as Mr Fosdyke the owner of the store. It turned out he'd come looking for his morning cuppa and spotted Dennis hanging from the lift.

"And you still didn't get the sack?" asked Stinky again.

"I expected to," Dennis said, "I told him what had happened and he apologised and said they had been meaning to fix the lift for ages. Then Mrs Ricketts came racing over and tried to blame me for everything, but he stopped her in her tracks and said it was Fosdyke's responsibility and I should get the rest of the day off to recover," Stinky shook his head in disbelief.

"It's amazing Ginge, I've never known a bloke who gets into so much trouble and yet always lands on his feet."

"You haven't heard the end of it Stinky, next pay day I received a bonus of two and sixpence; Mr Fosdyke had named me Employee of the Month," a beaming Dennis continued.

"Wow, so everything's okay now then," said his friend.

"Mostly," Dennis hesitated, "although Mrs Ricketts dislikes me more than ever, and I thought Mr Pike was going to have a heart attack the day he returned to work and spotted the remains of The Queen Elizabeth the

Second Memorial Tea Trolley. He started crying, I felt really bad about it."

"You're going to have to watch your step there Ginge," his friend warned him, "keep a low profile for a while." Dennis promised that he would, although they both had their doubts that it was possible for Dennis to keep a low profile for very long.

CHAPTER 11

For the next week or so Dennis managed to avoid Mrs
Ricketts. Mr Pike still wouldn't speak to him, he just
grunted and pointed if he wanted something doing. The
only time he perked up was when a brand new
replacement trolley arrived. It was even bigger and
shinier than the previous one. Mr Pike spent most of his
day polishing it and told Dennis he wasn't allowed
within six feet of it. This suited Dennis just fine, he spent
most of his day just wandering around the store,
delivering messages and helping out if someone was off
sick.

One morning as Dennis was sitting reading a comic
in the staff toilet, a voice suddenly boomed over the
Tannoy, "Battenberg, will Battenberg report to Mrs
Ricketts immediately." Dennis knew straight away that it
was he who was being summoned. He had a feeling that
Mrs Ricketts deliberately got his name wrong, just to
annoy him. He checked himself in the mirror,
straightened his tie and reluctantly dragged himself to
the office of his nemesis.

Dennis knocked on the door, listened for the "Yes!
Yes! Well, what is it? I haven't got all day," and entered.
Mrs Ricketts leapt from behind her desk and started

inspecting him. His stomach immediately started rumbling.

"Well, well, what do you want? I'm very busy you know, time is money," she screamed.

"I don't want anything, you sent for me," Dennis explained.

"Ah yes, quite right young Basket," she replied. "Now, today is a very special day. Mr Fudge has been with the store for 25 years, man and boy. After work we will be having a small celebration. Mr Fosdyke will obviously make a splendid speech and then, on my word of command, you, as Fosdyke's newest and youngest employee will enter the room with a large cake which is being prepared even as I speak."

Dennis, looked a bit vague, but Mrs Ricketts continued none the less… "You will push the cake in on the new trolley, and I don't need to tell you that Mr Pike will be watching you very closely." Dennis felt the need to interrupt, and asked "Excuse me but how will I know Mr Fudge?" Mrs R. gave him a look of contempt. "Oh come, come now Basingstoke, you've met Mr Fudge, head of Leatherwear and Wind Instruments, wonderful gentleman, tall, small moustache, always impeccably dressed, wooden leg, old war wound. Worked his way up from a junior, it's something you could aspire to my boy."

Dennis thought about this for a moment and then said "I don't think I want a wooden leg." She looked him up and down, it was the sort of look you gave the bottom of your shoe when something nasty attached itself to it.

"Mmm!" She finally said. "You're an idiot, Battleship. You might improve with age, like a fine wine or you might not. Now go and get the lunch orders, change that tie, comb your hair, polish those shoes and brush those teeth, it's like the Hanging Gardens of

Babylon in there." With that she turned away. He fled as quickly as he could before she could think of something else.

The next hour or so was spent delivering messages and mail to various departments and eventually Dennis found himself in the basement looking for Mr Pugh. He was not certain what it was Mr Pugh actually did but he never seemed to emerge from the basement. Dennis called his name without success; the place seemed deserted. He was just about to give up when he heard a strange noise coming from a closed door just ahead of him. He opened the door expecting to see Mr Pugh but instead, there before him was the wonderful Miss Perkins.

Dennis had met her a couple of days earlier, when he'd popped into the Confectionery and Military Equipment Department to buy a bar of chocolate. There in front of him, unpacking a new consignment of Flame-throwers was the most beautiful girl Dennis had ever seen. He'd stutteringly managed to introduce himself as "Dennis but my friends call me Ginger," but then Mrs Ricketts had screamed for him over the Tannoy system, so he'd disappeared quickly before Miss Perkins noticed his rotating ears.

They say things come in threes and the second thing Dennis noticed was that she was hugging a huge pig. The third was that judging by the state of the floor, the pig was not entirely yet toilet trained. A terrible smell filled the room which Dennis sincerely hoped had nothing to do with Miss Perkins to whom he had taken quite a shine. On realising that it was Dennis she cried out "Thank god it's you Ginger, you must help me save him."

"Are you mad?" shouted Dennis.

"Certainly not," said Miss Perkins indignantly.

"Not you," he told her, "I'm talking to the pig. If Mrs Ricketts sees the mess he's made there'll be hell to pay." He noticed that she had tears in her eyes when she replied "I think that will be the least of his worries; when Big Bill the Butcher gets back from his deliveries he's going to stick Bert the Pig on a spit for tonight's celebration, it's an old Fosdyke's tradition." Dennis tried to cheer her up by saying "Surely he'll kill it first," but it didn't seem to help. "No doubt he will, I've heard he strangles them with his bare hands" she told him between sobs. Dennis found this hard to believe and said "But look at the neck on that pig, you could strangle it for a week and not even make its eyes water".

"Yes but Big Bill is not like other men," sobbed Miss Perkins.

She's right, thought Dennis. Big Bill was nearly as scary as Mrs Ricketts. He had arms thicker than Dennis's legs and always seemed to be covered in blood. Once when he'd delivered a message to the meat department, he'd noticed that Big Bill was covered in tattoos saying things like "DEATH TO VEGETARIANS," and "A STEAK A DAY KEEPS THE DOCTOR AWAY".

He suddenly realised Miss Perkins was talking to him.

"I say Ginger, that's a very colourful tie you're wearing," she told him.

"Yes well, it's not quite what I had in mind but Mr Fish told me it compliments my ears," he explained.

"Mmm, I'd avoid Mr Fish if I was you Dennis, but the main thing is, will you help me save this pig?" she pleaded. Dennis couldn't refuse her and she was so pleased she jumped up and kissed him on the cheek.

"Wow", stammered Dennis, "I think I'm in love".

"Me too," she replied. "Have you ever been in love before, Dennis?" He thought for a moment before saying

"Not really although I did have a crush on Victor Sylvester when I was younger." She told him it might be best to never tell Mr Fish about that and then said she would tell him her first name as long as he didn't laugh. Dennis looked offended and told her he would never do such a thing.

Later when he finished laughing she'd explained that she was called Wensleydale because her mother had been very partial to that type of cheese when she was pregnant. Dennis told her he would call her Dale and they set about working on a plan to save the pig.

"You know Dennis, it just might work," she told him, "Might," he said, "there's no might about it, this plan is a work of genius." Dale laughed and patted Bert on the head; she had named the pig Bert after her young brother Camembert.

"We will need a vehicle," she suddenly realised, "I will ring my big brother Gordon, he'll help us."

"Just a minute," Dennis said, "you have a brother with a normal name like Gordon."

"It's short for Gordonzola," Dale replied, "and before you ask, Mum and Dad knew it should be Gorgonzola, but felt that Gorgon was a silly name."

"Boy, I thought my parents were a bit strange," Dennis said, "are there any more of you?"

"There's my young sister Ella", "Don't tell me," interrupted Dennis, "is it short for Mozzarella?" Dale nodded her head and continued, "Then there's baby Harold, he's named after Harold Higgins who owns the cheese shop."

They laughed and then Dale told him she would call Gordon and get him to park his van outside Fosdyke's at the appointed time, then they would stick Bert in the van and drop him off at Johnston's farm. "They won't notice one extra pig, but then I'm afraid you're on your own, Bert," she told him. Bert grunted and passed wind.

"Are you sure you can get him through the store Dennis?" she asked.

"Piece of cake," replied Dennis confidently, "although keeping him quiet could be a problem."

"I've thought of that," Dale told him, "I've got to pick up Mum's sleeping tablets from the chemist. If I give him a few he should sleep like a baby. Meanwhile he can stay here, Mr Pugh is off sick and no one else comes down here."

They arranged to meet later and Dennis rushed off, the last thing he wanted was to upset Mrs Ricketts again. Unfortunately, that's exactly what he was about to do, and as he happily ran up the stairs from the basement to the ground floor, he heard an approaching voice.

"Bushpole, has anyone seen Bushpole?" Dennis spotted a large cardboard box on the floor and picked it up to give the impression of someone hard at work. He rounded the corner and came face to face with an angry looking Mrs R.

"I'm right here Mrs Ricketts," he told her.

"Well I can see that Bisskit, my eyes haven't completely deserted me," she screamed.

"S-s-s-sorry" he stammered, "I thought you were looking for me."

"I'm not a fool, boy, obviously if I were looking for you I'd shout Bisskit, but as it is I'm looking for Mr Bushpole of Safari Suits and Superfluous Hair Products. Incidentally Biggles, what is in that box?" Dennis couldn't think of a good lie so just said "nothing". Mrs Ricketts looked him up and down and said "I see, and where might you be taking this empty box?"

"Nowhere," he admitted. She stared at him and appeared to be foaming at the mouth, "I'm keeping my eyes on you, young Bumfluff," she told him, "oh by the way", she continued, "When you walked around the corner you appeared to be in pain." Dennis thought back, "Oh no, I was just smiling" he explained, "I'm just so happy to be working at Fosdyke's". If Dennis was hoping that Mrs Ricketts would be impressed, she quickly corrected him.

"Smiling, smiling you say, it's impossible to smile and work at the same time young Bedpan. You never see me smile, the only time you would see me smile is when I'm tucked up in bed at the end of the day drinking a mug of Ovaltine and even then I'm only smiling because I'm thinking about how I can work even harder for Mr Fosdyke the next day." Dennis tried hard not to picture this happy scene.

"Now then Bunting, take your empty box to nowhere but at 16.00 hours precisely I expect to see you, the trolley and Mr Fudge's cake in my office." She turned to go then quickly turned back, "Oh, by the way, I don't suppose on your travels you happened to spot a large pig?" she enquired. Dennis could not speak but just shook his head.

"It's a bit of a mystery, Bamford, I think dirty work is afoot." Dennis hoped that she wasn't referring to the mess Bert had made in the storeroom, but she continued, "Bill the Butcher is a kindly, misunderstood man but he does like his roast pork and at the moment there is no consoling him. I'll tell you one thing, my boy, I would not want to be the one who came between Big Bill and his pig." Dennis gulped but felt that at this point it was best to remain silent.

Dennis spent the next hour assisting Mr Bent of the Fresh Fish and Gentlemen's Undergarments Department, but his heart wasn't in it. Now he'd found love, all he could do was daydream of a future with Dale. He imagined that one day, once he'd been promoted to Senior Tea Boy, with a small pay rise and the Brown Jacket, he would ask Dale to marry him. Of course she would immediately agree, crying tears of joy.

Dennis would use his old Scout Patrol Leader skills to build a small cottage in the country, with a back garden so that they could adopt Bert. They would get him a girlfriend, and hopefully before long there would be the patter of tiny trotters. They would name the little piglets after various cheeses from around the world.

His happy dreams were rudely interrupted by one of the scariest sights he had ever seen. Big Bill the Butcher was striding towards him, his white jacket was red with the blood of something recently slaughtered, his eyes were bulging and he didn't seem in a good mood. He stopped in front of Dennis; his fists were clenched as if he was about to throw a punch. Dennis had noticed before that it always took Big Bill a while to speak, it was as if he was struggling to get the words from his brain to his mouth.

Eventually he roared "PIG"! Dennis wasn't sure if he was being called a pig or if the game was up, either way he could feel his bowels starting to churn.

"P-p-p-p-p-p," he stammered. Big Bill just stared at him, and then said "Are you an idiot, boy?" It was the biggest speech Dennis had ever heard him make. It crossed his mind that Big Bill could be the love-child of Mrs Ricketts and Hitler. Now Big Bill had learned how to speak, there was no stopping him.

"Anyone who finds my pig, there's a couple of pork chops in it for them," he said. Dennis felt that now was not the time to mention his new vegetarian conversion, so instead said "O-o-o-o-o-kay." Big Bill stared at him as if trying to think of something new to say, but he'd obviously used up his entire vocabulary, so eventually he just shook his head and strode off.

At 3.30 that afternoon, Dennis made his way as quietly as he could down to the basement. As he pushed the brand new Queen Elizabeth the Second Memorial Tea Trolley in front of him, he dreaded walking into Mrs Ricketts and having to come up with some reason for being there. His only plan was to claim that he'd fallen over and banged his head and couldn't remember anything after that, but luckily he reached the basement without bumping into anyone.

When he opened the door to the storeroom, Dale was already there waiting for him. Next to her was a sleeping Bert, snoring away merrily.

"Perfect timing, Dennis," she said, "I rang Gordon, he will be waiting for us by the side exit, now let's get Bert onto the trolley." At this point Dennis's plan ran into its first major obstacle. Getting a comatose, 20 stone pig, onto the bottom shelf of a tea trolley is actually not as easy as you may at first think. The big problem was that Bert seemed quite happy where he was, snoring away with a contented smile on his face, with the occasional rumbling coming from his stomach, followed by a foul smell filling the room.

"I should have brought gas masks, we could be found dead in here," Dennis spluttered. Actually it was the smell that eventually solved the problem. It's amazing how strong you suddenly become when your life is in danger and after a great deal of pushing and pulling Bert lay sleeping on the tea trolley bottom shelf covered with a large white tablecloth.

Dale and Dennis took several moments to get their breath back. They then went over the rest of the plan. There was no way that they could get the trolley up the stairs, so, reluctantly he would have to use the lift and hope that no-one got in with them. Dale opened the storeroom door and Dennis, with some difficulty, pushed the trolley out of the room. The wheels creaked loudly.

"I don't think the trolley was built to take this weight," he told Dale, as they slowly made their way towards the lift doors. Dale ran forward and pushed the button to open the lift doors, then helped Dennis push the wobbling trolley into the lift, the wheels were squealing as if in pain.

Dennis looked distraught, "It's going to look terrible on my work record if I destroy yet another Queen Elizabeth the Second Memorial Tea Trolley," he muttered. Dale gave him a reassuring hug and asked him to wait there a moment whilst she retrieved her jacket she had left in the storeroom.

Dennis glanced at his watch, it was 3.50. He had ten minutes to get Bert upstairs, through the store into Dale's brother's van, then clean the trolley, collect Mr Fudge's cake from the canteen and get to Mrs Ricketts' office. He sighed and shook his head.

Just at that moment a large blast came from under the tablecloth on the trolley and within seconds the evillest smell Dennis had ever smelt filled the lift; tears filled his eyes and he started to choke. He heard approaching footsteps from behind him and said "Thank God you are here my darling." He wiped the tears from his eyes as he turned and nearly fainted when he spotted Mrs Ricketts, hands on hips, staring at him.

"Darling! Darling! I'm nobody's darling, Butternut. It's Mrs Ricketts. That was good enough for my late husband, Mr Ricketts and it's good enough for you my boy. Now I'm glad to see you have the trolley ready, let's go and collect Mr Fudge's cake from the canteen."

With that she stepped into the lift with Dennis and the sleeping Bert. Before she had even closed the lift doors, she started sniffing the air and looking around.

"Please tell me that smell has nothing to do with you Billingsgate," she gasped. Dennis was traumatised, he was stuck in a lift with Mrs Ricketts and a large comatose pig with flatulence problems.

"Mr F-F-F-Flange," he stuttered, "What about Mr F-F-F-Flange?" she enquired.

"Mr F-Flange of the Gentlemen's Toupees and Bakery Department," he continued.

"Yes, yes, I know who Mr Flange is, fine gentleman, always impeccably dressed, wears a monocle, member of the Freemasons, but what about him?" asked a, by now exasperated Mrs Ricketts. Dennis wasn't really sure since he was making it up as he went along, but continued none the less.

"Mr Flange could be responsible for the smell, he was just in the lift and told me he had a stomach upset, evidently he ate some prawns that disagreed with him." Mrs Ricketts shook her head sadly.

"Well there you go, that explains it," she told him, "you'd think a Freemason would know better. Personally I never touch seafood and let that be a lesson to you young Buttocks. My mother, God rest her soul, always used to say, if the lord had meant us to associate with fish, we would all have been born with a large fin on our heads. Anyway we will just have to put up with the smell, we have work to do."

With that she pushed the button and the doors closed but not before Dennis caught a glimpse of a concerned looking Dale peeping around a corner. The old lift creaked up to the next floor and suddenly stopped. The doors slowly opened and Mrs Crump from the Garden

Gnome and Archery Department stepped in; she glanced about and sniffed the air.

"It's okay," explained Mrs Ricketts, "Mr Flange...prawns." Mrs Crump smiled and nodded as if that explained everything. She turned and closed the doors and they continued to the next floor. Dennis was sweating so much, it was running down his legs and collecting in his shoes, he felt he might faint at any moment...

The doors opened on the next floor. Mrs Ricketts strode forward, shouting, "Follow me Buzzard, onwards and upwards." She suddenly stopped and turned as she heard the squealing wheels of the trolley; Dennis was struggling to follow her.

"Those wheels need oiling my boy, I'm surprised Mr Pike hasn't mentioned it and why are you puffing and panting?" She walked back and surveyed him for a moment.

"I've just got two words to say to you' she said to him, "Charles Atlas, now there's an example you could follow young Barrowmore, Charles Atlas. You don't see him puffing and panting because he exercises. Now hurry along, we have no time to waste, go to the canteen and collect the cake, then make your way to the reception area, where we are having the presentation." She turned and stormed off, and seconds later Dale appeared.

"Well done Dennis", she gasped, "I thought the game was up for a moment there." Dennis still felt faint but managed to tell Dale that Bert was starting to wake up and they had no time to lose. They started making their way to the side exit where Gordon would be waiting with his van. Dennis started giggling hysterically, as he always did when nervous.

"We are going to make it; we are going to make it" he said to no one in particular. He could see the side exit doors about 30 yards in front of him.

"I love it when a brilliant plan comes together" he shouted between giggles, then coming towards him he saw the last person on earth that he wished to see. He turned to tell Dale "It's Big Bill," but Dale seemed to have disappeared as if by magic and Dennis was on his own. Big Bill strode towards him. Dennis stopped giggling and started crying. Bert grunted from beneath the white tablecloth. Big Bill stopped in front of Dennis and said "Why are you crying, lad?" Dennis couldn't speak, he was shaking from fear; just then Bert grunted. Big Bill looked about him, "Did I hear a pig grunting?" he asked incredulously. Dennis immediately grunted and said "No, that's just me, I keep grunting hoping it will attract your lost pig." Bert grunted again, closely followed by Dennis. Big Bill just stared, the cogs in his brain slowly trying to make sense of it all, but just as he appeared ready to speak, a loud bell suddenly started ringing. Dennis heard footsteps behind him and Mrs Crutch from the pork scratchings and Dog Grooming Accessories Department ran past him.

"Quick lads, it's the fire bell", she turned to tell them. Big Bill sprang into action, "Quick lad, get out, I have to save my sirloin from the freezer". With that he was gone and before Dennis could move, Dale reappeared by his side.

"It's all I could think of, I saw Big Bill coming so I set off the fire alarm," she told him. Then she got behind the trolley alongside Dennis and started to push; "Let's move quick, before someone realises it's a false alarm". With two people pushing they picked up a bit of speed and raced along the corridor towards the exit doors. Just as they neared them and started to slow down, a figure ran around the corner, crashed straight into the trolley, shot into the air, and then landed unconscious on the floor. They rushed around to the front of the trolley.

"It's Mr Fudge, I think we've killed Mr Fudge on his 25th anniversary," cried Dale. She suddenly shot backwards and gasped, "Oh no! We've ripped his leg off," Dennis looked down and saw that Mr Fudge's left leg appeared to be back to front.

"No it's just his wooden leg," he told Dale, "it must have come loose."

"Quick," shouted Dale, "help me get him on the trolley." She grabbed him under the arms, whilst Dennis grabbed Mr Fudge's legs. Unfortunately, the wooden leg shot down Mr Fudge's trousers and Dennis fell backwards holding on to it. Dale also fell backwards with Mr Fudge landing on top of her.

It took several minutes to get him on top of the trolley. Dennis threw his wooden leg on top of him, Dale opened the exit doors and they pushed the trolley out into the sunshine. A white van was parked nearby and Dale shouted to the young man who was standing next to it, "Gordon, quick, open the back doors." Dennis lifted the tablecloth and Bert stared back at him and yawned.

With great difficulty, the three of them managed to get Bert into the back of the van, and Gordon drove off down the road, with Dale and Dennis promising to meet him as soon as they could get away. There had been one bad moment when Mr Fudge suddenly sat up just as they were guiding Bert into the back of the van. He pointed at Bert, tried to speak and then fell backwards again. Seconds after Gordon had driven away, several people including Mr Fosdyke and Mrs Ricketts ran around the corner.

"Thank God you're safe," Mr Fosdyke exclaimed, then he spotted Mr Fudge lying on the trolley. As usual Dale reacted the quickest.

"We found Mr Fudge collapsed on the floor so we stopped to rescue him' she said. Mrs Rickets gave them a look that suggested she didn't believe a word of it, especially when Mr Fudge suddenly shot up, pointed into the distance and shouted "PIG!" before collapsing again.

"I think he's hallucinating," said Dale, "he keeps imagining he can see pigs," Mr Fosdyke took control and told someone to call for an ambulance for Mr Fudge. Then he turned to Dennis and Dale and told them that they were heroes and had shown great leadership under stress.

"I think we should arrange for some sort of medal," he told Mrs Ricketts. She reluctantly agreed, unable to take her eyes off the bottom shelf of the tea trolley.

"I think Mr Fudge may have severely soiled himself on the trolley," she muttered to no-one in particular.

TWO WEEKS LATER

Stinky shook his head in disbelief. He'd known Dennis for years but never failed to be amazed by his best friend's ability to get into so much trouble and yet somehow come out on top.

"I can't believe it Dennis," he exclaimed, "They actually gave you a medal?"

"Well not really a medal," Dennis laughed, "It's just a piece of paper recognising our heroic deeds. Luckily Mr Fudge couldn't remember much; occasionally he asks if anyone saw a pig but we just tell him he must have imagined it. We dropped Bert off at Johnston's farm. Dale visits him every now and again."

"And what of your nemesis Mrs Ricketts?" asked an amused Stinky.

"She suspects something happened but she's not sure what," Dennis told him, and then broke into his, by now legendary Mrs Ricketts impersonation, "There's something going on, Butterdish, I don't know what, but once I find out there'll be trouble with a capital trouble. I'm not the person to be messed with, Badminton, not the person at all." They both fell about laughing and then Stinky suddenly looked a bit serious and said, "Well you're not the only one with news, Ginger, I have some big news myself." He told Dennis his big news and Dennis was unable to speak for several moments, he felt his eyes begin to water.

"Wow, that's come as a shock Stinky, the army? I didn't know you were even interested in the army. When do you go?" asked a stunned Dennis.

"Well, it's something I've been thinking about for a while, Ginger, I won't join until my 18th birthday, so we'll still see plenty of each other," Stinky told him, "I'm just sick of doing a boring job. I want to travel and have a bit of excitement," he continued, "remember the fun we used to have on Scout weekends? I should imagine the army is very much like one long Scout weekend, Ginger."

Dennis couldn't speak for some time. Not only did he remember those old weekends when he used to lead his Scout Troop, he often thought of them and wished he could have that time all over again. He was starting to get bored himself pushing the tea trolley around all day. Things were still going well with Dale, but she was now talking about leaving Fosdyke's to do a hairdressing apprenticeship.

"Are you sure the army is the same as the Scouts, Stinky?" he asked.

"Well, from everything I've read, it's very similar, Dennis," his friend told him confidently.

Dennis thought for a bit longer and then made a decision.

"Now look here Stinky, my old friend," he announced, "I'm not saying you couldn't manage on your own but in all honesty, if things get tough you're going to need me by your side to sort things out, how about we join together?"

Now it was Stinky's turn to look stunned but after a moment he said, "I was hoping you'd say that, my old mate." He tapped Dennis's glass of Dandelion and Burdock with his own and said "Here's to the new Scout Troop." Dennis thought for a moment and added, "The only trouble is, how do I manage to work with Mrs Ricketts for another year without going crazy?"

CHAPTER 12

Dennis pushed the tea trolley around at Fosdyke's for a few more months, getting more bored by the day. Mrs Ricketts suspected that somehow Dennis and Dale had got the better of her during the Bert the Pig saga, and every time she bumped into Dennis she would raise her eyebrows and say "I've got my eyes on you Bainbridge", or whatever she was calling him that particular day.

Dale left after a few weeks, for her dream job as an apprentice hairdresser at HAIR TODAY, GONE TOMORROW. She kept telling Dennis he should get a more modern style like Elvis, but Dennis stuck with his old short back and sides. As he'd told her on more than one occasion, "If it's good enough for Boris Karloff, it's good enough for me."

One day Dennis was talking to Stinky and started discussing how fed up he was with his job.

"You only need to last out for another nine months and then we'll be off to join the army," his friend told him, but Dennis was adamant.

"I can't last that long, Mrs Ricketts will drive me mad," he told Stinky, "they will lock me up in a padded cell and I'll be screaming, "Its Bisskit! It's Dennis Bisskit!"

Stinky laughed but then suddenly a thought occurred to him.

"I have the very job for you, and you wear a uniform so it will be good preparation for the army." He explained how he'd been talking to a lad he knew recently who was leaving his job because his family were moving to London.

"You remember Jimmy Biggins?" Stinky asked him. Dennis thought for a moment and suddenly nodded his head, "Chubby lad, with bad acne and a lazy eye".

"That's him," his friend replied. "Well he's been bellboy at The Victoria Hotel in Wolverhampton, he's just handed in his notice and they asked him if he knew anyone who could replace him."

"Bellboy," Dennis said. "What does a bellboy actually do?"

"Nothing much," Stinky told him, "carry people's bags into the hotel, a bit of light maintenance work, polish people's shoes, that sort of thing, but he said you meet loads of interesting people and get plenty of tips if you look after the guests. One man gave him a ten-shilling note once."

A few days later Dennis waited nervously to see Mrs Ricketts. He had visited the Victoria Hotel the previous evening after work, and been interviewed by a very nice lady who was standing in for the hotel manager, who was away that day. She had explained what his duties would be if he got the position and gone on to say that if he did a good job as Bellboy, one day he could go on to be Bellman. Of course Dennis didn't mention that he would be leaving in nine months to join the army, as he felt that could go against him. At the end of the interview, she had told him the job was his if he wanted

it, and all she needed was a reference from his present job.

"Leaving! leaving Fosdyke's, have you taken leave of your senses, Bottlebrush," Mrs Ricketts was foaming at the mouth, "in all my years of service to this magnificent store, I don't think I've ever heard such a thing. Do you realise all the hours that have been put into turning you into a half decent tea boy, time that can never be recovered?" She stopped momentarily to catch her breath. Dennis had realised a long time ago, that when Mrs Ricketts asked a question, she didn't require you to interrupt with an answer.

"Well," she continued, "I'm disappointed Biggles, you've let me down, but more importantly you have let this great institution down, and let me say this: One day Bradford, you will probably be doing some boring job and you will look back on this moment as a major turning point in your life," she took a quick breath. Dennis stared out of the window.

"Yes, you will think, I could now be Senior Tea Boy wearing the coveted brown jacket, if only I had listened to that wise Mrs Ricketts." Dennis could feel himself losing the will to go on, so for the first time since he had met Mrs R. he actually interrupted her.

"I need a reference," he told her. She just stared at him for a moment and then said "Come and collect it after work Barrymore, I can't waste time on that sort of thing during working hours." Dennis turned to leave but then turned back and said, "Please, Mrs Ricketts, just for once could you get my name correct on the reference letter?"

That evening Dennis called around to Stinky's house. He was holding an envelope with TO WHOM IT MAY CONCERN written on the front.

"Quick, Stinky, put the kettle on to boil," he shouted.

"I don't think we have any milk until Mum gets home," his best friend told him, but Dennis explained, he didn't want a cup of tea, he wanted to steam open this envelope.

"She was too polite when I picked up the reference," he told Stinky. "I don't trust her, she even got my name right. She shook my hand and said all the best for the future."

"Maybe she was just being nice," Stinky said, but Dennis explained to him that Mrs Ricketts didn't understand the meaning of the word nice and the fact that she was pretending to be nice, meant something was going on. He held the envelope over the steam, until he could carefully prise it open. He removed the folded letter from inside, read it and smiled.

"You may think you are very clever, Mrs Ricketts, but you have to get up extremely early in the morning to get the better of Dennis Bisskit," he muttered, and then passed the letter to his friend who read it aloud.

"TO WHOM IT MAY CONCERN. DENIS BUMSTEAD HAS WORKED (and I use the term loosely) AT FOSDYKES FOR THE LAST 12 MONTHS. HE SETS HIMSELF A VERY LOW STANDARD AND CONSTANTLY FAILS TO ACHIEVE IT."

It was signed, yours faithfully Gladys Ricketts. Dennis held out his hand, "Pen and paper Stinky, I'm fairly confident that I can write myself a much more flattering reference than this one."

Dennis was forced to work a week's notice and spent the majority of it avoiding Mrs Ricketts.

The following week, he was escorted into the office of Mr Morris Plumb, owner of The Victoria Hotel, who took the offered letter of reference from Dennis and told him to be seated. Dennis was slightly nervous as Mr Plumb read the letter, wondering if he might have got a bit carried away. Mr Plumb muttered to himself as he read, "outstanding worker…totally dedicated… always impeccably dressed…possibly the finest person I have met in all my days in retail…" The hotel owner looked him up and down and finally said "Well, my boy, you certainly seemed to have made an impression on this…" he looked at the reference letter again, "Ricketts woman". Dennis looked suitably embarrassed.

"I had no idea she would write that sir," he said, "it's very moving to hear you read that sir, as Mrs Ricketts is the most inspirational and hard working person I have ever met." Just to emphasise the point, Dennis removed his handkerchief from his top pocket and was just dabbing his eyes when Mr Plumb suddenly shouted "Went!". Dennis looked up and said 'Who went, sir?" Mr Plumb ignored him and shouted again "You there, Went". Dennis was a bit confused by now, so asked Mr Plumb, "Who there went where sir?" but then he realised that the hotel owner was waving his hand at someone on the other side of his glass office door, the door opened and a short, severe looking man in a fancy suit and bow tie entered the room. He had a small clipped moustache.

"Good morning Ronald, good to see you back," Mr Plumb said to him, "let me introduce me to our new bellboy Dennis Bisskit, and I'd be careful Ronald, he comes with such glowing references he could soon be

189

after your job." Dennis stood up and turned and the man shook his hand and said "Ronald Went, Hotel Manager".

The last thing Dennis wanted was to get off to a bad start like he had with Mrs Ricketts, so he quickly said, "Very pleased to meet you, Mr Went. I just hope I can do my best to uphold the tremendous reputation of the Victoria Hotel sir". Mr Went seemed suitably impressed.

CHAPTER 13

Dennis stared at his reflection in the mirror. He did a complete circle, glancing over his shoulder as he went, trying to see what he looked like from behind. He could not believe the transformation. In his young life he had already worn several uniforms, the wolf cubs' uniform, the school uniform, the scouts' uniform, and before long he hoped to be wearing an army uniform, but he doubted that he would ever look as impressive as he did now. Dark blue trousers with a red stripe running down the side. A short red jacket, with blue epaulettes and gold buttons, and the crowning glory, a small, round blue hat with VH printed on the front and a blue strap which went under his chin. Mr Went had told him there were several uniforms in the storeroom and to try and find one that fitted him.

The amazing thing was that he'd managed to find one that fitted as if it had been tailored especially for him. All his life Dennis had had trouble with clothes. Trousers were always too long, or too short or too baggy. Jackets and shirts likewise. It was partly because Dennis was short for his age, but also due to his family, like many others, being short of money after the war. Money was spent on important things and clothes were a luxury.

Often Dennis wore hand-me-downs, mainly from other family members. In fact, for the first five years of his life he was usually dressed in his cousin's old clothes. He wouldn't have minded so much but she wasn't even his size. Still, all that was in the past. Dennis was just disappointed that Mr Went had informed him, he could not take the uniform home. He had to change into it at the hotel. This was due to the fact that once, when Jimmy Biggins had walked home wearing it, he'd been attacked by some ruffians, who'd thrown mud pies at his uniform. When Dennis had later mentioned this to Stinky, his friend had looked a bit guilty and said "I wouldn't know anything about that." Dennis had one last look at himself in the mirror. He gave himself a little salute and muttered, "Okay, it's time to make my entrance".

The first week, Mr Went and Molly, the woman who'd interviewed him initially, showed him what his job consisted of. There were two bellboys, the other was Jack, who'd worked at the hotel for a few months. They did alternate shifts: one week, 7am until 3pm and then the following week 3pm until 11pm. Dennis had been worried about missing the last bus home but luckily it pulled up right outside the hotel at 11.05 every night. As Stinky had said, his main job was to look after the guests' luggage, escort them to their rooms, keep the lobby clean, and also help out with some maintenance when it was quiet. On the evening shift guests would leave their shoes outside their rooms and the bellboy would polish them. He was required to work some weekends, and on those weeks he would get a day off during the week instead. He was so busy that it was a couple of weeks before he managed to catch up with Stinky and let him know how things were going.

"You remember when we saw James Stewart in that movie Strategic Air Command, and we said how dashing he looked in his uniform?" Stinky had his mouth full of cake but nodded. "Well," Dennis told him, "In my uniform I look very like he did, in fact I'd say that from a distance many people could very easily think that I was James Stewart."

Stinky wiped the crumbs from his mouth, and said "It would probably have to be quite a large distance Dennis, since he's about twice your height and doesn't have ginger hair. Anyway, enough about you, what is the hotel like?"

Dennis took a sip of his tea, put the cup on its saucer and said "Well, put it this way, in the foyer is a large painting showing the Coronation of Queen Victoria, and I suspect that's the last time the hotel was decorated. I spend most of my time mending stuff that's falling to pieces. The other day I was polishing a door knob and it fell off. Still, at least I haven't got Mrs Ricketts screaming at me all day; Mr Went is a real gentleman, he even calls me Dennis."

"Well, that's a big improvement," Stinky said. "It's normally Badger, or Bumfluff or Basingstoke." Dennis laughed and ordered more cake.

Dennis was exhausted. The Victoria had a spectacular wooden staircase, it commenced near the reception desk, and then swept around in a big circle until it reached the top landing where most of the guest rooms were. There was a lift, but it was often out of order and even when it was working Dennis was reluctant to try it, still mindful of his disasters with the lift at Fosdyke's Department Store. Some of the guests seemed to bring a ridiculous amount of baggage with them, which Dennis was expected to carry to their rooms. It reminded him of his mother when she went on holidays, in fact he often thought how happy he was that his mother didn't come and stay at the hotel. He could imagine having to carry sofas and dining tables up the big staircase. He'd be saying, "The rooms already have furniture in them Mum," and she'd be telling him, "You can't be too careful Dennis".

His thoughts were interrupted by the bell; this meant his services were required. He straightened his cap and strode to the reception desk.

"Never run," Mr Went had told him, "just a smart, purposeful stride, and always a smile on one's face, as if one is delighted to get the opportunity to assist a guest."

Dennis strode purposefully and smiled, although when he saw the size of the suitcases next to the couple booking in he didn't feel especially delighted to be getting the opportunity to assist them. Fifty-five steps, Dennis counted them out, as he struggled with a case in each hand and a hat box wedged under his arm. He staggered to the room door whilst the guests meandered behind him. When he reached it, he put down the luggage by the door and said "I'll just pop down and get your other case". He raced back down the fifty-five steps, grabbed the suitcase and raced back up. His legs were shaking. The couple were still standing next to the door looking a bit unhappy and when Dennis reached them, the man said "About time, lad; now do you mind opening our door? Those cases aren't going to walk in on their own". Dennis carried the cases into the room and turned to leave, he hesitated slightly just in case, but the woman said "I hope you're not expecting a tip after leaving us waiting outside our room like that".

The wages were not high for a bellboy, in fact he was on slightly less than he'd earned at Fosdyke's and now he was doing shift work, but Mr Went had assured him that he could make plenty of extra cash in tips. Jack the other bellboy, whom Dennis normally saw for a few seconds as they swapped over at the start and end of a shift, had told him that some weeks he had doubled his wages in tips. So far Dennis had received sixpence off one gentlemen who'd looked like a gangster, and then an elderly lady had shouted to him as he reached the bottom of the steps. He had raced all the way back up and she'd said "I forgot to give you this". She had placed a penny in his hand. Dennis had thanked her very much once he'd got his breath back.

One day as he was walking past Mr Went's room, he heard the hotel manager's voice calling him. The door was half open so he stepped into the room. Mr Went was the only member of staff who lived permanently at the hotel and Dennis saw he'd made himself at home. Flowers in a vase and several framed photographs on top of a writing desk. Dennis noticed one of Mr Went in an officer's uniform.

Mr Went was sitting at the desk writing something. He turned and said, "Dennis, how is everything, I hope you are settling in okay?" Dennis told him that he was. Mr Went pushed his chair back and stood.

"Now lad," he said, "you may have heard of Mr Wellborn in Room 39." Dennis nodded. Apart from Mr Went, Mr Wellborn was the only other person who seemed to live permanently at the Victoria. His room was right at the end of the corridor on the top floor, near the large storeroom. Dennis had heard his name mentioned but had yet to see him emerge from his room. Mr Went explained that Mr Wellborn didn't get out much due to a leg injury, so a couple of times a week, Dennis should knock on his door and check if he needed any shopping doing.

"He never needs much, sometimes some tobacco," Mr Went told him, and then as Dennis left the room, he added, "I know you are very sociable Dennis, but Mr Wellborn likes to be left to himself, so don't waste too much energy trying to get him to talk."

Dennis walked up to the top landing, down to near the end of the corridor and knocked on the door opposite the store room. After a few seconds he knocked again, and he heard a quiet voice telling him to come in. He entered the room, it was very small, much smaller that Mr Went's room. Just a single bed, a round table with two chairs, and a stand in the corner with various items of clothing hanging from it. On top of the table was a little television set, on the other side of the room was a wash basin with a mirror above it. There was also a shelf on the wall holding several photos and above it a framed picture of the Queen.

Sitting on the bed was a middle-aged man with short grey hair. Even though he didn't leave his room much, Dennis noticed how tidy he kept it, and the sharp creases on his trousers and the clean shirt and tie. Dennis held out his hand and said, "Very pleased to meet you, Mr Wellborn, I'm the new bellboy Dennis, just checking to see if you need anything."

Mr Wellborn looked surprised, he stared at Dennis's hand for a while and eventually gave it a weak shake. "You could get me some toothpaste, if you don't mind," he eventually said. He reached for a cane next to him and used it to slowly stand up, grimacing as he did so. Dennis realised he had some sort of injury and reached out to assist him, but the man waved him away. He slowly limped over to the stand and reached into a jacket pocket. When he turned he saw that Dennis had taken a photo off the shelf and was staring at it. The photo had obviously been taken some time ago, it was a view of a

196

beach; a little girl sat on a donkey, with a smiling man walking next to her. Even though it was an old picture Dennis was sure the man was Mr Wellborn. He knew exactly where the photograph was taken as he could see the well-known tower in the background.

"Blackpool," Dennis said, "I went there with my family once, I couldn't find the sea, is that your daughter?" The man angrily grabbed the photo from Dennis's hand and placed it back on the shelf. As soon as Dennis apologised the man seemed to calm down.

"I don't like people touching my stuff," he said.

The next time Dennis was alone with Mr Went, he asked him, how come Mr Wellborn lived at the hotel.

"We don't pry into the lives of guests Dennis," Mr Went told him, but if there was one thing that Dennis enjoyed, it was prying. A few days later he spotted Molly by the open fire exit door having a quiet smoke. She jumped when he approached her, "I thought you were Mr Went," she said. "He doesn't like me stopping for a smoke." Dennis smiled and then asked her about Mr Wellborn.

"He saved Mr Plumb's life during the war," she said, and then told him what she knew.

"Evidently, they were both in a tank. Mr Wellborn was in charge, he was a sergeant and Mr Plumb was just a…" she shrugged and then said "whatever you call them, anyway, they were at the Battle of Tobruk. The tank got hit by a shell, a couple of men were killed. Mr Plumb was knocked out and Mr Wellborn had a bad leg injury, but he managed to drag Mr Plumb out and somehow carry him to safety." Molly took one last puff of her cigarette and then dropped it onto the ground and stood on it.

"Wow' said Dennis, "so he's a war hero, but what's he doing here?" She kicked the remains of the cigarette away and continued, "I heard that they lost touch and then about ten years ago, Mr Plumb discovered he'd fallen on hard times, he brought him to the hotel and insisted that he have a room here at a low rent, he can stay as long as he wishes."

"That's an amazing story," Dennis told her and then asked, "Why would he not live with his family?"

"No idea," she said "but I did hear he had some sort of family tragedy before he even met Mr Plumb."

He knocked on Mr Wellborn's door twice a week, just to see if he needed anything. Then he started calling in sometimes during his lunch break. Gradually Mr Wellborn starting chatting to him, just general stuff, the weather, that sort of thing, and then one day when he called in during his lunch, Mr Wellborn made him a cup of tea and invited him to sit at the small table.

Dennis told him all about his trip to France with his granddad. He was very interested and for the first time since they had met, he actually laughed when Dennis told him about to trying to order a Full English Breakfast in a French café. Dennis never mentioned the photograph on Blackpool Beach. For some reason, probably because he'd spent so much time with his granddad, Dennis seemed to get on well with older people, for some reason he felt at ease with them and they with him. He knew that eventually, when he felt ready, Mr Wellborn would tell him about the photograph.

The weeks passed by. Luckily the lift was repaired and Dennis got over his fear of using it, this made life a lot easier. He did get one minor telling off when he came to work one day and Mr Went asked him if he'd polished the guests' footwear and put them back outside the correct rooms, the previous evening. Dennis assured him that he had. Mr Went said if that was the case how come the Pastor's wife in Room 12 had found a pair of red stilettos outside their room.

"She told me they do not belong to her and that they certainly do not belong to the Pastor," he explained to Dennis. Apart from this life carried on fairly smoothly. Several times Dennis tried to get Mr Wellborn to accompany him to the shops but he seemed scared to leave his room. Eventually though, one cool October morning, Dennis knocked on his door and there was Mr Wellborn wearing a smart suit and trilby, he had his cane in his hand.

"Let's give this a try Dennis," he said. They walked slowly to the lift and got in, Dennis stared at the floor and said a silent prayer, "please don't break down," the lift heard him and smoothly carried them to the foyer.

Mr Wellborn seemed to enjoy his brief excursion, although his leg was aching by the time they returned to the hotel. After that, at least once a week he would walk down to the shops with Dennis, his leg seemed to get stronger the more he exercised.

At home, Dennis and Stinky were busy preparing for Bonfire Night, November the 5th. It was a tradition that the Bisskits along with several neighbours, would build a bonfire on some waste land behind their houses. Dennis couldn't wait, his father had already bought two boxes of Standard Fireworks, as well as some rockets, but had hidden them away.

On November the 4th, he knocked on Mr Wellborn's door, it was his lunch break and he often popped in. "Have a seat," Mr Wellborn said, as he passed him a cup of tea. Then, as Dennis had known he would, he told his story, and a sad story it was.

Mr Wellborn's parents had died from influenza when he was young and he'd been brought up by an aunty but had left home as soon as he could.

"Times were tough in the early thirties," he told Dennis; he'd been in and out of work, when he met Shirley, the love of his life. He fidgeted and looked uncomfortable, then continued, "One thing led to another, and Shirley got pregnant." Dennis stared at the photograph of the little girl on Blackpool beach.

"Obviously I did the right thing and we got married straight away, I wanted to anyway." He was thoughtful for a few seconds and then carried on, "It was 1933, we didn't have much money, and Shirley's parents didn't want to know her. Eventually I got a factory job and things improved a bit." he looked at the photo and smiled.

"One weekend we went to Blackpool on the bus, it was the first holiday we'd ever had." He took the photo off the shelf and stared at it. "That's my Gloria, we named her after Gloria Swanson; I'm 50 years old Dennis, and that was the best day of my life." Dennis didn't speak, there wasn't much he could say and anyway he knew there was more to come and he had a feeling it wasn't going to get any happier.

That evening, Dennis told his mother all about Mr Wellborn, how he'd been married and had a child and how in 1937 his wife had died in an accident and how he'd been so depressed that he been unable to work and unable to cope and had eventually taken the decision to have Gloria adopted. He'd thought it was the only way she would get a decent life, and then by the time he got a bit stronger, WW2 had broken out and that was it.

When he came back from the war, he was injured and couldn't work. Eventually Mr Plumb gave him his room at the hotel. Mrs Bisskit had tears in her eyes.

"Has he never tried to get in touch with Gloria," she asked.

"That's what I asked," Dennis told her, "he said he'd thought about it after he came back from the war, but by then she would have been nearly a teenager, he didn't want to cause any upset, and he also said that she had probably never forgiven him anyway."

Mrs B. dabbed her eyes on the sleeve of her blouse and said "So he's no idea where she is now?"

"Not really," Dennis answered, "although an old neighbour told him she'd been adopted by a family named Johnson and they'd moved to Manchester. That was a while back though." Mrs Bisskit saw the look in Dennis's eyes and immediately knew what was going on in his mind and said "It's a very sad story but you know you can't go interfering in people's lives, Dennis."

Dennis and Stinky cheered as the flames shot into the air and the guy that was perched on top rapidly disappeared into a cloud of smoke.

"Not much of a guy," Stinky shouted, "not up to our high standard." Dennis nodded. For many years he had enjoyed building a figure of Guy Fawkes and standing on a street corner shouting "penny for the guy". Some years he had collected quite a sum of money. Of course he was far too old and mature for that sort of thing now but he was looking forward to the firework display. His father was guarding them as if they were the Crown Jewels, possibly because he knew Stinky was around.

"Another spud?" Mrs Bisskit enquired. They both immediately shook their heads and said they were full. This was another tradition. Potatoes and chestnuts were placed in the hot embers to cook and then handed around. The only problem with the potatoes is that they were black on the outside and uncooked in the middle. For some reason Mrs Bisskit never seemed to notice this, and no one liked to tell her. So for years' people had been accepting them off her and then throwing them back onto the bonfire as soon as her back was turned.

Mr Bisskit was busy attaching some Catherine wheels to nails on the fence. When lit these spun around and around throwing a shower of colourful sparks into the air. As soon as Mr B. lit them everyone cheered, except for Granddad; his stomach had been playing up, so he left them to it and positioned himself next to the outdoor toilet in case of emergency.

Mr Bisskit made the supreme sacrifice and handed over some bangers to Dennis and Stinky, giving them strict instructions to be careful. Dennis lit a couple and threw them on the ground, making people jump as they went off with a large bang. Meanwhile Stinky crept up behind Gladys and let a banger off right behind her.

Gladys fell over, screamed, got back up, and then chased Stinky all around the bonfire. Meanwhile Granddad suddenly clutched his stomach and raced into the toilet leaving the door half open.

Stinky arrived back alongside Dennis and said "I don't know where your Gladys gets some of her language from, she sounds like a coal miner."

Mr Bisskit shouted for everyone's attention. He had placed a rocket in an old milk bottle and was lighting the blue fuse.

"Watch this everybody," he shouted, but just as the fuse lit, the bottle tipped over, and instead of shooting high into the air, the rocket took off just above their heads. People dived to the ground as it shot across the wasteland and straight through the open door of the toilet.

For a few seconds everyone just stared open-mouthed, then all of a sudden Granddad shot out of the toilet, he had his trousers and underpants around his ankles; smoke and flames were coming from inside his pants. As he ran, his trouser braces dangled behind him and after running faster than Dennis had run in the World Record Mile attempt for about 10 yards, he suddenly tripped over his braces and slid along in the mud. This was actually a good move on his part as it helped to put out the flames, although a neighbour also helped by throwing a bucket of cold water over him.

Amazingly Granddad wasn't badly hurt, just some minor burns, all the hairs on his legs singed off, slight damage to his trousers and a large hole in his underpants that required patching. He quickly recovered. It was much worse for Gladys, who said it was the most horrific sight she'd ever seen and she would never be able to look Granddad in the face again.

Later, Dennis lay in his bed, he couldn't get to sleep. I'm not going to get involved, he thought, but, just if someone was trying to find someone, how would they go about it?

Christmas 1962 approached and with it, the worst weather anyone could remember, it was already being called The Big Freeze of '62, much worse than the previous Big Freeze of '55, The Great Chill of '49, The Big Wind of '37, and amazingly Granddad finally admitted that it was even worse than the Huge Blizzard of 1899. Dennis spent most of his time clearing the snow away from the front entrance of the hotel.

He asked his mother if Mr Wellborn could come to Christmas dinner and she agreed. Dennis could tell he was greatly moved when he invited him, but he told Dennis he felt more comfortable on his own for now and then he told Dennis to stop calling him Mr Wellborn and start calling him Ronald.

Despite the terrible weather, it was a wonderful family holiday. Six months from now Dennis would start Basic Training for the army so who knew what would be happening next Christmas. Granddad was in fine form. After a couple of sherries, he entertained everyone with a couple of George Formby songs. As they relaxed after a large dinner, Mum suddenly realised she had forgotten to send her cousin Maureen a Christmas card. Dennis immediately said "Of course, if only we had a telephone, we could just call her up and say Happy Christmas Maureen".

Getting a phone installed had been the cause of much discussion lately. Dennis and Gladys thought it was a great idea. Granddad couldn't see any need for one, Dad was worried about the expense and Mrs Bisskit thought they were the devil's work.

"We must be the only people left in England without a telephone," Gladys shouted. She was exaggerating but certainly the number of people getting phones installed was growing every day.

Granddad swallowed the remains of his latest mince pie and announced "I remember years ago, some chap invented a walking stick with a butterfly net attachment on the side. If you saw a butterfly, you could screw the attachment onto the end of the walking stick and catch butterflies. That never caught on." Dennis stared at him for a moment and said, "Well I'm not surprised, let's face it, if you are bad enough to need a walking stick, you are hardly likely to suddenly start leaping about trying to catch butterflies".

"You are missing the point," Granddad told him. "The point is, the telephone is just a passing fad. A few months from now, people will be throwing them in the back of the shed alongside their walking stick with butterfly net attachment."

Dennis laughed and shook his head, "In that case I take it you don't agree with the Professor's prediction that one day everyone will carry a little portable phone around with them." Granddad nearly spat out his sherry.

"That is conclusive proof the Professor is an idiot, I mean, how will they carry the telephone lines, will everyone drag a big trailer along, full of cables?"

Then the Queen's speech started so that was the end of the telephone discussion.

A few days after Christmas, Dennis managed to catch up with Dale. He had barely seen her lately, she always seemed to be busy with her new hairdresser friends. They went to see a new movie called *Dr. No*. It was about a British spy called James Bond. Dennis thought it was the best film he'd ever seen, although it did put him off a bit, when every few minutes Dale kept muttering about how good-looking James Bond was. He wondered if it was possible to dye ginger hair black. Afterwards he told Dale all about Mr Wellborn. She told him not to get involved in other people's personal lives.

If the weather was bad before Christmas, it got even worse as 1963 began. There were few guests staying at the hotel. Dennis continued clearing snow from in front of The Victoria and wondering how best he could get involved in another person's personal life.

Gloria Johnson, if that was indeed her name, would be about 30 now. He suspected that she would have kept the name Gloria. She was about five when she was adopted. She would have been used to being called Gloria, surely her new parents wouldn't have changed her first name. Of course, even if their name had been Johnson, there was a good chance that she was now married with a different name. She could be living in Australia for all I know, thought Dennis.

After shovelling snow for a couple of hours he was cold and tired. He shook the snow off his shoes, went back into the hotel and got into the lift. As he walked towards the staff bathroom to wash his hands, he suddenly felt exhausted and on the spur of the moment, he entered one of the empty guest rooms. It was one of the best rooms, bigger than the standard room. In the corner was a comfortable armchair. Dennis looked at it and thought, "Just five minutes wouldn't hurt." He sat down and closed his eyes. It only seemed like seconds later that he heard footsteps approaching and then voices outside the room door. Dennis jumped up and looked about him; next to him was a large wardrobe for guests to hang their clothes in. He opened the door and leapt in pulling the door shut behind him. Seconds later he heard Mr Went's voice. "I'm sorry about the delay, I don't know what's happened to the boy," then he chuckled and said "maybe he's got buried under the snow." A man said something Dennis couldn't hear and then he heard Mr Went say "Enjoy your stay at the Victoria," and then the sound of a door closing.

Dennis couldn't believe he had hidden in the wardrobe. He could have just made up some excuse for being in the room, like, he was just checking it was clean and tidy. Now he would have to hope the guests went straight out and also hope that they didn't want to hang their clothes up.

After about ten minutes he was starting to get cramp in his leg. He quietly opened the wardrobe door a fraction. Across the room he could see a man and lady sitting at a table drinking tea and mumbling to each other, they didn't seem in any hurry to move. Dennis couldn't wait any longer so he just opened the wardrobe door stepped out and strode across the room as if it were an everyday occurrence. Out of the corner of his eye he could see the couple watching him open-mouthed, their cups stuck in mid-air. He thought he had made it but all of a sudden the man said "You there, what are you doing?" Dennis turned and smiled as if he'd just noticed them and said, "Just checking the wardrobe, everything seems fine," he turned to leave again but the man wasn't going to let it go at that.

"Why were you hiding in that wardrobe?" Dennis put on a shocked expression and said "Hiding! Oh no, I was just checking the wardrobe, we have had a bit of trouble with that one but it's all fine now." He left the room as quickly as possible before they could ask any other awkward questions. He raced back outside picked up his shovel and tried to look like he'd been there all of the time.

"That was a close call," he thought, but well worth it because whilst passing the time standing in the wardrobe, he had come up with an idea.

Well, it wasn't so much an idea as a thought. As he squirmed around in the wardrobe trying to get the cramp out of his leg, he suddenly thought, "I wonder if the Johnsons have a telephone installed, or whether, like Granddad they think it's just a passing fad, much like the walking stick with butterfly net attachment".

In the corner of the foyer at The Victoria Hotel was a small cubicle containing a telephone, a chair and a phone book for the West Midlands area; not much use to Dennis, but he knew that behind the reception desk on the bottom shelf were some phone books of other areas if required by guests. As usual Molly was standing behind the desk. Dennis asked her if she had a Manchester phone book. She asked why, and he told her all about Mr Wellborn and his daughter. She told him he shouldn't get involved with guests' personal lives, he told that he got that a lot, she reached for the book.

Dennis couldn't believe it. He'd thought there would be one or two Johnsons. He counted them:14.

"And that's only the people who have a phone, there may be hundreds of others called Johnson who don't," Molly reminded him. He thought about it, hundreds of Johnsons.

"Manchester must be the Johnson capitol of Great Britain," he said. Dennis felt a bit deflated, but then thought, he could only do his best. Molly didn't say anything, she just tore the page of Johnsons out of the phone book, folded it up and handed it to Dennis. The following Saturday, Dennis had the day off and called around to Stinky's house.

His friend had just got back from a run around the playing fields and was still dressed in sweaty shorts and top when Dennis turned up. Every time he saw Stinky lately he was running or exercising.

"Only a few months to go," he reminded Dennis, "I want to be as fit as I can for Basic Training, you should be doing the same thing." Dennis looked surprised and said "Plenty of time for that, anyway as you should know I'm a natural athlete, remember those times I was doing when I practised for the World Mile record?"

"Yes, I do remember that," Stinky told him, "I seem to recall your final time was just over twenty-six hours." Dennis shook his head; "As you well know Stinky, there were extenuating circumstances for that." Stinky wiped his sweaty face on his mother's tea towel and said "That's another thing Ginge, when we start Basic Training, try and avoid saying things like 'extenuating circumstances.' Remember, even though we have a Dudley education, some of the other lads come from up North, they can probably barely spell their names, so god knows what they would make of 'extenuating circumstances.'" Dennis didn't seem convinced, so

Stinky added, "Remember the advice your dad gave us, to try and keep a low profile." Dennis shrugged and said "Well, I shall bear that in mind, but don't expect me to lower my standards. Anyway I came around to tell you something."

He told Stinky all the latest news on Mr Wellborn and his daughter, and then added "Everyone keeps advising me not to get involved". Stinky filled a large glass of water from the tap, gulped it down, wiped his mouth on the back of his hand and then said "But obviously you will take absolutely no notice of all that advice and you will get involved".

"Naturally," Dennis replied.

Dennis had had a lot of expenses lately and was also saving up for his mother's birthday in April. Since he didn't know when he would be at home for future birthdays, he wanted to get her a special present. So after giving it plenty of thought, he decided that he would use his tips to make phone calls. Every time he got a tip he would ring up a Johnson.

"Hope I get plenty of tips," he thought to himself, "because time is running out".

Two days later, during his lunch break, Dennis entered the cubicle, sat down and placed three pennies next to the phone. He had used the phone in a telephone box in Birmingham recently when he'd been out for the day with Stinky. Dennis had never used one previously and had been fascinated. Stinky had explained that you first had to lift the receiver, drop your coins in the slot then dial the number. Then if someone answered you pushed Button A. If no one answered, you pushed Button B and your money got returned to you. When they had first entered the box, Stinky had pushed Button B, because he said that sometimes people forgot to get their money back. They had no such luck on this occasion, but he suggested they had a practice run so that Dennis would know what to do next time.

He opened the phone book and chose a name at random, MR JACK SMITH, he dialled the number and seconds later someone answered but before they could speak Stinky said, in an official sounding voice, "Is that Mr Jack Smith on the line?" When a voice on the other end replied "Yes, it is," Stinky immediately shouted, "Well you better move there's a train coming." They both ran off down the road, laughing hysterically. Dennis chuckled again at the thought, although for a couple of days he had been worried that somehow Mr Smith could track them down and put the police onto them.

He made himself comfortable, took the torn piece of paper with all the Johnson names on it from his pocket and read the first name, MR A.K. JOHNSON. He took a deep breath, lifted the receiver, dropped the coins into the slot, dialled and waited. After what seemed like a long time, he heard the pips go, he pushed Button A and a man with a broad northern accent shouted "Alec Johnson here". Dennis steeled himself and said "I'm trying to find a Gloria Johnson; she'd be about thirty." Mr Johnson told him there was no-one of that name there. Dennis thanked him, put the phone down, took his pencil from his pocket and crossed the first name off the list.

Over the next fortnight he tried four more numbers. One man had never heard of Gloria Johnson, one man called him a rude name and told him not to bother him again. One elderly lady was so excited that someone had called her up that she wanted to tell Dennis her entire life story. He had to make some excuse in the end to get away. The other number he rang, no-one was at home. He wondered whether it was worth carrying on; it seemed like a chance in a million, and then even if he ever found Gloria Johnson, she might just tell him to mind his own business.

The following week, a life-changing event happened to Dennis. He had been building up to it for quite a while now and had decided that today was the day. As he walked down the street with Stinky he suddenly stopped, pointed at his top lip and said "Look at that". Stinky stopped, turned and looked for a second, before asking "it's your lip?"

"No, above that," Dennis told him. Stinky looked confused and said, "You mean your nose". Dennis pointed his finger again and shouted, "Come on Stinky, you're not paying attention, now look between my lip and my nose". Stinky moved to within a few inches of his friend and stared for several seconds before shaking his head and saying, "No, I'm not seeing it". Dennis gave up and said "Well, you may have poor eyesight my friend, but from a certain angle I'm beginning to look like Lord Kitchener," suddenly Stinky caught on, "Oh you mean you're growing a moustache". He had another look and added "I still can't see it".

"Well, you certainly won't see it after tonight," Dennis told him proudly, "because I'm finally having my first shave. Dad's bought me my own shaving equipment, and tonight is the big night." Stinky held out his hand and said "Well, let me be the first to congratulate you Ginge, on this big occasion and of course, if you need my expertise, I'll be pleased to help because as you know I have been shaving for nearly a year now". Dennis shook his hand but then told him, "Thanks for your kind offer Stinky but some things a man has to do on his own".

That evening his father solemnly handed him a tea tray holding a mug, a shaving brush, a bar of soap and a silver razor.

"I've put a Gillette blade in there, it should last you a year or so," he told Dennis. His mother dabbed her eyes with a handkerchief and then loudly blew her nose into it. Granddad patted him on his back and said "We'll be right here if you need us lad". Dennis turned and walked into the bathroom.

He stared at his reflection in the mirror. He looked like Father Christmas, soap covering most of his face. He took a firm grip of the razor and commenced shaving. Within a couple of seconds, he had nicked his ear and blood started running down his face. He stuck some toilet paper on it to stem the flow; next he nicked his chin and more blood appeared, then under his chin, and then the door flew open and Gladys walked in. He turned and shouted at her, nicking the end of his nose as he did. A few minutes later he walked into the dining room. Blood-stained toilet paper covered most of his face, including a large piece hanging from his nose; his white T-shirt was covered in flecks of blood. His father walked over and shook his hand, "Congratulations son" he said "You are now officially a man".

Dennis pushed Button A and eventually a child's voice said "Hello, this is Noreen, who's that?" Dennis told her his name and asked if he could speak to Mum or Dad. She told him that they were having a lie down and she'd been told not to disturb them. Dennis asked if she knew anyone called Gloria and after thinking for several moments she said, "My friend is called Barbara". Dennis told her to have a nice day and not disturb Mum and Dad, then he crossed another name off his list.

Towards the end of April, Mrs Bisskit had a wonderful birthday, except for when Dennis tripped over carrying her birthday cake and landed head first in the cake. Luckily the candles only singed his eyebrows. Mrs B. wasn't too upset though because Dennis had bought her an amazing birthday present, a Goblin Teasmade.

"Just think," he told his mother, "you don't have to get out of bed now to make a cup of tea; you'll just be able to lie in bed like Queen Elizabeth." Mr Bisskit looked confused, and said, "Well, she'll still have to get up, or else who's going to make my toast?"

Later on Granddad said to him "That was a very nice thought. But I've got a feeling it will end up in the shed next to the walking stick with butterfly net attachment".

Dennis stepped dejectedly out of the telephone cubicle. Mr Went strode towards him.

"Mr and Mrs Dawkins from Room Seven just left," he told him, "and they were full of compliments about you, they said you could not have looked after them any better." Dennis smiled, he'd thought they had complained about something.

"You are very highly thought of at the Victoria Hotel Dennis, you could go far," Mr Went added. Dennis felt terrible, he knew he couldn't put it off any longer. He told Mr Went that he would be leaving soon to join the army.

"I was coming to see you later," he told the shocked hotel manager, "I was going to give you two weeks' notice." Mr Went seemed very disappointed but eventually said that if ever the army didn't work out, he was always welcome back here. He turned and walked off leaving Dennis feeling quite sad, but then he suddenly turned back and said "I notice you've been using the telephone a lot lately Dennis, is there a problem?"

Dennis decided to tell him all about Mr Wellborn's daughter and how he'd been trying to get in touch with her.

"I thought I mentioned to you to never interfere in guests' personal lives," he said. Dennis just stood there looking guilty, until Mr Went asked how many numbers he'd called.

"Eleven," Dennis told him.

"And how many more numbers are there," Mr Went asked.

"Three left," Dennis said. Mr Went fumbled in his pocket, took out some coins and handed them to Dennis.

"You may as well finish what you started," he said, then added, "don't take too long, your lunch break is nearly over."

Dennis studied the three numbers left, wondering which one to call first, and then he suddenly noticed a number near the top of the page not crossed out. He suddenly remembered, he'd called it a couple of weeks ago but no one had answered. He lifted the receiver, put some coins in the slot, dialled the number, and waited. Someone picked up the phone at the other end so he pressed Button A. Just silence, and then a woman's voice said "Hello, who is this?"

"I'm looking for a Gloria Johnson," Dennis told her. More silence, but it didn't matter because in that silence, somehow Dennis was absolutely certain of one thing, Gloria Johnson was on the end of that phone line. He never understood why he was so certain, but he knew that he only had a second. If she put the receiver back on the cradle she was lost. So he blurted out, so loudly that Molly looked up from the reception desk, "I know your father". Still silence, so he hurriedly added, "He keeps a photograph of you sitting on a donkey on Blackpool Beach, you were about four years old". Silence, he felt exhausted, and then a quiet voice came down the line to him all the way from Manchester, "I wasn't sure if that was just a dream," the voice said and then asked "Who are you?"

Four days later, on his next day off, Dennis checked himself in the mirror, "I reckon another week or so and I'll be needing another shave," he told his mother, "the wounds have nearly healed." He put on his jacket and checked he had some money in his pocket.

"I don't know why you have to go all the way to Manchester," his mum said, "Why couldn't you just explain it over the telephone?" Dennis looked at her and replied, "I told her the basics but it's too much to hear from a stranger over the phone, I need to tell her face to face."

"But Manchester, is it safe?" she asked. Dennis laughed and said, "Mum, I'm not off to Russia to fight the Communists, it's just an hour or so by train, then I'm meeting her in a café opposite the train station, so I can't get lost." Mrs B. stared at him and said "Yes well, you got lost running the mile so anything is possible." They both laughed, she gave him a hug and said "You're a good lad Dennis Bisskit".

A FEW DAYS LATER

The woman followed Dennis's instructions. The lift was out of order, so she walked up to the top landing, down the long corridor and knocked on the door of the room opposite the storeroom. Her legs were shaking.

Dennis pretended to sweep the front steps of the hotel, but eventually he couldn't stand it any longer. He raced back inside; the hotel seemed deserted. He ran up the stairs to the top landing and along the corridor. As he got closer, he slowed down and tiptoed towards Ronald's room. He couldn't hear anything. He noticed that the door to the storeroom was slightly ajar, so he looked inside. Behind the door Mr Went and Molly were listening intently.

"Anything?" Dennis asked. Mr Went put his finger to his lips and shushed him, and then whispered, "She was already inside when we got here; we can't hear a thing." Dennis wedged himself behind the door with the other two and tried to think if the fact they hadn't heard anything was good or bad.

"Maybe she's stabbed him," he said quietly. Then all of a sudden the door to Ronald's room opened. Ronald and his daughter stepped out into the corridor and stared at each other and then Gloria threw her arms around her father and hugged him for a long time. Through the crack in the door Dennis could see tears in Ronald's eyes.

Gloria finally stepped back from her father, grabbed his hand and they walked off down the corridor. Dennis leaned out of the storeroom door to get a better view, slipped and landed with a loud crash on the floor of the corridor. Gloria turned and said "Oh Dennis, it's you, we are just going for a walk."

Ronald came back to help Dennis to his feet and whispered so quietly that no one else could have heard, "Thank You." When the couple had turned the corner at the end of the corridor, Mr Went and Molly emerged from the storeroom. Mr Went stared after them, and said "You did a good thing Dennis," and then a moment later, "Okay, back to work, a hotel doesn't run itself you know".

The following Friday at three o'clock in the afternoon, Dennis removed his bellboy's uniform for the final time. He hung it in the Staff Room wardrobe and took one last look.

"I hope I look as good in my army uniform," he muttered to himself. It was time to leave the Victoria. He had made good friends there and wasn't looking forward to saying goodbye. He walked along the corridor to Mr Wellborn's room.

Amazingly, his daughter Gloria had told Dennis that she had married several years ago and had only happened to be at her adopted parents' house by chance the day Dennis had rung up. They had gone away on holiday and asked her to check their letterbox. She had told him that she was just leaving the house when she had heard the phone ring.

He knocked on Ronald's door, but there was no answer. He walked back down to Mr Went's room and knocked on his door, but again no answer. Confused, he walked downstairs. Halfway down the steps he heard cheering and looking up he saw Mr Went, Molly, some other members of staff he become friendly with, and Ronald, all waiting for him.

Everyone shook his hand and Molly gave him a big hug. Then Mr Went, said "Quiet everyone, I'd just like to say a few words about this young man." Dennis had never felt so embarrassed in his life. Mr Went told some stories about Dennis's short career as a bellboy and then said, "In his short time with us, we have all become very fond of Dennis and wish him all the best in his new career fighting for Queen and Country".

Dennis hoped that was it, but then Mr Went continued, "Myself and the staff wanted to get you a small token of our esteem to remind you of your stay here. I asked around but we had no idea, so one day, whilst you were hard at work, I popped around to your house hoping to get a clue. Luckily your granddad was at home and he told us there was something you had been looking for." He paused for breath whilst Dennis tried to think what his granddad could have told him.

"It's very lucky I saw him, because we would never have thought of this, in fact, in all honesty, I'd never even heard of it; we were just fortunate that Molly found this one in an antique shop." He called Dennis forward and handed him a long thin box. As Dennis opened it, he looked up, everyone was leaning forward, waiting to see the look of delight on his face. He tore open the box and looked. There inside was a walking stick with a butterfly net attachment. Dennis smiled and held it up, "Amazing," he said "It's just what I always wanted."

THE EVEN LATER THAN THE EVEN LATER THAN THAT YEARS

CHAPTER 14

JANUARY 1964
JUST OUTSIDE KAMPALA,
UGANDA

Dennis carefully placed the hat on top of the snowman's head, and then stepped back to admire his handiwork.

"There you go, all finished and it's a beauty, though I say so myself," he said so to himself. Suddenly he heard a loud noise coming from nearby, he couldn't quite place it, but it sounded oddly familiar. When he looked back at the snowman he couldn't believe his eyes. It had half melted already. A blazing sun had appeared above it and within minutes it had completely disappeared, leaving a puddle of water with a hat floating in it.

"Come back, come back," Dennis shouted, then he shot up in bed, he was soaked in sweat and as usual had managed to get himself tangled up in his mosquito net. He realised the strangely familiar sound he'd heard was the bugler, who shouted a chirpy "Wakey, wakey, rise and shine," before quickly disappearing to avoid the torrent of abuse coming from inside the tents.

Dennis eventually managed to disentangle himself from his mosquito net and sat on the side of his bed, yawning and stretching his legs. He was wearing his army issue jungle green underpants, which like the rest of his army kit, appeared to have been designed for a person at least twice Dennis's size. Most of his body was its usual snowy white colour except for his face, neck, arms from the elbows down and legs from the knees down, which were burnt bright red.

Dennis had initially thought that a beautiful tan would impress people when he got back home, but after about ten minutes of scorching heat and high humidity, he had suddenly realised that a ginger, freckly person was designed to avoid sunshine at all costs. Not only were parts of him semi-cremated but most of the rest of him was covered in red, itchy mozzie bites. He slapped his leg, as he felt another bite, and not for the first time muttered to no one in particular, "I was quite happy in Dudley, how did I come to end up in the middle of Africa?" and then "Why do they pick on me, I've never done them any harm?"

"It's because they sense fear," a voice replied, closely followed by Stinky Blackshaw entering the tent. As usual Stinky looked immaculate, already washed and shaved. He was possibly the only person in the British Army who appeared to have been fitted for his uniform by a Savile Row tailor. They had not been in Africa for very long but already Stinky had a golden tan, with, as far as Dennis could tell, not a single mozzie bite. He couldn't understand how, despite the heat and humidity, Stinky always looked like he'd spent the night in a five-star hotel, instead of being wedged into a steamy tent alongside three other sweating soldiers. Dennis slowly got up and walked to the tent entrance, lifted the flap and stared outside. Already the camp was a hive of activity, with half-dressed soldiers rushing to and from the latrines. The sweat was already pouring off Dennis.

"How can it be this hot, so early in the morning?" he asked Stinky, who'd joined him. "I haven't sweated this much since I first met Mrs Ricketts, and another thing whilst you're here; explain to me once again, how is this anything like the Scouts?" Stinky smiled but didn't bother answering as this was about the hundredth time Dennis had asked the same question since that morning they had got off the bus and begun basic training with the Staffordshire Regiment.

SIX MONTHS EARLIER... Whittington Barracks, Lichfield, Staffordshire.

Dennis opened his eyes, glanced out of the bus window and read the sign; "Two miles to go lads." he shouted. He'd just been thinking about his granddad, Dennis had thought he would be delighted when he'd told him that he was joining the army, just as his granddad had all those years ago, but all he had said was "Are you sure Dennis, are you sure it's the life for you?" As the months passed by his granddad had accepted the idea, but still occasionally would ask Dennis if he was still sure he was doing the right thing. Dennis would always say "Sure I'm sure, Granddad," but now as the bus got closer he was not sure that he was so sure. Turning to Stinky, he asked "what do you think the camp will look like?"

"Oh, I should imagine very much like a Butlin's Holiday Camp," Stinky replied confidently, then noticing Dennis was putting his trilby on his head, said "are you really going to wear that hat Dennis, you do realise that the world has moved on, no one wears a trilby anymore."

Dennis looked shocked, "I'm surprised at you Stinky, the trilby is quintessentially English, just mark my words, everyone will be wearing one again soon, it's just a passing phase".

"That's another bit of advice I'd give you," Stinky told him, "apart from not wearing the trilby, I'd do away with words like 'Quintessentially'. Remember what your father said, the best way to get through basic training is to keep a low profile."

"Yes well," Dennis mumbled, "I think we've already established that my dad knows even less about basic training than we do. Anyway, I'm quite capable of keeping a low profile." Stinky wasn't convinced, he looked at his reflection in the coach window and sighed.

"I'm really looking forward to joining up," he said, "but it nearly broke my heart having my hair cut. I'd been developing that quiff for about a year now. Several people have told me that I looked a bit like your heart throb Elvis." The sarcasm went over Dennis's head and he said "That man is no heart throb of mine, in fact I hold him personally responsible for the moral decline of this country." Stinky smiled, he loved setting Dennis off on one of his rants about society.

Dennis continued, "Since Stone Age times, man has had the same haircut and been very happy with it, and now this man comes along and suddenly men want hair sticking out in all directions." He calmed down and then asked Stinky why he hadn't waited to get a free haircut on the camp.

"Well," his friend replied, "I thought if I have to get it cut, I'll get it done properly. Someone told me that the Regiment hairdresser only got the job because he owned a pair of scissors and not only that, he's blind in one eye. He cuts half your hair and then you have to turn around and face him so that he can cut the other half." Dennis wasn't sure whether to believe this story or not, but Stinky added, "You don't have to worry for a while anyway, I see you already went and got a military haircut." Dennis smiled and said "No, this is just my normal haircut."

"I know," Stinky told him, "I was just being sarcastic." Dennis was just about to tell his friend that sarcasm was the lowest form of wit, but by now the bus was slowing down as they approached a large sign with WHITTINGTON BARRACKS, HOME OF THE STAFFORDSHIRE REGIMENT written on it, then they turned left, through large metal gates, passed several blocks of buildings, drove across a massive concrete parade square and came to a halt opposite a huge imposing brick building.

Dennis stared through the window and got the first inkling that Stinky's description of the army being just like the Scouts may not be quite correct. He pointed at the grim building that stood before them and said, "I put it to you Stinky, it's not so much Butlin's Holiday Camp, as Victorian Hospital for the Criminally Insane".

There were about twenty other lads with them on the bus. Most had looked nervous and deep in thought on the journey, all wondering how they would cope with the next twenty-six weeks of basic training. Now, as the time came to get off the bus, some of them looked even more nervous. No-one seemed keen to be the first one to leave the safety of their seat. Stinky jumped up and grabbed his suitcase off the rack above his head.

"Come on, Dennis, let the fun commence," he announced, and with that he marched down the aisle, skipped down the steps and stepped down onto the concrete to begin his new life. Dennis followed close by, holding onto his trilby as a gust of wind met them. The lads stood in a circle wondering what to do next, when suddenly they heard a loud tapping noise approaching them from across the parade ground. A large, immaculately uniformed man was marching towards them, tapping out his steps with a wooden pacing stick. Even from a distance Dennis could see the sun shining off his glass-like boots.

"It's a Colour Sergeant' whispered Stinky, "remember what I said, low profile." Before Dennis could answer, a gust of wind swept his trilby off his head and it flew away, bouncing across the square towards the approaching soldier. Without breaking stride, he stood on it and carried on towards them. Dennis looked distraught and opened his mouth to say something but Stinky immediately said "Don't".

The large man came to a halt several feet in front of them. As he came to attention, his left foot slammed into the ground with so much force that the earth seemed to shake. He stared at them for a while which did nothing for Dennis's bowels. He had a massive head and appeared to have no neck; his head just balanced on his shoulders. This was their first impression of the man who would forever after be known as Buckethead.

"Welcome, welcome bonnie lads, welcome to my world," he shouted. They would soon come to realise that he always shouted, even when he was whispering.

"Let me introduce myself," he continued, "I am Colour Sergeant Plunkett. If you have something vital to say and wish to convey it to me, you shall come to attention and address me as Colour Sergeant and nothing else, do you understand?" He must have assumed that they understood because he didn't stop for breath, "When we've known each other for twenty years, and we are old friends and I'm best man at your wedding and we've had a few drinks and I'm in a very good mood, you may address me as Colour. Nothing else, not Sergeant or Sarge, or Your Royal Highness, and especially not Sir. I have a chin, I don't have a double-barrelled name like Ponsonby-Smythe and I can read a map, so definitely not SIR! Is that clear?"

He stopped for a second and a couple of lads muttered "Yes Colour Sergeant," but he hadn't finished.

"Turn to your left, lads and look over your shoulder. You see those gates you came through," they nodded. "The other side of those gates is the world...the other world...the old world, but see this," he tapped the parade square and looked lovingly at it, "this is my world, this is Planet Plunkett and on Planet Plunkett I am God but as we have already established, you don't need to call me God, just Colour Sergeant. On Planet Plunkett I will turn you sad, pathetic lads into soldiers. Well, some of you anyway. Of course, some of you won't make it, you will run back to the old world, back to your mothers." He suddenly put on an upset child's voice, "Mummy, mummy I went to Planet Plunkett and the naughty man shouted at me."

Then something amazing happened, in the split second Buckethead stopped to draw breath, a plaintive voice was heard. It was Dennis, who obviously hadn't been paying a lot of attention, "Excuse me sir, may I retrieve my trilby, before it blows away?"

The silence was deafening, the other lads, even Stinky, stared at their feet, anxious not to be associated in any way with Dennis. After a moment, Buckethead marched over and stood right in front of him, then he leaned forward so his face was only inches away from Dennis.

"Well, well," he shouted, "well, well, well, what have we here then, are you deaf, lad, trouble with the old ears?"

"No," Dennis replied.

"No what?" said, the by now fuming Colour Sergeant.

"No, I'm not deaf, Colour Sergeant," said Dennis. Buckethead took a step back and then shouted "What's your name lad, because I'm going to be keeping a special eye on you". Stinky groaned inwardly as Dennis replied "Dennis Bisskit, Colour Sergeant".

"Dennis, Dennis," shouted the agitated Buckethead, "I don't need to know your first name, we're not on first name terms, next thing you'll be inviting me around for tea and scones, where's it all going to end? I'm not on first name terms with anyone, even my wife calls me Colour Sergeant. Now you've got off to a very bad start, young Bisskit, I think the wise thing for you to do is get down and give me 20". Dennis was confused, "20 what Colour Sergeant?" he asked.

"20 push-ups, you idiot, what do you think I mean, 20 bags of cheese and onion crisps?" Buckethead was almost foaming at the mouth, so Dennis quickly got down on the ground and struggled through two push-ups before collapsing face down.

"Have you fallen asleep?" asked the fuming Colour Sergeant.

"No," panted Dennis, "that's all I can do."

"That's all you can do!" Buckethead shouted incredulously, "My great grandmother can do five push-ups and she's 92. Seeing that pathetic effort makes me feel like crying, Bisskit, and I've never cried. Even when I was born, the midwife slapped my backside for nearly two hours, she had to give up in the end, her arm got tired, but I never cried, and do you know why, Bisskit?"

227

Dennis had no idea but was fairly confident that Buckethead was about to tell him, "Because even though I was only a few minutes old, even then I knew I wanted to be a soldier and soldiers don't cry."

He calmed down for a few seconds and then said in a surprisingly softer voice, "Push-ups are all in the mind lad. I'll tell you where you are going wrong. You're showing Planet Plunkett your fear, you're trying to push away from Planet Plunkett. Instead of that, imagine you're super strong and push Planet Plunkett away from you, try that, lad".

Dennis wanted to tell Buckethead that he thought he was mad but instead said "I think that's a scientific impossibility Colour Sergeant." The Colour Sergeant gave this some thought and then replied, "Well it's probably a scientific impossibility for me to boot you so hard up the backside that you land on the other side of the parade square but I'm still inclined to give it a go. Now get back in line before you bring me to tears again."

Dennis stood up, shaking and feeling at least as close to tears as Buckethead. The Colour Sergeant moved back and addressed them all.

"Well Bisskit's off to a bad start, still it's early days. Now, you're all off for a medical, where the doctor, and I use the term loosely, will inspect you naked from head to toe, no particular reason, he just enjoys that sort of thing; then off to the canteen for a fresh, healthy lunch, the chef is no doubt opening the cans even as I speak. Following that you will collect your kit which has been hand tailored by some of the finest blind tailors in the country. Everybody happy, okay, form up three abreast and follow me, no talking." They formed up as requested and attempted to follow Buckethead's "Left, right, left, right, left," but most were right when they should have been left and had to do constant little skips to try and correct it. From a distance it looked like a team of drunken Morris Dancers.

"So much for the low profile," Stinky whispered, "Yes, and so much for it being just like the Boy Scouts," Dennis replied, adding "Surely Buckethead must be related to Mrs Ricketts".

Suddenly Buckethead's voice boomed out "Halt," the lads at the back cannoned into the lads at the front and several fell over. "It appears that young Bisskit is still having hearing problems, I said NO TALKING!" he shouted at Dennis, "okay, lad, down and give me three of your best push-ups and let's feel Planet Plunkett move downwards."

JANUARY 1964, UGANDA

Dennis waved a greasy sausage around on the end of a fork, took a bite and mumbled "I don't even understand what we are here for". Stinky wiped bits of egg yolk off his face and answered "The natives are revolting". Jimmy Grimshaw immediately said "Oh, I don't know, I've met a couple and they seem okay". They all chuckled despite having heard the same joke for several days now.

Stinky took a large gulp from his mug of tea, that tasted less like tea than any tea he'd ever gulped and said, "I'll try and explain it again for those not paying attention", he stared at Dennis as he said this.

"The Ugandan Rifles are sick of bad conditions and wages, whilst all the white officers are getting good pay and top jobs, and now they are threatening mutiny, and that's why we are here, to sort it out." The lads quietly contemplated this for a moment, and then Dennis put into words what they were all thinking, "Well, how is that any different from us, we are on rubbish wages and conditions, compared to our officers".

"Exactly," agreed Jimmy, "I bet our officers aren't attempting to chew these concrete sausages for their breakfast, they are probably getting fresh salmon and champagne."

"I'm not sure they have champagne and salmon for breakfast", Stinky told them, "I think that's more of a lunch thing, anyway, it's not just that that's causing the trouble, also the northerners and the southerners don't get along."

"Well there you go", chimed in Rusty Balls, "that's something else we have in common. Birmingham born and bred, I've got no time for northerners or southerners." They all nodded in agreement.

Wandering back to their tent, Dennis suddenly turned to Stinky and said, "You know, it occurs to me that it's all a laugh and a joke but we may have to do some actual soldiering here".

"Don't worry, old mate, I'll watch your back," Stinky told him. Dennis smiled and said, "Well, it's only fair, after all that time I looked after you in the Boy Scouts". They both laughed at the memory, but Dennis knew that their roles had reversed. Stinky was undoubtedly a leader now, and a better soldier than Dennis could ever hope to be.

FIVE MONTHS EARLIER...BASIC TRAINING

George "Rusty" Balls, stared at his reflection in the mirror and ruefully shook his head.

"I can't believe what that butcher did to my head," he muttered, "it's as if he cut my hair with a knife and fork." Dennis who was standing next to him brushing his teeth, pointed his toothbrush at George and said, "That, young George, is a perfectly good haircut, it was good enough for our fathers and good enough for their fathers." He stopped for a moment, gargled with water, spat it out and continued, "You blokes should be glad at least you got a free haircut, he wouldn't even touch mine".

"Well of course he wouldn't," replied George. "There was nothing to touch. You were the only bloke who still has a 1920s' haircut, the butcher was well impressed." Stinky, who had just walked in with his towel around his shoulders, looked at George and said, "The thing you have to understand about Dennis, is that, if it happened after about 1958, he isn't interested in it".

"Well, I may be a bit old-fashioned," Dennis told them "but there's nothing wrong with that. I just like to maintain standards and standards are starting to slip in this country and I blame those Beatles people. Have you heard of them Stinky?" Stinky looked at George who was shaking his head in amazement.

"Of course I've heard of The Beatles," Stinky exclaimed, "everyone has heard of The Beatles." Dennis was in full stride now, there was no stopping him.

"Stupid songs and have you seen their hair, it's almost down to their collars, where's it all going to end? If it carried on like that, in a few years you wouldn't be able to tell a man from a woman. No wonder not as many men are wearing the trilby, it's because they can't fit it on their head."

"Well you better get used to it" Rusty told him, "The Beatles are going to be huge." Dennis reached into his back pocket, pulled out his tattered leather wallet and extracted a ten-shilling note.

"Well," he told them, "as a man with a well-documented knowledge of music, I'm willing to bet you big money that six months from now these Beatles people will be finished. You will say to people, 'do you remember the Beatles?' and they will say 'Who?' And another thing I can say with full confidence, the short back and sides and the trilby will be just as popular as ever. Any takers?" Stinky, Rusty and half a dozen other lads rushed to place bets.

"Hurry up, Dennis," Stinky shouted, "let's grab some breakfast before room inspection."

Dennis adjusted his beret and looked in the mirror. Somehow he always seemed to look a mess, especially when he stood next to Stinky, who had taken to army life like a duck to water. He raced after his best friend. They had completed the first phase of basic training, which had consisted mainly of cleaning their rooms, drill, basic weapons instruction and lots of fitness training. Dennis had definitely improved but still came last or near last in most things he did.

The previous week they had completed a series of tests and Dennis had not only come last in the one and a half mile run, but, as Buckethead had taken great delight in telling them, he was the first person in the history of the Regiment to actually get lost on the one and a half mile run.

"Not only are you rubbish at running, you have no sense of direction," he'd shouted at Dennis in front of the parade, "my granny could run a faster time than that carrying me over her shoulders." Dennis had seriously doubted this but felt it wise to say nothing, anyway he always knew what came next.

"Drop down onto Planet Plunkett and give me 20." Dennis seemed to have spent the majority of the last six weeks on the floor staring at Planet Plunkett. He caught up with Stinky, and as they rounded the corner to the canteen, he heard him say, "Watch out, it's Buckethead, with Major Tomkins."

Dennis looked up and sure enough, his mortal enemy was heading towards them with their section commander by his side.

"Remember to salute as we walk past," Stinky whispered. Dennis felt his bowels begin to churn. He had done plenty of drill, including saluting practice but until now had always managed to avoid actually having to do it for real. As they got closer, he went over it in his head, "Fingers tightly together, take the arm the longest way up and the shortest way down."

By now they were getting close and Dennis followed Stinky's lead. As with everything else he did, Stinky's salute was immaculate. Dennis's salute started out fine, "I'm looking good' he thought, but then it all went wrong. His hand came down next to his right eyebrow, fingers together, palm facing outwards, but for some reason he forgot to stop, his hand carried on, crashing into the bridge of his nose. Dennis let out a cry, put both hands over his nose and sank to his knees. He suddenly remembered where he was and rose to his feet, he had tears in his eyes and blood poured out of his nose and down his chin.

Stinky had carried on marching and glanced back in horror. "S-s-s-sorry sir, my hand wouldn't stop," Dennis blurted out to Major Tomkins, spitting blood in his direction. Buckethead and the officer just stared in amazement for several seconds, before the Major said, "Well, I'm off to clean blood off my tunic, Colour Sergeant, I will leave this in your safe hands." With that he turned and marched off.

Buckethead just shook his head and said "You know what Bisskit, you make me believe in reincarnation, because no-one could achieve this level of stupidity in one lifetime. Have a guess what I'm going to say next". Dennis didn't bother waiting, he leapt down onto Planet Plunkett and proceeded to push as hard as he could, whilst spitting blood from his mouth. He reached quite a respectable eleven push-ups before collapsing. When he looked up Buckethead had long since gone.

Dennis slowly walked into the canteen. He had a long piece of screwed up, blood-stained toilet paper dangling from each nostril. He couldn't see Stinky anywhere but hoped that he had kept what had happened to himself, and was reassured when no-one mentioned it as he joined the breakfast queue. He piled bacon, baked beans and what was laughingly referred to by the chef as scrambled eggs, onto his plate. Nearby a large pot of porridge was bubbling. It didn't really matter whether you had the porridge or the scrambled eggs with your bacon, they both tasted the same.

Suddenly a loud voice came over the Tannoy system, "Important Message for Private Bisskit, important message for Private Bisskit! When saluting, always stop the hand before it batters the nose". Dennis turned towards the chef's office and saw Stinky with the microphone in his hand, then looked around and realised everyone was convulsed with laughter, some of the lads were on their knees. After several seconds even Dennis saw the funny side and joined in the laughter.

For several weeks after this incident, every time someone walked past Dennis, even lads he'd never met before, would salute and pretend to hit their noses. It was funny for a while but was just starting to wear a bit thin, when luckily, Taff Evans accidentally shot himself in the foot on the rifle range and the lads had something new to amuse them.

JANUARY 1964 UGANDA

Winston expertly flicked the hamburger and it fell back into the frying pan, sending fat flying in all directions. He lived in a nearby village, and though the lads had been here several days they had yet to see Winston change the fat or wash the pan. Still, it didn't seem to affect the taste of the burgers. He looked up and smiled; Winston had the whitest teeth they had ever seen.

"Nearly there Mr Stinky, would you like an egg with that, sir?" he shouted happily.

"No, that's fine Winston, just the fat and the burger, thank you," Stinky told him. Winston reached up and turned on his old transistor radio and immediately the sound of The Beatles filled the room. Showing perfect timing, Dennis walked through the door. As soon as Winston spotted him he shouted, "They are playing your song, Mr Dennis, She Loves You, yes, yes she does very much sir". The lads all joined Winston in a quick verse and shook what little hair they had as they reached the chorus, "She loves you yes, yes she does Mr Dennis, sir".

Dennis couldn't believe it, even here in the middle of nowhere, thousands of miles from home, there was no escape. A couple of days earlier he had paid out most of his savings to all the lads who'd made the bet with him. He'd finally had to admit that after six months, not only were The Beatles bigger than ever, but apart from in the army, the short back and sides, like the trilby, had all but disappeared.

"It's the end of life as we know it," he had told them. "Your usual, Mr Dennis sir?" Winston asked.

Dennis noticed that the cuff of Winston's shirt, which incidentally appeared to be his only shirt, was hanging in the frying pan, dripping fat over the stove.

"No, I'll just have a cold drink when you're ready, Winston," he told him.

As they sat chatting at one of the outside tables, a stern looking Corporal Jimmy Jenkins suddenly jogged up the steps and stopped in front of them.

"Keep it to yourselves, lads but I was just in Major Tomkins' tent and I heard some big news," he spluttered. They stared back at him and eventually Rusty said, "Well, come on what's your big news?" Jimmy got his breath back and announced "The natives are revolting". There was much groaning and Stinky said 'Oh come on Jimmy that's not even funny anymore". "No, they really are," Jimmy replied, "the Ugandan Rifles have taken over Jinja Barracks, shots have been fired. It's on lads." Jimmy turned and jogged off, then looked back and said "Remember lads, not a word until it's official".

There was quiet for a moment or two whilst the lads took the news in. It had all seemed like an exotic holiday up until now. It was Dennis who broke the silence.

"Well, personally I feel sorry for The Ugandan Rifles," he told them, "they think things are bad now, wait until they meet Buckethead and he has them all on the ground attempting to push Planet Plunkett away." Despite their misgivings everyone laughed.

FOUR MONTHS EARLIER…BASIC TRAINING

Buckethead stood so close to him that Dennis could smell the tobacco on his breath. He stared at Dennis's boots and muttered "not bad", then he slowly raised his eyes until he was staring at Dennis's face. A slight gleam came into his eyes and Dennis knew that despite his best efforts, he'd done something wrong.

"Did you shave this morning Bisskit?" Buckethead inquired gently.

"Yes Colour Sergeant," Dennis replied. Buckethead leaned even closer so that his nose was nearly touching Dennis's and screamed as loudly as he could "Well, next time stand a bit closer to the razor, lad". Then he turned and marched a few paces, came to attention, spun around and came to attention again, facing the troop.

"Well, bonnie lads, the good news is, you are halfway through basic training; the bad news is, the vast majority of you are completely useless and have no place on Planet Plunkett." He paused for breath and looked from one to another.

"Still, let's not worry about that, lads because luckily you have one thing in your favour, me. Believe it or not I've taken lads who were very nearly as useless as you and I've turned them into professional soldiers, unrecognisable from their former useless selves. These lads have gone home on leave and their mothers have said "Who are you? where's my little Tommy?" and they have had to say, "It's me Mummy, I was little Tommy but now Colour Sergeant Plunkett has turned me into a professional soldier, worthy of standing on Planet Plunkett," and I will do the same for you lads". He stopped and stared again and then his eyes fell on Dennis and he continued "Well, most of you anyway, some of you may never be worthy of standing on Planet Plunkett".

They did some drill on the parade ground for about thirty minutes and then Buckethead brought them to a halt and removed a piece of paper from his shirt pocket. "Well lads, we have a bit of a dilemma. As you know, much of the regiment is away on exercise and I have a top secret task, so important that I'd normally only use an experienced professional, but in the circumstances I will have to use one of you." He stared along the ranks until his eyes settled on Dennis, and glanced at the paper in his hand.

"Now lads, I've been looking through the questionnaires you all filled in on your first day. Remember the question on previous work experience you'd had?" He looked up and some of the lads nodded whilst others just looked bewildered.

"Young Bisskit, it would appear that you're a bit of a dark horse, been keeping something to yourself, a secret talent. Well not any more, lad, it's time to put this secret talent to good use." Dennis was totally lost, he felt strangely proud that out of all the troop, he, Dennis Winston Bisskit had been chosen for this top secret task, it was just that he had no idea why he had.

"Right," shouted Buckethead, 'Fall out, Private Bisskit, back to your billet, get changed, T-shirt, shorts and black plimsolls will do for this task, report to me under the clock tower in ten minutes and I shall escort you to Lance Corporal Clive, where you will begin your top secret task. Quickly now, at the double!"

Dennis raced off; all he could think of was that Buckethead had noticed on the form that Dennis had been a Scout Troop Patrol leader and this top secret task, whatever it was, required a man of his great leadership qualities. But what the task was and who Lance Corporal Clive was, he had no idea.

Dennis quickly got changed, tied the laces of his plimsolls and stared into the mirror. "This is it Dennis", he said to his reflection, "this is your chance to shine, this is where all that time spent studying the great military strategists finally pays off." He glanced at his snowy white legs and hoped that sometime in the future the regiment would go somewhere nice and warm where he could attain a golden tan. "I always knew I was destined for greatness," he continued as he tucked his T-shirt into his shorts and jogged from the building.

He raced to the clock tower just as Colour Sergeant Plunkett marched around the corner, "Fall in Bisskit, left, right, left, right, let's not keep Lance Corporal Clive waiting". Dennis quickly fell in next to Buckethead and after a bit of shuffling managed to get in step. Without looking at him Buckethead shouted "I'm taking a big chance using you for this special mission Bisskit, I hope you won't let me down." They marched on, moving to an area of the camp Dennis was unfamiliar with.

"I will not let you down on this mission Colour Sergeant", he said, then hesitatingly asked "what exactly will I be doing?" Buckethead appeared to consider the question for a moment and then replied, "Your main task will be to escort Lance Corporal Clive wherever he wants to go, don't let him out of your sight, his safety is your top priority". Dennis couldn't believe it, this sounded like a mission for highly trained Special Forces and yet he was being entrusted with it.

"Will I need my rifle, Colour Sergeant?" he asked. Buckethead just shook his head as they arrived at a small brick building, opened the door and strode in.

"Lance Corporal Clive, allow me to introduce Private Bisskit, Private Bisskit, this is Lance Corporal Clive." Dennis looked around the dark interior of the room. In the corner sitting on a woolly blanket was a stocky looking Staffordshire bull terrier chewing on a large bone. Dennis carried on looking about the room but could see nothing else.

"Is Lance Corporal Clive working out the back?" he asked. Buckethead pointed at the dog, and said "This is Lance Corporal Clive, the finest Regimental mascot we have had since his predecessor, lovely temperament, always well behaved. His handler is away on a course until 4 o'clock, so I have chosen you to look after him. It's a great honour Bisskit, don't let me down."

Dennis couldn't hide his disappointment, "I thought it was a top secret mission," he mumbled.

"Well it is, lad, I wouldn't trust just anyone with this task, it's just lucky I spotted on the questionnaire you filled in, that you were an experienced dog walker in your younger days before you arrived on Planet Plunkett."

Buckethead showed him where Clive's food, cleaning equipment and dog leash were kept and then as he turned to leave he said "You haven't got off to the best of starts, young Bisskit but a good job here could get you right back in my good books." With that he left, slamming the door behind him leaving Dennis to his top secret mission.

Dennis turned back to the dog, sighed and said "Well, Clive it looks like we are stuck with each other for the day". Clive suddenly seemed to realise that he was not alone. He dropped the bone and started a low growl, not taking his eyes off Dennis.

"Now, now, Clive, be nice," Dennis told him, "I've heard you have a lovely temperament." With that Clive raced forwards and then launched himself into the air, heading straight for Dennis.

JANUARY 1964 UGANDA

As the sun blazed down, sweat dripped off the end of Dennis's nose, but for once he wasn't complaining about the heat. Like the rest of the lads he listened intently as Major Tomkins explained the situation to them.

"As you know the Ugandan government invited us here following the army threats of rebellion," he told them, "well now things have taken a turn for the worse. Members of the Ugandan Rifles have mutinied and taken control of Jinja Barracks; they are holding their officers' hostage until their demands are met." He paused for a moment and then said, "This could turn very nasty but we are going to make sure that it doesn't. I'll leave Colour Sergeant Plunkett to brief you". With that he turned and marched off.

Buckethead wiped his brow and then gave them their orders. At 04.00 hours the following morning, when, as he put it, "The Ugandan Rifles will be tucked up in bed with their teddy bears", the Staffordshire Regiment, would march into the barracks, surround the armoury before anyone could get at the weapons, and put down the mutiny. It all sounded fairly simple when Buckethead said it but most of the lads were fairly certain that it wouldn't be quite as easy the next morning.

FOUR MONTHS EARLIER...BASIC TRAINING

Dennis staggered along the road holding onto the dog leash with all his strength. His T-shirt hung in tatters, flapping around in the wind as he walked. There was a huge tear in the back of his shorts and a flap of material hung down his leg. He glanced down at Clive, who trotted proudly alongside him. A long black lace from one of Dennis's plimsolls was stuck between the dog's front teeth and hung down his chin like a very thin, long beard. More than once Dennis had attempted to remove it, but it seemed that Clive had taken a liking to it, so Dennis had decided to leave well alone.

"You may be a Lance Corporal, Clive," Dennis told him, "but I think we need to establish just who is in charge here." Clive suddenly stopped, turned to face Dennis and let out a low growl, then turned and carried on walking.

"Well," Dennis mumbled, "it seems like we've already established it." Dennis walked Clive past the stores area and onto the playing field, or rather, Clive walked Dennis. Clive had decided that he wasn't keen on Dennis's slow pace and had sped things up a bit, with the result that the walk had turned into a steady jog and then a fast run. Dennis attempted to slow Clive down but the dog was having none of it and Dennis was now starting to have a lot of trouble hanging on to the leash, especially with the lace missing from his plimsoll.

All of a sudden the plimsoll slipped off.

"Stop Clive, stop now," Dennis shouted, and amazingly Clive stopped and commenced sniffing a fence post.

"Good boy," said a relieved but out of breath, Dennis. Clive seemed fascinated by the fence post, so Dennis tied the leash to it and ran back to reclaim his plimsoll. He tugged it onto his foot, shouting over his shoulder, "Okay lad, we'll try again but this time at my pace". As he turned he saw the most horrendous sight he'd seen since meeting Mrs Ricketts on his first day at Fosdyke's. Well, actually it was what he didn't see that was horrendous, and that was Clive. He ran back to the fence post to make sure he wasn't seeing what he wasn't seeing and sure enough there was just a fence post with a dog leash tied to it. Dennis picked up the other end and found that someone or something had chewed through it. Putting two and two together Dennis guessed that it was probably Clive.

He looked around but there was no sign of the dog, Dennis couldn't believe it, he shook his fist at the sky and said "Could this day possibly get any worse?" and it immediately did. Buckethead suddenly appeared as if from thin air and marched towards him. He stopped in front of Dennis and looked him up and down, shaking his head as he took in his tattered clothing.

"Is that some sort of new fashion statement, Bisskit, because we are not having it, there may be all sorts of strange new fashions going on out there," he pointed off into the distance as if discussing another country, "but here," he said pointing at the ground, "there is only one fashion, and that's my fashion, the army fashion, Planet Plunkett fashion." He suddenly stopped and stared at the remnants of the dog leash in Dennis's hand, and for a moment something unique happened: Colour Sergeant Plunkett was lost for words. Eventually he slowly shook his head and said "Don't tell me Bisskit, please don't tell me," but Dennis had to tell him.

"I stopped to put my plimsoll back on and he ran off, he bit through this," he held up the leash.

"You left Lance Corporal Clive on his own?" Buckethead asked incredulously.

"Only for a second," Dennis muttered.

"You know, Bisskit, your brain must be in pristine condition," Buckethead announced. Dennis couldn't believe he was being complimented at a time like this, but realised he wasn't, when Buckethead continued, "let's face it, it's rarely been used, do you know what happens on Saturday, Bisskit?" Dennis thought for a moment and then remembered.

"Her Majesty the Queen is visiting, Colour Sergeant."

"Yes she is, lad and I know for a fact that she is very much looking forward to meeting Lance Corporal Clive.

I think she will be devastated when she finds out what's happened, lad and you will have to explain it to her. You will have to say, "I'm sorry, Your Majesty, but Colour Sergeant Plunkett put me in charge and I let him down. I let myself down, I let Your Majesty down, I let the regiment down, I let the country down but most importantly I let Planet Plunkett down." There was no stopping Buckethead now so Dennis had to shout to be heard.

"I'll find him, Colour Sergeant, give me one more chance, I often used to lose dogs when I walked them and I always managed to find them." Buckethead stared into space, not looking happy with life.

"Sometimes I fear for the future of Planet Plunkett," he muttered, but suddenly appeared to perk up.

"Find that dog, lad, and all could be saved. Of course, if you don't, you will be doing push-ups for so long, you will wear a large hole in Planet Plunkett." He came to attention, spun around and marched off.

JANUARY 1964 UGANDA

That evening rifles were cleaned, maps of Jinja Barracks were studied and live ammunition was issued. The lads were anxious but excited. After all their months of training, this was the real thing. Dennis and Stinky were sitting in their tent drinking mugs of tea, when Buckethead suddenly appeared through the tent entrance.

Dennis was so shocked he leapt up and spilt boiling tea all down the front of his shorts, he yelled and hopped around the tent for a few seconds, before tripping over a rubbish bin and crashing towards the bed of George Balls, where he became entangled in George's mosquito net.

Buckethead waited patiently until Dennis had managed to extricate himself from the net and then said "At ease lads, no need to stand up". Dennis sat back down on his bed, steam rising from the front of his shorts.

"Just wanted to check, everybody is set for the morning;" Buckethead told them, "you'll be representing the Regiment lads so don't let me down." Stinky stood up and said "We can't wait to get stuck in, Colour Sergeant". Buckethead nodded and said "That's the spirit young Blackshaw, in fact it was you I wanted to talk to," he cleared his throat, "you and Private Bisskit".

Stinky didn't like the sound of this. Much as he was Dennis's best friend, he tried his best not to get too associated with him in Buckethead's mind. Buckethead continued, "Whilst the rest of the lads will be retaking Jinja Barracks, I have another task for you and Bisskit", he smiled, it was only the second time Dennis had ever seen him smile and it wasn't a pretty sight, "let's call it a secret mission," he told them. Dennis groaned, remembering the last time he'd been given a secret mission.

FOUR MONTHS EARLIER...BASIC TRAINING

Dennis raced around the camp, shouting Clive's name, his tattered clothing flapping behind him in the breeze. Eventually he stopped, exhausted. He leaned against a wall, sweat dripping off him, as he tried to get his breath back. He couldn't believe he had failed the top secret mission. He dreaded having to tell Her Majesty that he, Dennis Winston Bisskit, had somehow lost the Regimental Mascot. It was enough to bring a tear to his eye, but just as he was feeling sorry for himself, he suddenly heard the sound of shouting coming from the building behind him. He turned and realised he was at the back of the cookhouse. Looking further along the building, he noticed a door was open so he ran towards it and looked inside. There was Clive with a sausage in his mouth, in fact as Dennis grew closer, he realised that it was a string of sausages and holding onto the other end of it was Corporal Pods, also known as Senna Pods because his food had the same effect.

"Don't just stand there", he screamed at Dennis, "help me, he's got hold of Plunkett's personal pork sausages." Dennis shouted at Clive to let go but he was having none of it.

"Plunkett will go mad, I have to get these especially for him," Senna Pod explained to Dennis through gritted teeth. Dennis tried to get behind Clive but he kept moving around.

"You must have more in store, what about our breakfast?" he asked Senna, who answered "Don't be daft lad, you'd need a microscope to find any pork in the pork sausages you lads get". Just then the string broke leaving one sausage in Senna Pod's hand and the rest dangling from Clive's mouth. He immediately took advantage by racing around and around the kitchen rapidly eating them. Eventually when they were all gone, he sat down licking his lips and wagging his tail. Dennis immediately grabbed hold of him and attached the remains of the dog leash to his collar. Meanwhile Senna sat down on a box with his head in his hands.

"Don't worry about it," Dennis told him "Plunkett will be so glad to see I've found Clive, he'll forget all about his sausages. By the way, if it's not pork, what exactly goes into our pork sausages?" Senna slowly stood up and said "you really don't want to know".

Dennis thought he was probably right, so he said "Come on, Clive, let's try again", and slowly walked him back to his kennel. He washed him, and brushed his coat. Just as he finished, the door opened and Buckethead strode into the room. He actually smiled.

"Well done, lad, you've redeemed yourself, he looks has good as new. You better get back and get cleaned up, his handler should be back soon. I will wait with Clive."

Dennis walked out, but as he closed the door, he glanced back and said "Oh, by the way, Colour Sergeant, there was a slight problem with your personal pork sausages." Buckethead just nodded and said "that's fine," but a few seconds later realised what Dennis had said. He rushed for the door but when he looked out Dennis had disappeared.

JANUARY 1964 UGANDA

It was 03.15 am by the time Stinky and Dennis reached the summit. An hour earlier a Land Rover had dropped them at the bottom of the hill and they had followed a narrow track to the top. There was enough moonlight that they could find their way quite easily. It was a cool night but they were still panting and soaked in sweat by the time they reached the peak, especially Stinky who was carrying the radio. They put their rucksacks and rifles on the ground, carefully crept forward to a large rock and looked down on Jinja Barracks, it stood about half a mile away but even in the middle of the night they could clearly make it out in the moonlight.

"Wow, we will have a great view," Dennis whispered.

"I didn't want a great view," Stinky replied, "I wanted to be down there in the action." Dennis kept quiet.

Buckethead had described it as a Top Secret Mission. They were to observe the fight from the top of the hill and maintain radio contact. If they saw any rebels trying to escape or launch a sudden attack they could immediately report it via radio. It was an important job but Dennis knew that Buckethead had given him this task to keep him out of the way and unfortunately Stinky, who was a fine soldier, had the misfortune to be his friend.

"Sorry mate, I know you're only up here because of me," he sadly told Stinky as they walked back to unpack their equipment. Stinky didn't turn but just muttered, "Let's just get on with our job". He set the radio up on the ground, extended the antenna, and turned it on. Nothing. The radio was completely dead.

TWO MONTHS EARLIER…BASIC TRAINING

"Pass me the entrenching tool, Ginge," shouted Stinky.

"You mean the little shovel?" Dennis asked him.

"Yes, the little shovel," a clearly exasperated Stinky answered.

"Well, why don't they call it a little shovel," Dennis continued, "that's the trouble with the army, they always have silly names for things." He passed Stinky the little shovel, and watched as he started digging the trench.

They had been on exercise for the last few days, map-reading, night patrols, some shooting on the nearby range and as usual a great deal of marching mainly up and down hills. Slowly but surely Dennis was getting fitter and stronger. When Buckethead screamed "down and give me 20," he had no problem getting down and doing a quick 20 push-ups. It was just as well because he still seemed to get in trouble more than anyone else in his troop and by now Buckethead only had to look at him and he dived down onto Planet Plunkett before he was even ordered.

A few minutes earlier Sergeant Jackson had told the troop to commence digging two-man trenches. Stinky measured out theirs, and commenced digging. "Don't get too comfortable Dennis," he shouted over his shoulder, "it's your turn soon."

JANUARY 1964 UGANDA

Stinky made several attempts to get some life out of the radio, then shook his head and said "I can't understand it, the battery must be dead. I'm sure I checked it out before we left. Pass me the spare, Ginge". Dennis stared back at him for a moment and then said "the spare what?"

"The spare battery", Stinky told him, "remember, it was the last thing I said to you last night." Dennis didn't speak for a moment and Stinky started to get a bad feeling.

"I thought you said, don't forget the spare bathroom key," Dennis said quietly. Stinky couldn't believe it.

"Why would you think I said that, we haven't even got a bathroom, yet alone a door, so why would we have a spare key to it? We just have a hole in the ground, there is no key." By now Stinky was shouting.

"Keep your voice down," Dennis said, "we don't want someone to hear us." Stinky put his head in his hands, and muttered, "Well that's the only way they will hear us; they certainly won't hear us on the radio".

Dennis felt it was best to say nothing, and they both sat in silence for a minute before Stinky continued, "Well did you bring the spare bathroom key?" Dennis shook his head and said, "Now you are just being sarcastic, as you quite rightly point out, there is no bathroom or spare key, but I assumed you had made a mistake due to stress". Stinky just sat on the ground shaking his head, then looked up and said, "So let's just get this straight, we are sitting on a hill in the middle of nowhere, in the middle of the night, with a completely useless radio. If I wanted to use the toilet and I turned around and by some miracle there was a bathroom behind us, I couldn't get in because you didn't bring the spare key that doesn't exist. Somewhere down there," he pointed into the night, "Buckethead is trying to contact us and no doubt saying, 'What have those idiots done this time?" Once again Dennis decided it was best to say nothing.

In the darkness some distance from them, Colour Sergeant Plunkett kneeled behind a bush at the side of a track and looked again at the soldier next to him as he listened to the radio. The soldier looked up and shook his head, "Nothing Colour Sergeant," he said. Buckethead looked up through the gloom in the general direction of the hill but could see nothing.

"What have those idiots done this time?" he said, then continued, "Oh well, we can't wait for them." he gave a quick signal and as if by magic, soldiers suddenly appeared from behind bushes at the side of the road. He gave another signal and they cautiously proceeded down the track towards Jinja Barracks.

TWO MONTHS EARLIER...BASIC TRAINING

Stinky pulled Dennis up out of the trench. They were both exhausted. He then paced around it.

"Perfect' he told Dennis, "Six foot by two foot by four-foot-deep, even Buckethead couldn't find fault with that."

"Oh don't worry' said Dennis, "he'll find something to moan about." Moments later Sergeant Jackson approached them, stared at the trench for a couple of seconds and said, "That will do lads, now fill it in". The lads couldn't believe it.

"We've only just dug it," cried Dennis.

"Look," the sergeant explained to them, "we are moving on soon and you can't leave a big hole in the countryside. What if a little old lady came by walking her dog and fell in it? Now quit complaining and get it done, then you can grab a cuppa," with that he strode off. Thirty minutes later Stinky stamped down the last bit of soil, the trench was no more. Dennis lay flat on the ground panting and wiping sweat from his face.

"I'll never understand the army," he muttered.

"Come on," said Stinky, "grab your rifle and kit and we will go and get a mug of tea." He walked off but suddenly realised his friend wasn't following him. Turning he saw Dennis staring at the ground with his mouth wide open.

"Oh no", he cried, "I don't believe it, did I have my rifle with me when I was standing in the trench? Pass me the little shovel, Stinky." Thirty minutes later Stinky shouted down into the hole, "Come on Dennis, it's not there, you've dug down further than we dug in the first place, any deeper and I won't be able to pull you out".

Dennis reached up and with some difficulty his friend pulled him to the surface, where he collapsed onto the ground. He looked like he was close to tears.

"Well that's it for me old friend," he gasped, "I think losing your rifle is still a hanging offence. If I don't get time to write a will, do me a favour, Stinky, tell my family I'm sorry, I did my best. Tell Dale to forget me and move on with her life..."

Stinky interrupted him, "Cheer up, it won't come to that, Dennis," but it was in vain. Dennis added, "You've always been my best friend, Stinky, I'd like you to have my autographed copy of Victor Sylvester's Greatest Hits, it's my most treasured item, look after it..." Just then George "Rusty," Balls came running towards them, carrying a rifle.

"Dennis, you idiot", he shouted. "You left your rifle next to our trench when you came over to borrow that chocolate bar." Dennis leapt up and hugged a shocked looking Rusty yelling, "I'm saved, I'm saved," but suddenly stopped, turned and looked at the big pile of soil next to the trench and cried "Oh no, not again". But before he could do anything, Buckethead suddenly marched towards them. Rusty rapidly disappeared, leaving Dennis and Stinky to it. Buckethead stared at the trench and screamed, "What have you two idiots been doing? This trench should have been filled in ages ago". Before he could continue, Dennis stood to attention and said, "I accept complete responsibility Colour Sergeant, we did fill it in but I was not completely satisfied with my first trench, so I remembered what you always tell me". Buckethead looked confused and said "just remind me Bisskit, what is it I always tell you?"

"You always tell me Colour Sergeant, that practice makes perfect, so I dug my trench again for the practice. I think you'll agree it's much better this time."

Buckethead was taken aback by this turn of events. He stepped forward and had a better look at the hole in the ground.

"Well, it's not bad Bisskit, perhaps slightly deeper than is necessary, still a highly commendable effort. It took a while, Basic Training is nearly over, but good to see you're finally getting somewhere, lad."

Dennis looked pleased with himself, until Buckethead got back to normal and screamed, "Now fill it in, and smarten yourselves up, we leave soon." Dennis happily started filling in the trench but suddenly stopped and told Stinky, "Sorry, but I'm afraid this means you don't get the autographed copy of Victor Sylvester's Greatest Hits."

"That's a shame," Stinky told him, although he didn't sound too despondent.

JANUARY 1964, UGANDA

Dennis and Stinky stared through their binoculars and watched helplessly as their comrades, led by Buckethead, approached the camp. Sunrise was yet to have any effect but there was still enough light from the moon to see what was unveiling beneath them.

"I hope it all goes well," whispered Stinky, "I just wish we could get in touch with them."

Fifteen minutes later they realised that they needn't have been concerned. Jinja Barracks had been retaken without a shot being fired. Buckethead had led some of his men through the main entrance, whilst others entered at various points around the camp. Heavily armed and expecting resistance, they were amazed to find most of the rebels asleep. Even the few guards at the main entrance were shocked to be woken by men with camouflaged faces pointing rifles at them. Other troops quickly took over the armoury, and moments later Dennis was relieved to see the captured officers being let out of a locked building.

"Wow, that didn't take long," Stinky said, "looks like we didn't miss much after all." Then out of the corner of his eye, he noticed some movement at the rear of the camp. He quickly trained his binoculars on the area. Just as he was thinking he'd been mistaken, he spotted three Ugandan soldiers run for the trees at the back of the camp. They were carrying weapons and in front of them they pushed a man in officers' uniform.

"Look over there, Ginge," he pointed, and Dennis shifted his binoculars in that direction. He couldn't believe his eyes.

"We have to do something Stinky, there's no way to let Buckethead know." They leapt up, grabbed their kit, including the useless radio, picked up their rifles and raced down the track towards the escaping rebels and their hostage.

ONE MONTH EARLIER...BASIC TRAINING

The big day was finally here, after nearly six months of hell, it was Passing Out Parade day.

Dennis felt he had never looked smarter as he stared at his reflection in the mirror. He was wearing his best uniform and his boots were so shiny you could see your face in them.

"Just think, Stinky", he told his friend, "another half an hour and we will be proper soldiers."

"Yes, congratulations Ginge," Stinky replied, "I must admit there were times when I didn't think you were going to make it."

Dennis looked surprised, "Really," he said "personally I thought it was never in doubt, it was only old Buckethead, holding me back." Just at that moment a familiar scream came from behind them.

"What's that, Bisskit, about something holding you back?" They spun around and immediately shot to attention. Dennis's nemesis stared down at them, looking as immaculate as ever. His boots were so shiny that they made Dennis's look dull by comparison.

By now Dennis had got used to thinking quickly and said "Colour Sergeant, I was just telling Private Blackshaw that you are always telling me to hold my back straight." Buckethead stared at him for a moment and murmured "Mmmm!" is that right?" then he proceeded to look Dennis up and down.

"Mmmm," he said again, "not bad Bisskit, I may have finally made a soldier of you. Who knows, one day you may yet be up to Planet Plunkett standard." Just then his gaze reached Dennis's face and he took a step back.

"Do you use a safety razor, lad?" he asked surprisingly quietly.

"I do, Colour Sergeant," Dennis answered.

"Well, next time take the safety catch off," Buckethead screamed, turned and strode off.

"I'd swear he is related to my old boss, Mrs Ricketts," Dennis told Stinky.

JANUARY 1964 UGANDA

They ran all the way down the track until they reached a clump of trees, where they stopped to get their breath back. Hiding their kit behind a large tree, they cocked their rifles and crept forward. Not far in front, they could see another track that ran to the left of them and to the rear entrance of the camp. When they got there, Stinky peeped through the shrub, and immediately stepped back.

"I can see them coming this way," he whispered, "They are about 100 yards away." Dennis had a quick peep and suddenly recalled what his granddad had said to him when they had visited France and Dennis had asked him how he managed to climb out of that trench and go over the top.

"You just somehow manage to find the strength inside of you," he'd replied. Dennis took a deep breath and said "You stay here; I will sneak along the tree line until they go past me. When they get close you, challenge them and I'll step out behind them". Without waiting for an answer, Dennis disappeared into the trees.

Stinky waited for several minutes until he could hear voices getting closer. He had a quick glance and could see the captured officer being pushed along the track by the three rebels, they were only about 20 yards away. Stinky took a deep breath and hoped that for once Dennis had managed to not get lost. He raised his rifle and stepped out into the open.

"Halt," he shouted in a loud voice, "drop your weapons," but one of the rebels immediately fired a shot in his direction and Stinky fell to the ground.

ONE MONTH EARLIER…BASIC TRAINING

The Parade had gone brilliantly. Dennis had never felt so proud, as a large crowd, including his parents and Dale, had applauded their every move. There had been one unfortunate moment when, at some point, the troop had come to a halt, Buckethead had screamed "Eyes right", and Dennis, trying to impress, had shot his head around to the right with so much force, that his peaked cap had spun around on his head and he was forced to finish the parade with his peak facing backwards. As they marched off the square, Buckethead marched past him, did a double take and said "Bisskit, your head's on back to front, fix it".

JANUARY 1964 UGANDA

Dennis had crept forward some distance keeping low to the ground. He heard voices pass close by. When he risked a quick look, he saw he was now behind them. He quietly stepped onto the track just as Stinky shouted "Halt", then he heard a shot, and saw Stinky fall to the ground. Dennis immediately shouted. "We have you surrounded, throw down your weapons". One of the rebels started to turn, so Dennis fired a shot over their heads and screamed, "Do not turn around or we will shoot, throw down your weapons," It did the trick, the rebels dropped their rifles onto the ground and raised their arms into the air.

The relieved officer immediately picked up one of the discarded weapons and trained it upon the captured rebels. He glanced up to thank his rescuers and was amazed to see just one young soldier walking towards him.

Dennis shouted "Watch them sir, I have to check on my friend," but just as he ran anxiously towards the spot where Stinky had fallen, his friend emerged from behind a tree holding his head; blood ran down his face. "It's okay, I dived down and hit my head on a rock," he shouted, then he spotted the captured rebels and said "Well done Dennis, you did it".

Just then they heard a vehicle approaching. A Jeep sped towards them, and skidded to a halt. Buckethead and three other armed soldiers jumped from it and ran towards them. The freed officer looked up and said "Good to see you, Colour Sergeant, I take it these two superb soldiers are yours. I probably owe them my life. I shall certainly be mentioning them in my report".

Back at Jinja Barracks a medic applied a dressing to Stinky's wound, whilst a concerned Dennis looked on. Buckethead entered the room and said "Well done lads, I never doubted you for one minute". He clapped Dennis on the back and said "Good lad Bisskit, I think you are now worthy of Planet Plunkett". He turned to walk out but suddenly stopped, turned and said "Of course, later on we will discuss why your radio wasn't working".

ONE MONTH EARLIER…BASIC TRAINING

There was a jubilant mood amongst the lads as they changed into their civilian clothes. Basic training was over. Four weeks' leave coming up. Dennis couldn't wait.

"Can't wait to taste some decent cooking, Stinky," he said, "Christmas with the family, it's surprising how you can't wait to leave home and then you realise it wasn't so bad after all."

Stinky was just about to agree when Jimmy Jenkins raced into the room.

"Big news lads, everyone's got to be on the parade square in 15 minutes," he shouted "don't ask me why but something big is going on. I just ran past Buckethead and he couldn't even be bothered to shout at me." Jimmy raced back out and the lads stared at each other.

"What's going on?" Stinky said to no-one in particular. Fifteen minutes later they found out.

"You've been training hard for the last few months' lads, and it looks like you are going to put it into practice a bit sooner than you might have thought," Buckethead told them.

"There's some sort of conflict going on in Uganda. Their government have requested assistance and luckily the Staffordshire Regiment have been chosen to go over there and help out. Now personally I'd like to get started right now, after all who needs Christmas leave when you could be preparing for some action, but unfortunately, the powers that be say you can have a few days' Christmas leave and then report back here on December the 29th."

There was complete silence in the ranks, everyone was stunned at this sudden turn of events.

"Cheer up lads," shouted Buckethead, "just think, if you were a civilian, you'd have to pay good money to go somewhere sunny in winter."

JANUARY 1964 UGANDA

Tents were starting to be pulled down as the temporary billets were cleaned up. Dennis and Stinky were the talk of the camp. It turned out that in all the retaking of Jinja Barracks and freeing of the hostages, Dennis had been the only soldier to actually fire his weapon.

Of course every time they told the story it got more exaggerated, there had been five rebels, then ten and then 20. Dozens of shots had been fired at Stinky, one of which grazed his head.

The medic had tried to put a plaster on his wound but Stinky had insisted on a huge bandage, as it looked more impressive. Even Buckethead was full of new-found respect for "his boys" as he now called them. Luckily he seemed to have forgotten about their lack of radio contact. 'Rusty' Balls dragged a huge old dustbin into their tent and said, "Stick any rubbish in here, lads". Tommy Devlin walked over holding something in his hand, looked at Dennis and Stinky and said, "Well, you two may be the big heroes but you're not that clever, it turned out I didn't need these after all." With that he dropped a set of chopsticks into the bin.

ONE MONTH EARLIER...BASIC TRAINING

The troop stood there in shock for a while. Tommy Devlin turned to Stinky and said, "Uganda, where the hell's that? Is it in China?" Stinky said, "Yes that's right Tommy. It's right in the middle of China."

"You better get some chopsticks," Dennis added quickly, "they won't let you eat food there without chopsticks." Tommy wandered off, confusing anyone he met by asking "Where do I buy chopsticks?"

EPILOGUE

ONE MONTH LATER

Dennis woke with a start. For a moment he couldn't remember where he was, but then he glanced through the window and saw the sign, WHITTINGTON BARRACKS 2 MILES. It all came back to him. The regiment had returned home from Uganda and the lads had been sent on three weeks' leave. Now it was over and he was on his way back to camp.

In the seat next to him Stinky sat yawning, "Are we nearly there?" he asked.

"Yes," Dennis replied, "I was just thinking, it doesn't seem five minutes since we were first arriving here, and yet so much has happened since then."

"I remember it well Ginge," Stinky laughed, "You were wearing that stupid trilby."

Dennis groaned, "I certainly got that wrong, I don't think I saw one trilby whilst I was on leave, all my old friends had hair down to their collars, all I could find on the radio was bad music, The Beatles and the Rolling Bones or whatever they are called. It's amazing, it's like we went away and when we came back the world had changed. I'll tell you one thing, Stinky, it's not looking good for The Victor Sylvester Orchestra".

Stinky laughed and then said, "So, what did you get up to?"

"Well, it may surprise you, Stinky," he told him, "but I decided to write my autobiography."

"You're right," said his friend. "I am surprised. Don't people normally wait until they have actually done something before they write their autobiography?"

Dennis tutted, "You may mock, young Stinky, actually that's what I thought at first but once I started writing, I realised I'd had quite a few adventures."

"Do I get a mention?" Stinky asked.

"You certainly do," Dennis told him. "In fact I've dedicated it to: MY BEST FRIEND STINKY, WITHOUT WHOM I'D HAVE GOT INTO A LOT LESS TROUBLE OVER THE YEARS."

His friend laughed and then said "I notice you haven't mentioned Dale; did you see her at all?" A sad look came over his friend's face.

"Yes I bumped into her in town," Dennis told him. "She was hand in hand with her new boyfriend, he's got hair down to his eyes, plays guitar evidently. I wished her the best, I suppose we just drifted apart."

"You certainly did drift apart," Stinky told him, "about 10,000 miles apart, all the way to Uganda."

"Anyway," said Dennis, "I'm told this is the swinging '60s, so why should I restrict myself to one girl?"

Stinky stared through the window. "It may be the swinging '60s out there," he told Dennis, "but I very much doubt if there's any sign of the swinging '60 s on Planet Plunkett."

The bus pulled into the camp, the lads grabbed their bags and started walking towards their billet. The camp was unusually quiet, but then just as they approached the NAAFI, they heard a familiar scream.

"Get down, give me 20!"

They looked up and saw Buckethead standing over some poor, unfortunate new recruit, who was struggling to complete one push-up.

Buckethead glanced up and seeing Dennis and Stinky he almost broke into a smile.

"See these two lads here!" he shouted at the recruit, "Believe it or not, they were once like you, unworthy of Planet Plunkett, but I turned them into heroes of the regiment."

Dennis could resist it no longer and asked what he'd wanted to ask ever since he'd first met the Colour Sergeant.

"Excuse me Colour Sergeant, I was just wondering, do you happen to know a Mrs Ricketts from Wolverhampton?"

Buckethead looked surprised and asked, "Do you mean Aunty Gladys, works at Fosdyke's Department Store, wonderful woman, an example to us all?" Then he turned his attention back to the recruit who was stuck mid push-up, wondering whether to carry on or not. The lads left them to it, all they could hear was, "My Aunty Gladys could do better push-ups than that, now stand up, get down again, stand up."

They managed to turn the corner before they dissolved into fits of laughter.

THE END

263